Where the Pieces Land

A Novel by
Claire Addington

Copyright © 2023 Claire Addington

The right of Claire Addington to be identified as the Author of the work has been asserted by her in accordance with the Copyright, Designs and Patents Act 1988.

First published 2023

All rights reserved. Apart from any use permitted under UK copyright law, this publication may only be reproduced, stored, or transmitted in any form or by any other means, with prior permission in writing of the publisher or, in the case of reprographic production, in accordance with the terms of licences issued by the copyright Licensing Agency.

All characters in this publication are fictitious and any resemblance to real persons, living or dead, is purely coincidental.

Front cover image by ANKBookDesigns

Dedicated to my eldest son Brandon who was my muse, my cheerleader, my patient editor and companion during testing rewrites - I'm forever grateful to have you on my side

Living in your dreams meant bitter disappointment when you woke up
– Ilona Andrews

Chapter One

'Here's to surviving the week and making it through to Friday in one piece.'

'I'll raise a glass to that,' exclaims Michelle, her north London accent getting stronger as the evening proceeds.

'Cheers.'

'Cheers, honey.'

We chink glasses. My best friend and upstairs neighbour is always happy to be my celebration or commiseration companion. Especially as Andy, my current partner, is the subject up for discussion. I aim to see the best in everyone. The place that I do this most is in relationships. However, they don't always have the best of intentions for me. Thankfully Michelle is willing to point this out.

'I'm sure they're just busy. That job is really high pressure.'

Even I don't believe this as the words fall out of my mouth. Michelle somehow manages to raise her eyebrows and frown at the same time at my reasoning.

'And?'

'Well, I can't expect a reply straight away every time I message, can I? We don't have that kind of relationship.'

This sounds vaguely viable.

'Babe, don't be a div! You need to sort it out.'

I screw up my face as I take a glug of my wine. She's right of course but the words seem harsh.

'It takes seconds. It's not as though there's quill and ink required to compile a perfectly calligraphed love note. Or having to find the best carrier pigeon this side of Surrey and needing to await the perfect weather conditions before sending it on its way to you.'

The image of Andy in a big old manor house, finger held out the window testing the wind direction, with a pigeon tightly held underarm makes me laugh. The mouthful of wine nearly escaped. Somehow there is something kind of sexy about this image.

'Maybe that's what happened. Maybe the pigeon got caught up with his mates in Piccadilly and forgot he had a job to do.'

We both laugh as we refill our glasses. I love having Michelle as my best friend. She is a no-nonsense kind of girl. At just a few years younger than me - twenty-nine - she takes no shit. She was also not about to sit here supporting me taking any either.

'When did you last hear?'

Michelle drained the last of the bottle of wine into our glasses.

'Erm,' I picked up my phone, pushing my long chestnut hair out of the way. 'Last Tuesday.'

I have no idea why I bothered to even refer to my phone at this point. I'm fully aware of how long it has been. I could reel off how long to the minute.

'See you next Tuesday, Andy!'

Michelle literally rolls off the sofa as she laughs so hard at her own joke.

Once I realise what she meant I'm cackling loudly along with her.

From her new spot on the floor Michelle announces, 'Hang on, that was ages ago.'

'I know. We're supposed to be meeting up tomorrow night to celebrate my birthday. Urgh my birthday...'

I bury myself in the sofa cushions and groan. I'm feeling old and this neglect from my current partner is not helping.

'If we are still going, I need to find something to wear. I don't even know if we're going to McDonald's or the Hilton.'

'The dress code is very different.'

'Exactly.'

I sat back up and pulled a strained face as I mentally worked my way through my wardrobe. In my head I see a vision of myself in front of a full-length mirror, aged and wrinkled and with no partner to love me. My Mum would class this as me overexaggerating. I know my thirties are supposed to be the best years of my life. Apparently I'm in my prime. Yet with the day looming I'm allowing myself to wallow in my own self-pity.

'Oh my god, let's call her now!'

Michelle makes me jump by sitting up at super fast speed, only to fall back against the sofa again, somehow saving her dregs of wine.

'No, I couldn't.'

'What?' She says too loudly, as she clambers back up to sitting, 'You have every right to phone.'

'It's nearly eleven o'clock.'

'On a Friday. It's not a school night and supposedly she's "working all the hours"!'

The put-on voice is hilarious. There are even air quotes and everything.

Michelle's logic filters through the fog of excuses.

'Okay, how about I just message?'

'Wimp.'

At work I'm the complete opposite of this drunken, whiny mess. As an event planner I'm usually the one ensuring that people in my current state don't ruin the carefully executed plans of others.

'Do it, do it! I'll find more wine.'

She scrambles up, arse in the air. The word 'Juicy' flashing in front of my eyes from the back of her grey joggers. Luckily, she has the kind of bottom that looks good in anything.

'I don't think there is any,' I call over my shoulder, holding up the other empty bottle.

Michelle crawls out from the array of furniture and uses the back of the sofa to bring her up to full height. I try to focus on my phone screen as it swims around in front of my eyes. All I can see in my peripheral vision is the word 'Juicy' wiggling around. Why am I so ridiculously nervous? My stomach is in knots and I know it's not just from the consumption of wine. Andy and I have been together for almost a year. Well, on and off for a year. As even just my friend, I should be able to make contact no matter the time. I give up trying to message and ring the number.

'No answer,' I shout in the direction Michelle went.

Now even Michelle isn't answering me. The overwhelming, drunken feeling of desertion is threatening to take over.

'Aha!'

Michelle reappears at the front door proudly holding a fresh bottle of wine above her head like a trophy. I hadn't even heard her leave the flat. Just stealthily making her way up to her flat and back in one piece was an achievement in itself. Finding more wine was impressive. I cheer her return and commend her hunter gatherer skills. She staggers her way over to me, taking the phone from my hand.

'Hey. NO!' I shout. 'Don't.'

It appears I've managed to sink further into the sofa with each glass of wine. I'm not fast enough to haul myself out to stop her.

'It's gone to voicemail,' Michelle stage whispers.

'Hang up!'

'Hold on. Very professional sounding,' she sniggers as she listens to the voicemail. She clears her throat. 'Andy, it's Michelle,' she slurs. 'Hayley wants you to ring her back as we can't go shopping for clothes until she knows where you're taking her tomorrow night. Plus, it's mean of you not to have rung her back and you are being very rude. In fact...'

I lunge, and this time successfully grab the phone. I cut her off just before she goes into a full-on rant. I knock the phone out of her hand.

'Well, that was rude.'

We both stand, swaying slightly, staring in the direction of the sofa. The phone has disappeared into the deep ravine I'd just escaped from. We are silent for a few moments and then we look at each other and start laughing. We are interrupted by the phone ringing. We pause. Then laugh harder. Michelle is faster once more as she jumps over the back of the sofa and digs into the cushions trying to find it. Her mission fails as it stops ringing.

The ringing starts again. Michelle shoves her hand down again, finding it straight away this time.

'Hello,' she says, putting on a posh voice.

I've got the giggles but I'm covering my mouth to stifle them.

'Hayley? Is everything okay?'

'This is Michelle. How can I help you?'

She covers the phone as she cackles.

'Put Hayley on the phone.'

'Please hold.'

She hands me the phone. I abruptly stop giggling.

'Hello?'

'What the hell was that about?'

'What?'

'You know what! The message Michelle left.'

'Oh. That.'

'Yes that.'

'I was wondering what to wear tomorrow.'

'How should I know?'

'I mean, for our meal?'

'Oh well... I meant to message to say I'm working all weekend now. It's just so busy that...'

'So we're not going now?' I pause, straightening my spine.

'Hey, I can't help it if my job is...'

'I think that's the point. I've been looking forward to spending my birthday weekend with you.' I take a short breath and wait for her reply. I can practically see her running her fingers through her short fire engine red hair. Silence stretches out on the other end.

'Hayley? You still there?'

'Yea,' I say quietly.

'We can still go babe. I do want to, I was just saying that it's super busy at the moment.'

'I know. The problem is you're always too busy. I'd kind of hoped you'd blocked this time out for us.'

'I did. Well, I tried but then the clients wanted a rework at the last minute and...'

'And you told them you had plans.'

'Don't be like that. You know it's not that easy for me. I don't have anyone I can hand things over to.'

'I know but I hoped this would be the one time you could take a night off so we could enjoy some time together.'

'I'll get through it as quickly as I can. Shall we say 8pm?'

'Sure. So do you have a place in mind?'

There is a pause and I can hear her typing on her phone.

'Are you literally Googling it right now?' I ask.

'No... I was thinking Farmacy. Shall I book it?'

'Good luck getting a reservation this last minute.'

'I'm sure it'll be fine. I'll message you with what I get,' she says, her voice tense. Then when I don't answer straight away she adds in a smoother tone, 'is that alright?'

'Sure.'

'Great. Night babe. See you tomorrow.'

I hang up. My hands are shaking. My skin is burning. I'm just standing, holding the phone in my hand. Michelle is kneeling down by the coffee table, the bottle of wine held tightly between her knees. She appears to be channelling her irritation towards the corkscrew. This works as she pops the cork.

'Well done,' she says.

I flop back onto the sofa while she refills our glasses.

'So,' she says conspiratorially as she edges closer. 'Are you going?'

'Yea, I think so.'

'Good.' She takes a large glug of her drink. 'Well, at least you sort of know now.'

We both lean back into the sofa and quietly sip our wine.

'You still up for a shopping trip tomorrow?' Michelle says, turning to me excitedly, not even turning to look in my direction.

'Absolutely.'

Chapter Two

Michelle loved clothes shopping. For someone who spent most days in joggers, she in fact had an impressive eye for fashion. What pleased her even more than shopping for herself was dressing up others. When it came to shopping she was fast and hit with precision. Her skills were especially useful on a sunny Saturday morning like this one when Notting Hill was at its busiest.

Living within walking distance gives us the perfect selection of shops for all occasions. It also puts us in a tourist spot. As locals we know how to avoid these bits whilst still attaining our objective. We start our mission in Westbourne Grove. The boutiques here are divine. Clean, slick and tranquil.

'Miss Jordan. Lovely to see you again.'

'Thank you, Janet. Are you well?' Michelle asks the boutique owner.

'Very. How can we help you and your friend?' She smiles politely at us both.

'You're alright. I've got this.'

Janet smiles and knows Michelle well enough to understand she's not just being polite. Within minutes I'm in the changing room with an array of items to try on.

'Nope,' Michelle says to my reflection.

'You're absolutely right.'

I removed the frumpy trouser suit and am trying to wrestle it back on the hanger. Another elegant shop assistant silently appears behind me, saving me from this Mensa task.

'Thank you. I'd have been here all day.'

'There's a knack,' she kindly reassures me.

That was the last of the first batch. Janet was at the till desk compiling them into neat piles of those to buy and another to be hung back onto the sparsely arranged rails.

'Anything else?' I call over to Michelle.

'Try this.'

'I'm not sure if this is quite the look I'm going for.'

'Not for tonight. I think it will be perfect for your trip to Italy.'

I slip the dress on and step out to show her. The assistant has zipped it up before I even ask. This is why we come here.

'See.'

'You're right. It's perfect.'

'Yep. Simple, yet flattering.'

'It feels like it will keep me nice and cool too. I Googled it yesterday and it said Tuscany in May is the equivalent to our summer.'

'Raining?'

'Funny. No, hot.'

'I love these,' Michelle exclaims, joining me in the changing room.

She hands me another dress. This time it is a stunning purple patterned skater dress. She is now trying on a black jumpsuit. We stand in front of the mirrors, me twirling and her posing.

'Yes, to both,' she confirms.

The assistant takes these and a few other bits we found to the till to start packing while we get dressed.

After a couple of the other boutiques, we make our way over to Portobello Road, starting in the vintage clothes stores and working our way up to the market.

After missioning through and finding a few bits we're super happy with we decide to stop for a break. We make our way through the crowded street, Michelle makes a beeline for our target restaurant. Even though I'm only a couple of inches off her five foot eleven, my legs seem so much shorter than hers. She receives admiring glances. A group of teenagers look up from their phones as we pass. One lad leans in to say something to his mate that I can't make out. The whole group turns our way now and I smile. Michelle is oblivious to it all. I find this amusing.

'How do you not even notice?'

'Notice what babe?' she asks, holding the door open for me.

The smell of burger and chips makes my belly rumble. There's a spare table near the back, so we weave our way through the busy resturant, trying to manoeuvre our bags without disturbing people's lunches. I feel liberated to not have my work messenger bag with me. That damn laptop satchel might look cool with its worn brown leather but it likes nothing more than to cause trouble. Especially in places like this.

'I'm really enjoying myself,' I say as I pull the chair next to me out to hold my bags. Michelle does the same and we sit down with a sigh, pleased to rest for a while.

'I've been so busy being busy that I forgot how fab these shopping trips are.'

'Well, it's lucky I remembered.'

She gives me a wink and hands me a menu.

'Honestly, it's been ages since we've had a girly day out.'

'Well, you were busy being swept off your Converse clad feet by Andy's charms.'

'Absolutely,' I chuckle. 'Trying to have any kind of a relationship with Andy is harder than the demands of my job.'

'The demanding job that is sending you swanning off to Italy.'

'Yea, that one,' I laugh.

'Talking of jobs. How are plans for your Netflix proposal going?'

'It's on my list.'

I pull a face.

'Don't worry it'll be done in time. If not, I know you'll help me put it together. It's more your thing than mine. My job is to look pretty.'

'You saying I'm not pretty?'

'You will be back to, no better than, your beautiful self by the end of the day.'

'Woo hoo!'

I think I said that a little too loudly as the couple next to us gave me a disapproving look. I'm saved by the waiter appearing and blocking their view of me. He smiles and welcomes us. He then looks twice at Michelle. Before he can try and work out where he might know her from, she puts him out of his misery by placing our order.

'A Malibu and pineapple juice for my friend here, with a side of fries and your biggest burger. I'll have a vodka and coke and the all day breakfast with extra bacon please.'

'Good choices. I'll bring your drinks over momentarily and your food won't be long.'

'Now what are we going to do with you?'

She pretends to check me over.

'How do you mean?'

'You're joking right?'

'What?'

'Right, young lady. You are miserable. And although you know I allow this for a second, enough is enough. You're in need of a pick me up and although the burger and Malibu will help, we need to sort you out.'

I laugh, mainly through nerves at what she has in store for me. It really could be anything from taking me for a full body wax to buying me a new floaty scarf. I can never tell just which direction her brain is working in. This is part of her charm - there are always surprises.

'Remind me, when do you leave for Florence?'

'Three weeks' time. But I've got to -'

She cuts me off, waving her hand dismissively and flicking her hair over her left shoulder. This is her signal, the one that tells me she is serious. I automatically move backwards to lean as far away from her as I can muster in this cramped space. I shift awkwardly in my seat and am relieved as the waiter returns with our drinks.

'Thank you,' we chorus.

Michelle is not so easily distracted.

'Okay, so three weeks.'

She mulls this over as she sips from her glass. I take a gulp of mine, nearly choking it back out again. She's making me edgy, which has made my throat tighten.

'For now, let's get you ready for tonight. We'll deal with the trip another day.'

'Sounds like a plan.'

'I'm gonna miss you,' she says, pouting.

'I'm only away for a few days. It's not like I'm moving there. You'll be fine.'

'Will I though? I feel I'd die without you,' she says in a fake American accent.

There are theatrical arm gestures to show the depth of her despair, gaining us more disapproving glances from the couple next to us, Michelle doesn't seem to notice which I find all the funnier.

Our food arrives, interrupting Michelle's dramatics. Instead she smiles charmingly at our waiter. I wink. She's still smirking as she pulls out her pink, diamante covered phone and starts scrolling. I try to crane over and see what she's looking at, but she tilts it away. She is expertly typing between mouthfuls. I, however, am only managing to get sauce everywhere.

Michelle hands me her unused napkin without removing her eyes from her phone. I normally find it rude if people are on their phones all the time, especially when eating. Yet, with Michelle I let it go. It gives me the chance to catch up on some work emails. I take my phone from my bag once I've finished wrestling with the burger and am just picking at the salad.

Michelle is rarely off her phone. She's quite internet famous. She's got a couple of million followers on YouTube. She'd struggled to hold down jobs back in her early years and had become part of a troublesome crowd. Her Mum had stepped in and had the talk of 'sort it out or else'. At that time, she'd found gaming to be a good distraction. She found herself to be surprisingly good at it and had jumped on the YouTube trend and started a channel doing gaming walkthroughs. As much as her Mum was unsure this was a viable pastime, she was relieved that Michelle was not out at all hours dabbling in god only knew what.

As a female, she quickly built up a following and sponsorship followed not long after. Although she didn't have a fancy set-up in the beginning, her and her Mum used their creative flair and enthusiasm to make-up for it. Before long, she had the dream set-up. Companies wanted her to be using their products and promoting them to the growing community of female gamers. Michelle broke the mould and has made a lot of money doing so. I find it awesome to actually know someone who has done this in real life. Apparently, her Mum now considers it a bona fide career.

'What?' Michelle looks up at me.

'Nothing. Now what have you got in store for me?'

I dip a fork full of lettuce in the sauce.

'There's a place round the corner that we're booked in to in half an hour.'

'Well, I guess with only a few hours until I'm meant to be meeting Andy, I can do nothing but trust you.' I smirk.

I settle the bill while she nips to the toilet. I might not be anywhere close to as wealthy as her, but I like to pay my way.

'Ow,' Michelle exclaims as we are fast-pacing it towards the hairdressers with all our bags.

'What's up?'

'Stitch!' She grabs her side. 'I haven't had one of these in years. No, that's not true - we took that stroll in Richmond Park and I got one then too.'

I smile at the memory as I link my arm through hers and assist my lovely friend.

'Here we are,' announces Michelle as she opens the door.

'Aw fancy!' I say as I follow her.

'Good afternoon, ladies. Appointments for Hayley and Michelle?' says the immaculately attired receptionist with a welcoming smile.

'That's right,' confirms Michelle.

I scan the hair salon for a sneaky tattoo chair. All clear so far as I can see.

'Please come this way. You can pop your bags here if you'd like.'

'See you on the other side,' says Michelle, as she's led to a chair by the window.

My stylist, Chelsea, is friendly and bubbly, instantly putting me at ease. So much so that as she massaged the shampoo and conditioner through my hair, I found myself having to stifle a contented yawn. Once seated in front of the mirror I try not to scrutinise myself under the bright lighting. No-one looks good at this stage.

'So what are we going to do for you today?'

She runs her fingers through my brown hair, squeezing the ends with the towel around my shoulders, as she waits for my reply.

'I'm happy with the length. I think it just needs some shape.'

'Would you like layers through it, to take some of the weight out? And some feathering around your face? That'll be flattering.'

'Sounds perfect.'

'Let's get started, shall we? Would you like a drink?'

'Coffee would be great. Milk and two sugars please.'

The receptionist is on hand and nips off to make it for me. Chelsea and I easily drop into conversation and it soon turns to the subject of what I do for a living.

'Wow, you get to go to Florence?'

'Yes. I'm very lucky. Sometimes it really doesn't feel like work.'

'I bet. I love Florence. My fiancé proposed to me there. So romantic.' She smiles.

'It really is beautiful. Unfortunately I have yet to see much of it. Last time I was based just outside Florence, so I only saw the train station. However, as I'll be more central this time I'm planning to get a good look around.'

'I hope you do. If not, maybe you and your partner could go another time.'

I follow the direction of her head nod. I realise she is gesturing towards Michelle. I smile at her and say nothing. It was a very fleeting moment of passion for each other when Michelle and I first met. However, we soon decided we were better as just the closest of friends. We often joked about how we'd have nothing to moan about if we were still each other's partners, thus spoiling our Friday night bitch sessions. Ironically, Andy wasn't even my first thought when Chelsea said partner. I quickly correct her, probably more to ease my conscience.

I was occupied Googling my client's website so I could show Chelsea the Hotel I'm planning the event for in Italy when I hear a shrill voice cut across the salon. I look up from my phone and see Debbie waddling towards me.

'I'm in desperate need of getting my roots done,' she tells me before I ask, running her hand down her blond bob. 'I didn't know you came here.'

She looks almost put out to see that I'm in 'her' hairdressers, yet for the benefit of the people around us, she's acting as though we are the best of friends.

'Yes, spur of the moment.'

She shuffles slightly as though I've ruffled her feathers.

'Really?'

'I have mine booked months in advance. They're so popular it's hard to get in otherwise.' She leans nearer with her hand shielding her mouth so no-one can see what she's saying. 'Especially closer to Christmas.'

'I'll try to remember that.'

'Do.' She winks conspiratorially and stands proud, pleased that she knows something I obviously didn't.

'Debbie, would you like to come over?' calls across a more mature stylist with a similar bob in a shimmery grey.

She shuffles away. Chelsea raises an eyebrow as she catches my eye in the mirror.

'We work together,' I responded to her silent question.

I purse my lips. That was the politest way I could answer the question to someone who also seemed to see her regularly. Neither of us elaborated. Instead we returned to our conversation.

'Here you go - this is Hotel al Cioccolato.'

I hold my phone so she can see as I scroll through their gallery.

'That's beautiful.'

'The photos don't do it justice to be honest. We're arranging a Summer Ball for them to launch their new chocolate factory that they've moved into one of the renovated barns.'

'That sounds more idyllic by the second. I'm not gonna lie, I'm jealous. How do I get a job at your place?' she whispers.

'I'll keep you in mind,' I mouthed.

'Did you say you're actually staying in Florence?' she enquired. When I nod, she continues, 'If you get a chance while you're there you should visit Ponte Vecchio.'

'Is that the bridge?'

'Yeah, it has all the jewellery shops on it. I think you'd love it.'

'I'll have to add that to my list.'

'No worries. I really do hope you get a chance to explore this time. I'd love to go again.'

I smiled at Chelsea in the mirror. Her liveliness was infectious and with the relaxed atmosphere in here, I'm feeling blissful. Michelle had, as always, done the right thing in booking us in here. I glance over to where she and her stylist are chatting away animatedly.

Chelsea effortlessly teased my hair into big chunky ringlets.

'Ta da!' she exclaimed, as she held up a mirror so I could see the full effect.

'Thank you so much. It looks fabulous.'

'It really suits you.'

Michelle bounces across to me.

'Sweetheart, you look superb. Yay!'

'As do you, my lovely!'

Her stylist has created a wonderfully flattering updo for her. We are both grinning from ear to ear. We hug and giggle, chuffed to bits with our glamorous new looks. Both our stylists and the receptionist are beaming at how excited we are. We detach from each other and as I turn to go and pay, I spot Debbie giving us a reproachful look. It's of no surprise to me. This is a standard expression for her. I simply wave goodbye to her. She forces a smile and vaguely lifts her hand from under her cape. Seizing the opportunity of my momentary pause, Michelle dashes to the till.

'Birthday treat.'

I can't argue that and she knows it. The receptionist laughs at our escapades and hands us our bags.

'Thanks. Bye,' we call over our shoulders.

'You're very welcome. Have fun in Italy.'

'I certainly will try.'

'BYE see you Monday,' hollers Debbie from the back of the salon.

I wave a quick farewell to her. Michelle holds open the door while I get through with all the bags.

Chapter Three

'I'm so pleased to be home.'

I open the door to my flat, dropping the bags and removing my Converse in the small hallway. Michelle kicks off her high tops and places her bags next to mine.

'Me too,' she says.

I love my flat. It's one floor of a converted Victorian town house. The selling point of this flat for me had been firstly the fireplace in the lounge. It reminded me of my grandparents. It was the epitome of home. Hours can disappear while I stare into the glowing coals. This is magical to me as I find it hard to switch off, especially from work. Although Michelle is here most of the time, she actually lives in the apartment above. Our landlady, the lovely Mrs Temple, and her cat Tiddles live below. The other resident is Joe, on the top floor. He's recently divorced and works in finance. He has a couple of grown-up children who live with their Mum in Kensington.

I love my job. I'm confident in the service I provide for our events. I'm highly commended for my precision in executing the plans. However, I get obsessed. No one other than Michelle really sees the part of me where I'm up until all hours going through the finer details. I trawl through websites until I find what I believe to be the perfect table setting. It is both a blessing and a curse to be so invested in my job. I am trying to master the art of taking time to relax. To be able to just allow myself a moment to do nothing is something I have started to implement. Even in summer I will aim to light a few logs in the grate.

'Right, before we settle down and have coffee, I'm gonna go upstairs and jump in the shower,' says Michelle. 'Meet you back here in a bit.'

'Yep, good idea. I'll go do the same.'

I grab my dressing gown from my bedroom as she heads towards the door. She gathers her bags ready to leave, but stops and turns.

'I'll leave this one here. No peeking.'

'Guides honour.' I salute.

My next favourite room when I viewed my flat was the bathroom. It has a roll top bath with a shower over. After a long week at work it is my salvation. I've created my own spa here with my collection of pillar candles, bath salts and bubble baths. The thing that gets me through stressful days is the thought of coming home to soak. It's the place where I do my best brainstorming.

I've tied my hair up loosely so as not to ruin the style set out by Chelsea and have lowered the shower head over the bath so it only hits my body. This shower feels amazing and is helping me to wash off the day's antics. That's kind of metaphorically how baths and showers make me feel; as though they are washing away the shitty feelings I seem to take on from the outside world. Michelle and I have spoken about this often, that weird feeling when you know that these emotions and reactions are not yours. Michelle just says that's why she tries to avoid people, especially mardy ones.

I exit the bathroom wrapped in my dressing gown just as Michelle comes back through the front door the same way, making me jump. I'd momentarily forgotten I'd popped the door on the latch in case she was back before I was out of the shower.

'Lord, calm down. It's only me,' she giggles.

'I know. I was miles away.'

'Right, we have a date to get you ready for,' she says as she takes the bottle of wine through to the kitchen to open. She passes me a glass. I take a mouthful of the wine and smile.

'Perfect. Thanks.'

I sit on the edge of the sofa, adjusting my dressing gown so I don't get a draft.

'Are you going to show me what's in the secret bag?'

'Absolutely!'

She places her drink on the coffee table and skips over to the bag tucked behind mine. She's smiling widely as she lifts up the bag and hands it to me. I put my glass on the other coaster and take the bag from her, smiling quizzically. I gasp as she lifts the most stunning dress from the bag. I jump up, and grab my towel tight in one swift move. I run my hand down the dress, the fabric feels delicious.

'How did you -' I didn't finish my sentence, my throat contracted with emotion.

'I knew you loved it when you tried it on.'

'But I put it in the pile not to buy.'

Once I'd clocked the price tag. I love to buy beautiful clothes and don't mind paying good money for them. This dress, however, was far more than I was willing to pay.

'Yes, you did.'

She sips her wine. I look up from the dress to her.

'You deserve it. It's your birthday.'

She grins from ear to ear.

I imagine it against my skin and the thought sparks anticipation in me. Far more than I'd previously had for the idea of spending the evening with Andy. Michelle hands me the hanger so I can hold it up against me. I swish it around. It's perfect. The deep purple makes it feel regal. I dash it to the bedroom to try it on. The excitement is electric. I don't remember ever feeling like this about a piece of clothing. I can almost imagine how people feel when they find the perfect wedding dress.

I lay the dress carefully on the bed as though it might break. I put on my favourite underwear, the ones that make me feel extra sexy. I step into the dress and pull it up over my shoulders. I shiver as the fabric brushes my skin. This is a dress to go out-out. This dress deserves to be seen, with me in it. It is my right to ensure it has a bloody good time. I zip it up as far as I can and survey myself in the wardrobe mirror.

I feel ridiculously giddy. I look like a new me. A happier, sexier version of myself. I release my hair and sigh as it topples over my shoulders. The me reflected back right now is the person I was meant to be. This is me. I smile broadly as I twirl and twist, trying to see myself from every possible angle.

'It fits me like a glove and the length is perfect,' I call through to Michelle, 'and my boobs look incredible.'

Michelle appears in the doorway, a matching pair of shoes in one hand, a clutch bag in the other. She stops in her tracks and just stares, mouth agape.

'I must look good. Michelle is speechless,' I narrated while giggling.

She silently, her mouth still open, hands me the shoes and bag. It's her turn to run her fingers over the dress. I find it mildly erotic to have the dress fabric being pressed against me as she moves her hands across it. I'm reminded of the way I felt when we first became friends. I break the moment by sitting back onto the bed and slip my feet into the purple platform shoes.

'What do you think?'

'What do I think? You know what I think. You look incredible, stunning, gorgeous.'

'Is that all,' I giggle.

'Don't be a div. You look divine! Almost edible.' She winks.

'Seriously though - thank you so much.'

I hug her close.

'Hey, I don't want to crease it.'

She pulls back from me but I know the real reason why. I felt it too, the electricity that sparks every once in a while. The thing we promised each other we'd ignore.

She claps her hands together in excitement. She has such an energy about her when she's this enthusiastic. I love seeing her like this; at other times she has a tendency to drop into deep, dark moods that can linger. Especially if she's left to her own devices for too long. Thankfully it has been a while since she's had one of her 'episodes'. She's been busy working and moments like this help keep it at bay. I'm happy to be part of her distractions and appreciate her keeping me buoyed up too. I smile widely and kiss her on the cheek.

Chapter Four

I'm already seated at our table as I see Andy enter Farmacy. I've been here only long enough to have a bottle of wine brought over. I take a sip from my glass as I watch her swish sway through the tables. Our eyes meet as she nears me and I can't help but match her smile. It was her smile that first caught my attention, the way it lit up her whole face. I was there overseeing the event for the company she worked for. Each person who greeted her automatically smiled. I was mesmerised as I stood to the side of the room ensuring everything was running like clockwork.

Later that evening she had approached me at the bar, dropping straight into conversation with me as though we were old friends. She had leaned against the bar next to me, run her slender fingers through her red hair, which magically fell straight back into place. Then when she'd locked eyes with me I caught my breath. She was even more stunning up close. In that non-assuming, confident way. We spoke for a few moments and then the bartender had arrived to take her order and I'd been swept towards the CEO by my boss, Bob, something to do with the lighting being the wrong shade of purple. I'd kept looking out for her throughout the night but it was a packed event and she was nowhere to be seen.

It was as we were leaving that I bumped into her again, literally. We'd apologised and she'd asked if I was leaving already. I'd looked at Bob who had winked at me and stepped away to look as though she was doing something important on his phone. She and I exchanged names and numbers and I was smitten from that moment on. And still now, all these months later, after all the ups and downs, she still has that same effect on me. I believe I do love her, I'm just not sure we love each other enough to work through our issues. I push the thought from my mind as I stand to hug her and give her a quick kiss.

'I love your hair like that,' she says, beaming.

'Thanks,' I say and pat my hair slightly, 'Michelle took me to this fabulous place...'

I trail off as Andy pulls a face. I want to say something but I don't want to spoil the night before it's started. We've finally got an evening together away from our work commitments. I fiddle with my glass and try to look interested in the menu. She takes a deep breath and plasters her smile back on.

'Everything here looks so good,' she says.

'It really does. It's so hard to know what to choose.'

By the time the waiter comes to take our order we have decided to go for two dishes which we can both share.

'Happy birthday, sweetheart,' she says as she produces a small gift bag.

'Thank you so much,' I say with genuine glee.

I love receiving presents. It is all I can do to stop myself clapping my hands together like a seal. I dig into the bag and pull out the small jewellery box inside. Excitement swells and I look up at her. She has her elbows on the table and is resting her chin on her steepled hands, smiling in expectation of my reaction. My hands are shaking slightly as I untie the box and lift the hinged lid. I gasp as the stones glint from the light of the candle between us. She reaches her hand across and takes my hand in hers.

'I love you.'

'I love you too,' I say, my voice almost a whisper.

'What do you think? Will you marry me?'

I look from her to the ring, my cheeks burning, my mind whirling with a thousand different thoughts. She squeezes my hand to bring me back into the moment. As I look into her eyes she's expecting an answer. The right answer to such a gesture. I have to say something. But there is something stopping me, holding me back. It has not been an easy relationship so far and I'm not sure either one of us are ready for this. But sitting here in the dimmed light of this fancy restaurant, it would be all too easy to forget those other things and say that one word. But I can't because it's stuck in my throat. I let go of her hand and grasp for my drink, sipping it as a distraction tactic.

She moves her hand away too and fiddles with her napkin. Her eyes lowered, her lips pouting. I want to say the right thing so she is happy again, so that smile I love shines again, but it would be wrong of me at this point. Not so long ago this moment would have been a dream come true. My heart feels heavy. I want so much for things to return to those first few months, the ones where we couldn't see enough of each other. When we exchanged constant messages back and forward. When we didn't care if we arrived at our desks in last night's clothes and having had all of two hours sleep if we were lucky. Back to when I'd think of her and my belly would ripple with memories of our time together. My cheeks burn even at the thought now but my insides are churning with anxiety rather than exhilaration.

The waiter arrives with our meals and I move the box to the side to make room. He glances at it and then at me and I assume from doing this job long enough he knows to not pass comment. Instead he gives me a half smile and says he hopes we enjoy our meals. I'm not sure we will now. I feel I have spoiled the evening. Yet I feel that in saying yes I would spoil much more than that.

The conversation is non-existent and we don't end up sharing our food. Andy is pissed off, and probably with good reason. Obviously we are both in different mindsets about where we are at in our relationship. It is for me to break the ice.

'I'm sorry,' I say. She looks up at me from under her eyelashes. 'I just don't think I can accept your offer at this time.'

She sits up now. I brace myself. I can feel her blood starting to boil from across the table. She has a fierce temper when she blows and I'm willing with all my might that she holds it under wraps until after we have left. Yet with all the will in the world I don't have that power.

'I thought that was what you wanted. Commitment.'

'But we don't need to be married for that.'

'Fuck's sake, Hayley. Make up your mind,' she says, rolling her eyes.

'You can't just throw this at me out of the blue and expect me to say yes.' My voice is shaky.

'Even a maybe would have been something. Instead you turn me down as though it was a business offer that isn't worth your investment.'

'Don't be like that. You know that's not how I meant it.'

'Do I?' she asks, looking straight into my eyes. I can see hers are brimming with tears and I swallow the lump rising in my throat.

'Would you rather I just said yes and we regret it later?'

'Why would we regret it later?'

'Because we hardly see each other and when we do it's...' I pause to choose my words carefully and to lower my voice, 'difficult.'

'Difficult!' I obviously didn't choose the right word as her voice went up a good couple of octaves. 'Difficult? You know what's difficult, Hayley?' I don't like hearing my name when she says it in that tone. It sounds more like an insult. 'What's difficult is you spending so much time with Michelle!'

'Hey! Don't bring her into this. She has nothing to do with it.'

'Really?' she asks, sitting back and crossing her arms.

'Yes. Michelle and I were over long before we met.'

'So you say, but you live as though you're a couple, doing everything together.'

'We're friends!' I say, throwing my hands up in exasperation. 'That's what friends do.'

Not convinced, she takes a breath. Not a calming one. The kind that is her refilling her lungs ready for the next verbal attack. I top up my glass from the bottle they left for us. I refuse to deal with this sober.

'So what is it then?' she demands.

'It's not just one thing. It's many little things.'

'Is it the man thing again?'

'The man thing?'

'The fact that you like men too. Am I not enough for you?'

I feel stung and my own anger begins to rise.

'Being bi doesn't mean that I can't be fulfilled by one or the other. What a stupid thing to say.'

'Then what?'

I take a deep breath and rub my hand over my face, forgetting momentarily that I have full make-up on. Although at this point who cares. This evening is now ruined.

'I just wonder if we are trying too hard to make this work,' I say in a low voice. 'Perhaps we should take a bit of a break.'

At that point she snatches the bag and box from the table, snapping the box shut sharply. The action makes me jump and the people who weren't already looking at us turn as the sound breaks through the relaxed atmosphere. My cheeks are burning and I take another mouthful of my wine, keeping hold of my glass like a life raft. It was a good move, as moments later she pushes out her chair, knocking the table as she does so. I steady her glass before it lands on my plate and by the time I look up to say something she is already marching with purpose towards the exit.

I lower my head and just as I'm about to get my phone out to message Michelle the waiter arrives at the table. I force myself to look up at him as he places down a birthday cake with one single lit candle on it. I clock the other waiters making their way over but he shoos them away and

I'm exceedingly grateful that I'm not going to be subjected to a chorus of 'happy birthday'. He smiles apologetically.

'Make a wish,' he says with a weak smile.

I close my eyes, wish with all my might to be far away in Florence, and blow out the candle.

Chapter Five

It turns out that last night's wine did not like me as much as I liked it. It could also be the fact that it was mixed with the earlier drinks of the day. However, it turned out that my bathroom floor is far more comfortable than I would have imagined. It was not so much fun seeing the regurgitated wine and meal swirl before my eyes as they disappeared into the toilet bowl and the pain in my head this morning is harsh. This feeling very much takes me back to my uni days. My feet seem to have stopped throbbing and just ache. I crawl over to the bath and put the plug in ready for a wonderfully soothing bubble bath. The noise of the water in this echoey room is splitting through my head. I head off to find coffee and aspirin while it runs.

My mission is interrupted by the sound of my phone ringing. I have no idea where it is. I can hear it so it can't be far away, but every time I think I'm going in the right direction it sounds further away. I have no idea where the clutch bag is that I can only assume is housing my phone. Before I can locate it, the ringing stops.

I swear and nip to stop my bath running so I can concentrate on finding my phone. The last thing I need is it overflowing. Thankfully the caller is insistent. Well, I'm not thankful because it's hurting my head but I'm grateful that I finally found it outside my flat door. I can only assume that I dropped my bag while locating my keys. Who knows? Right now I also no longer care as the missed calls are from Andy. All four of them. I shut the door and slide down to sit on the floor. My purple dress no longer feels wonderful against my clammy skin. I want to cry and scream and throw my phone at the wall, but for one I don't want to break it and with my throwing skills it would probably bounce back and smack me in the face.

As I sit staring at the phone a message notification bings loudly, making me jump. All I can do is stare at it. I don't want to know what Andy has to say to me. The rest of last night was a blur. I start to giggle as I remember the kind waiter bringing me my cake and another bottle of wine on the house. I laugh harder as I imagine what a state I must have looked as I worked my way through the cake and wine. Before I know it the laughter has turned to tears. I curl up on the floor and cry. The tears shake my whole body with the force and my head aching even more than before.

It's silly. I know it's silly. Andy, as it turned out, wanted to marry me. That had been the last thing I'd expected. Yet I can't help feeling a sense of loss, regret, and foolishness at having turned down the offer. But I know that it was the right thing to do. We were nowhere close to that point - well, I didn't believe we were. Did she only propose because she felt it was the only way to save our relationship or did she truly love me that much? My mind races through all the other issues we had come up against; how hard it was to find time to see each other and how awkward it was when we did was just the tip of the iceberg. She'd caught me off guard straightaway with her greeting me with a kiss. I don't think she's ever allowed that in the whole time we have been together. She's not one to show affection in public, including brief kisses and holding hands. I, on the other hand, struggled to flip the switch from friends to lovers on a whim upon returning home so most nights together ended in arguments instead of cuddles on the sofa or sex.

Plus, I know that she would never have joined me on my travels. I'd invited her to come to Florence this time, I had thought it would be fantastic, romantic, and idyllic to be there together. But, as ever, she had claimed to be too busy to come, even though she can work from anywhere as long as she has WiFi which Italy has - especially in the city. It has been hard enough to get her to leave the district for even a weekend away, let alone any further afield. I'm not sure it was ever gonna work between us. I yearn to travel and spend time in new places, especially Florence. Andy seemed satisfied to stay in London. I really wanted to share Italy, a place that I love, with the person I love, but she was having none of it.

The crying escalates into heaving sobs and I grab a tissue from my work bag next to me. I surprise myself with the intensity of my woes. I don't believe it was because she was more invested in the relationship than me. I was invested but I struggled. Possibly with being capable of loving in return. Openly, honestly. Not forced as it is often felt but the kind of love that grows organically over time. Not dwindling out after the first few months of lust have passed.

Who am I kidding? I've only personally experienced glimpses of this kind of love, and then I blinked to find myself here on the morning of my birthday, not just loveless but literally on the floor in last night's clothes. This dress, last night's escapades, was all supposed to be my rising from the embers like a phoenix. Instead I'm extinguishing my own flame with my tears.

I'm not doubting the fact that suggesting we take a bit of a break was the right thing to do, but I regret the time and energy I wasted trying to make it work. I was clearly trying to make it into something with a person who had a very different idea of what a relationship was. Or what kind of relationship I wanted. I wanted love. True love. The kind they write sonnets about, make movies about, sing about. The kind that has yet to exist in any other form for me than those - created from the reality or imagination of others. A huge sob escapes me once more as my dream shatters around me on the floor of a rented flat in Notting Hill.

I sink down deeper into the carpet and close my puffy eyes. My clumpy mascara lashes feel too heavy to hold up any longer. Darkness falls behind my watery lids and I carry on crying silently letting the carpet soak up my despair. Fuck this. Fuck this bullshit crap. I'm worth more than this. More than this self-inflicted guilt-trip. I sit up sharply, open my eyes wide and use the doorframe to haul me up. As I do, I have to grab it to balance as my head splits with the hangover that was holding back to knock the last of my strength. No. I close my eyes for a second until I feel steady.

I slowly, with the guidance of the back of the sofa, the wall, the kitchen side, make it to the coffee machine. Salvation right here in the little pod I slot in and the Anadin kept in the cupboard above. I half fill the cup with water, take the tablets and put the cup back under to catch the golden nectar.

I slide down and lean against the kitchen cupboard with my knees up, cup cradled against them. I take my first sip just as I hear what sounded like a scream. Not in the distance, from the house next door or the street, but from in this building. I listen hard, holding my breath. As it comes again I realise it's from the floor below. Mrs Temple! I jump up, way too fast. I have to pause for a second to stop the spinning again. I sprint out of my flat, down the stairs and stop to listen at her door. My heart is racing. I can't hear anything. I knock, my worry intensifying. I pray that she answers. I listen intently. I knock again, slightly louder. I can hear movement this time. I breathe again now and stand back slightly.

'Morning, dear,' she says as she opens the door.

'Morning, Mrs Temple. Is everything okay?'

She looks at me curiously.

'I thought I heard a scream.'

'Oh that,' she chuckles. 'I'm so sorry. I tripped over Tiddles.'

'But you're not hurt?'

'Not at all. Tiddles ran out from under the table as I was passing and then again as I passed the sofa.'

I clutch my chest, relieved.

'She's not normally that energetic.'

'I know. That's why it shocked me so much. It's these,' she points to her feet. My granddaughter thought they were perfect for keeping my feet warm. I do feel the cold these days.'

I look down to see she's wearing big Nordic patterned slipper boots. She wiggles a foot and I see what all the excitement was about. Each boot has two pom poms hanging from them.

'See?' she chuckles. 'I really should cut them off but they are such fun.'

'Not if Tiddles trips you up again.'

She brushes away my comment with a wave of her hand. She seems to see me properly at this point and her smile fades to a look of concern.

'Would you like a cup of tea while you're here?'

I look around as if searching for the answer, before shrugging.

'Sure. Tea would be lovely.'

She moves aside to let me in and it is not until my feet reach her kitchen floor that I remember I'm barefoot. I ran out of the flat so fast I didn't think about shoes. I shiver as the chill from the floor runs through me. Mrs Temple pulls out a chair at her kitchen table and wraps the cardigan that was hanging on the back of it around my shoulders. She's the epitome of a kind grandmother. I sit and pull the cardigan closer across my chest.

'Thank you.'

She doesn't hear me as she's filling the kettle. The kitchen worktop has an array of ingredients out and I wonder if she's already made it to the shop and back this morning. My attention is brought back to her as she pulls up the chair opposite me, places her hands on the tabletop.

'Happy birthday, by the way.'

I smile weakly in response.

'I don't mean to be rude, dear, but you look a little bedraggled. Was it a messy night for you?'

I nod.

'I'm sorry to hear that. Although that's a very pretty dress.'

She touches me on the arm reassuringly and I feel the tears start to well up again. I swallow them back down as best I can. She rubs my arm, passes me a box of tissues, before standing up to go and pour the hot water into the teapot. Mrs Temple is always happily pottering about. In the years I've lived here I don't remember ever hearing her complain about anything - or anyone, come to that. She is a truly good person through and through. She places the tray on the red Formica table as I move the tissue box to one side.

'Would you like to talk about it?'

By way of an answer, I simply pull a pained face. She places the cups on the saucers. They're so delicate looking and just watching the process calms me. I can see why this is an English remedy for solving pretty much everything. She lifts the lid, the steam escaping, and stirs the water, the tea bags bobbing around as she does so. She puts the lid back on with a satisfying clonk.

'It'll be ready in just a moment. Would you like me to show you my latest achievement?'

'Very much so.'

Mrs Temple pushes on the back of the chair to assist her standing up. I rarely see her in her home. We are normally chatting in the hallway or at the front door. I never consider her to be elderly. She has such vibrance but here in her home I notice the little things she needs to do that help her manage. She makes no show of them - no huffing, puffing or wincing - just an odd hand on furniture to balance herself. We make our way out towards the back garden. It's not a big space, but for a house in London it's ample. Tiddles opens one eye to see who is disturbing her sunbathing. She doesn't move, likely too tired from her antics.

When I first came to view the apartment Mrs Temple explained how her late husband, Barry, and her had bought it when they first got married. She chuckled at the fact that a month's rent now would have paid for the whole house back then. After her husband had retired and their children had grown and flown the nest, they had considered moving to somewhere quieter; perhaps Devon, she had said. Yet the more they looked around and bounced their retirement plans about, they were less keen on the idea of selling this place. She recalled how they had sat at the Formica table over tea one day and, whilst dunking their rich tea biscuits, they stumbled over a better suited idea.

Barry had heard about how similar houses in the area were being split into flats. The idea was upsetting at first to Mrs Temple as she hated the thought that their beautiful family home would be ripped apart and instead of her children pottering from room to room it would be full of strangers. Yet the more they talked it through, and went to look at a couple to get an idea of how it worked, it started to seem quite exciting. Her face had beamed as she recollected the memory. The final decision was made when Barry had experienced a harsh flu that winter and it had become clear that they were most certainly getting older and he expressed his concern while he was in the middle of high fever. With tears spiking her eyes she told me how he worried that if he were to die she would be left with this huge old house to handle by herself. She said that although it had upset her at first, the realisation was there on both parts. Either one of them could be left without the other, next to no income and a big old house to rattle around in.

However, they had run the place as apartments for ten years after he recovered from the flu that year. The past five by herself after his move to Devon. It had been an amicable split. He wanted to go, she wanted to stay. He's now remarried. I have to admit that it was the combination of the fireplace, fabulous bathtub and her wonderful tale that had led to me accepting the place right then. Mrs Temple was such a caring lady and I felt connected to her and viewed her as a friend from that day forward. I'd never known anyone in my life who smiled so genuinely each time I saw them. She had a happy soul and looking after us all gave her purpose. I was forever grateful to her for deciding not to move to Devon. I had needed her as much as she had needed a paying tenant. Having Michelle as my neighbour had been a huge bonus. I was lucky to have found this place.

We made our way round the side of the house and out into the back garden. It was like an oasis right in the middle of the city.

'You really do have a gift, Mrs Temple.'

She smiled proudly, a slight glow of embarrassment to her cheeks.

'Thank you, dear. I do enjoy being out here.'

'I love sitting up at my window and staring down at the garden. It makes me so happy.'

'I'm so pleased it is enjoyed by you too.'

'Very much so, and I consider this tree my thinking tree,' I say as I run my hand along a low branch of newly budding cherry blossom.

'We planted this many years ago. It has thrived. My daughter bought it for us for our 30th wedding anniversary.'

I looked back at the tree and allowed her a moment with her thoughts. Being out here in the sun was making my eyes sting again. I turned to investigate the flower beds instead.

Mrs Temple nipped over to her potting shed and came back with a pot of compost.

'Would you please hold this for a moment?'

'Of course.'

From her apron pocket she pulls a pair of secateurs and takes a cutting from the branch I'd been stroking. She disappears back into the shed with it and returns holding it proudly, the base covered in white powder. I hold out the pot and she pokes her finger to make a hole in the middle of the compost and tucks the cutting in neatly.

'Rooting powder,' she clarifies as I look at it curiously. 'There you go. Let me get you a tray to sit it in.'

'Now if you keep this on your windowsill, it can learn from the big tree how to grow.'

Something in her words makes me feel emotional again. I feel as though that is like me learning from her.

'It just needs light and water and the odd chat if you feel the need to talk.'

At this a tear escapes and I wipe it away with my upper arm, not wanting to drop my little tree. I clear my throat.

'Thank you so much.'

'Think of it as a little birthday present.'

'I'm not the best with plants but I'll try.'

I place the plant next to me on the table as we have our tea. Mrs Temple doesn't push me as to why I was so upset. The gifting of the plant is her way of cheering me up and I consider it my talking tree. I remember a friend of mine telling me of worry dolls that she had. This poor tree might not thrive so well if I burden it with my current state of mind. Then again, Mrs Temple had told me that these are hardy trees. I feel a bit apprehensive about the responsibility of keeping this tree alive.

Mrs Temple offers me another cup of tea, breaking me out of my thoughts.

'Oh no, thank you. I'd best be off.'

I take off the cardigan, hanging it on the back of the chair as I tuck it in. As I go to reach for my cup and saucer to place them in the washing up, she stops me.

'Please, don't worry. It gives me something to do.'

She smiles kindly. Picking up the pot I thank her again and I head back to my flat. Thankfully the door hadn't closed behind me. I place the pot on my windowsill so it can see its mother tree. I smile at them sitting there and get my phone from where I'd left it on the floor so I can document the growth. I manage to get what I consider an arty image of my little cutting with the big tree behind it through the window. This gift has made me happier than Mrs Temple could have imagined.

I cherish the warm fuzzy feeling it's given me as I head to finally get in the bath.

Chapter Six

Wrapped in my cosy dressing gown, I curl up on the sofa, fresh drink in hand and a blanket over my chilly feet. The flames are finally taking to the fresh logs in the fireplace. I pull my cold damp hair out from my collar. I'm in a better head space now. I take a deep breath and wiggle my phone from my dressing gown pocket whilst ensuring I don't spill my drink. Open the home screen and see the many notifications waiting for me. I play safe first and open Facebook, grinning as I see Michelle has tagged me in a photo of yesterday's lunch. I pop my cup on the coaster as I go through liking all the birthday wishes on my timeline.

As much as pausing my relationship with Andy has temporarily rocked the boat, I am feeling relieved. Had last night not happened I would have possibly carried on pining for that mythical life that would 'get better when'. The illusive 'when'. Although it is not nice and I'm gutted that things turned out the way they have, I also feel as though it gives me the chance to think things through whilst I'm away. To perhaps discover how I truly feel about everything. I turn my mind to my upcoming trip to Florence. I reflect back to my conversation with Chelsea yesterday in the hairdressers. She was right. I needed to go and actually experience Florence. To go there purely on business, to see nothing but the inside of hotels, was sacrilege. I'm excited to see Hotel al Cioccolato since they have finished the renovations, but also I yearn to experience more of the city. To join the many other people from all around the world as they explore.

I gaze into my fireplace. Closing my eyes for a moment, I hear the fire crackling away, and smell my warm coffee from where it stands on the table. I drift off in my mind to the familiar daydream I've had since I was a teenager and watched 'Under the Tuscan Sun' with my Mum. The vision always starts with an image of me nestled in a home in the Tuscan Hills. The open fire warms the thick stone walls of the building that by day are heated by the sun. The smell of the fresh air from the open windows is tantalising my senses. I sigh contently as I stare out at the wondrous view. The cherry tree growing strong in the garden, the cypress and olive trees protecting it from the elements.

As I move towards the kitchen the tiles are chilly underfoot. I lift the lids from the saucepans simmering away on the aga. The tomato sauce spits at me, splattering my white top before I can replace the lid. I curse and smirk at the fact that, yet again, I'm wearing white while cooking.

This top already has faded orange marks on it from the many other times this has happened. I peek into the larger of the two saucepans, the pasta is bubbling happily. I envisage myself setting the huge scrub topped pine table, which was the perfect fit for this room. The mix match of chairs, salvaged and donated from random places. There is space for eight of us to sit around the kitchen table to enjoy the freshly prepared meals I'm learning to make. My Florence cookbook sits open on the table and I smile as I notice the corner of Fat Tony's menu poking out. I no longer consider his meatballs to be the best I've ever tasted. Now that I have tried true Italian food, there is no going back.

I imagine the way the tastes are enhanced by the air surrounding us as we eat, the company we keep, the ground we walk on. Here there is true connection to one's self and the earth. This version of myself has had her soul come alive. She 'felt' in a way I never knew was possible for me. Imaginary me experiences things rather than just going through the motions. I breathe deeply as I stand in my Tuscan kitchen, running my hand along the tabletop. It is as though I can feel the energy from the roots that grew the tree it was made from. I take the pasta bowls from the dresser. I love this dresser - I salvaged from the barn and lovingly restored it and painted a deep turquoise. This colour was purely by chance as the pot of paint was in the back of the shed. I had to strike a deal with many spiders in order to have it. In ode to the experience I painted a small spider on the bottom right side.

A breeze blows through the open Dutch door, the bottom of which is closed to stop the debris scooting across the floor. I had learned this trick early on. The footsteps behind me make me smile. I pop the bowls on the table and turn. Their presence causes a warmth to run through me like I'd never known actual life.

My phone rings and I physically jump. Wow, I was miles away.

I huff as I glance at the screen. Of course Andy would be the one to break the spell. I know we will have to talk things through at some point but I'm not ready yet. I'm sure me turning down her proposal was harsh for her but to me it would have been worse for me to simply say yes while I still have concerns. I'm upset to have been snatched from my daydream. It had felt more real and wondrous than ever before. Perhaps this is the point - mine and Andy's relationship would not have led to me living out my dreams. I feared it would instead, as it had already started to become, turn into a constant waiting game. Waiting to have time together. Her waiting for me to be ready. Me waiting for her to venture out and wish for more than her job.

I stared into the fire once more, still halfway between the present and the imaginary world I had slipped away to. I had felt so at peace, so content, so happy. It was as though every part of this world, from the trees outside the window to the table I served food on, existed in reality. I'm curious to know if there are actually people who feel this connection to themselves and the places they occupy.

Forcing myself to move from this spot, I walk slow and steady, feeling quite odd. I've just finished drying my hair when there is a knock on my door. I place the hairdryer down, retying my loosened dressing gown cord as I walk to open it. I poke my head round.

'Hello.'

'Hello to you.'

Michelle makes her way in and takes in my appearance. Her eyes scan over the cold coffee, the fire and my phone sitting abandoned on the sofa.

'You okay?'

'Yea sure. Why?'

'There was no noise from down here so I thought I'd come and check you're alive.'

'You listened for me?'

'Sure,' she says, as though laying on her floor with her ear literally to the ground is normal.

I offer her a drink whilst collecting my cold cup on my way through.

'Joe said there was drama earlier.'

'Drama?'

'Yea.' She looks at me with genuine concern. 'Are you sure you're alright?'

'Yea I just dozed off on the sofa for a minute.'

That was not good enough for Michelle.

'Joe said you were running through the house barefoot with last night's dress on.'

'How did he - I didn't even see him.'

'So you were.'

'Not in the way it sounds. Mrs Temple screamed so I was checking on her.'

'See - you were listening in on your downstairs neighbour too,' she jests. 'Sorry. Seriously though, was she okay?'

'She was fine Tiddles was chasing her around the flat cos of the pom poms on her slipper boots.'

'Oh, bless her,' she says, disappearing into the kitchen. 'Anyway, happy birthday,' she calls through.

'Did you not wish me a happy birthday enough times yesterday?'

'Not even close. Your birthday treat will be arriving soon. But before that tell me, how did it go with Andy? Your text last night was quite cryptic.'

'Not so well,' I say as I scoop up my cold coffee cup ready for a refill. 'She proposed.'

'She what?'

I wait a beat.

'She WHAT?' Michelle yells as she thrusts her head back through the doorway.

'Yep.'

'She didn't!'

'She did.'

'Well, shit.' She runs her hand through her hair, the coffee forgotten. 'You didn't say yes, did you?' she demands, striding forward and grabbing my hand in search of a tell-tale glint of jewellery.

'Of course not!' She drops my hand, relieved. 'I said I thought it would be better if we took a break to both think things through - or something along those lines. Either way, she stormed out and I've been avoiding her calls ever since.'

'Shit,' she says again.

'Yep.'

'So what did you do after she stormed out?'

'I stayed and ate my birthday cake and washed it down with the bottle of wine they gave me.' I can't help but grin slightly.

'Good girl!'

She hugs me and takes the cup out of my hand.

'I'm going to finish getting dressed.'

'You don't have to.'

She winks at me before returning to the kitchen to finish making the coffees.

I snigger and carry on through to my room to change. I throw on jeans and a hoodie. I find that covers most possible scenarios. After all Michelle's not dressed up.

She's in one of her signature tracksuits, today her arse reads 'bite me'.

The buzzer rings before I have time to sit back down. Michelle turns excitedly to watch over the back of the sofa as I go to the door. I'm watching her suspiciously as I do so and the person simply says it's a delivery through the crackles. I wonder if tattooists do home visits?

'Just buzz them in,' she says impatiently.

I do as I'm told and stand by the door ready. The knock still makes me jump and I open the door warily.

'If it's a tattoo artist, I'm not letting them in.'

'Surprise!'

There in the hallway is Mario, the delivery boy from Fat Tony's, holding up two heavy bags. Joe is on one side of him and Mrs Temple on the other.

'You guys are the cutest.'

'Happy birthday,' they all chorus.

Mario has a massive grin on his face.

I go to find my purse but Michelle jumps in to tell me it's all paid for. Instead I retrieve the bags from Mario, the smell of which is divine.

'Happy birthday Hayley. Enjoy!'

I close the door and turn to see my three neighbours huddled round the bags, removing each delicious serving and placing them in the middle of the white kitchen table. I help Michelle to get the plates and glasses as I spot a couple of bottles of champagne being taken out of a blue carrier bag by Joe. The bustle in my flat is welcomed and momentarily reminds me of my Tuscan daydream.

Joe is folding out the three chairs that pretty much stay living under the fold up table. When I moved in I saw this more as a work desk than a table at which to entertain. It's nice to see it be used like that.

Once we are seated, we each raise our glasses to each other, clinking them together and laughing as Mrs Temple nearly spills hers into the spaghetti. She quickly sips it, claiming that the best way not to spill it was to drink it fast. We all join in, downing our first glasses and thanking her for her wisdom.

We dig in and pass each dish round to each other. I look about this diverse group of people huddled around my precarious table. Everyone is smiling and chatting and all here for me. I got a lump in my throat. Champagne has always made me emotional. I take a big gulp to get myself to the merry stage quicker - I've done enough crying for one birthday.

The aroma of the food on my plate is tantalisingly. Vera, Mario's Grandmother, really is the best Italian cook this side of London. I can imagine us all transported into my Tuscan dream. The four of us are celebrating my birthday, possibly with me not doing the cooking.

'So, are we allowed to ask your age?' Joe asks cagily.

Michelle jokingly whips at him with her forkful of sauce covered tagliatelle. He ducks just in time to miss the splatter.

'Whoa,' he says. 'No need for that.'

Mrs Temple has the giggles. It appears it only takes her half a glass to reach the point of tipsy. I put my arm around her shoulder and hug her close.

'Mrs Temple, you are wonderful.'

'I know,' she laughs.

'I'll clean that up,' Michelle mouths to me while she and Joe are still bickering. Joe is still going but Michelle quickly loses interest and is gobbling down her food as though she hasn't eaten in a year.

'Now, now children,' I say across the table. 'Play nice.'

'Never,' retorts Michelle through a mouthful.

Joe has shoved two meatballs into his cheeks and is doing Godfather impressions. I'm unsure if these are actual quotes from the films or Facebook memes. Either way it's hilarious and we are all trying to see if we too can fit meatballs in our cheeks. My eyes are watering from the effort and the laughing. I fear I may choke at any moment and decide that I'm not cut out to be a mafia boss. Instead I start chewing them, but it's impossible to keep my mouth closed. Mrs Temple does an even better impression than Joe. We all give her a round of applause and cheer.

'I just realised that we don't need to worry about the neighbours. We're all here,' I say to the group.

'That's true,' Michelle chimes in.

As the two middle neighbours, we do occasionally worry we disturb the others when we have one of our evenings together. I'll be even more aware of it now I know my crying on the floor can be heard by Mrs Temple and that Michelle keeps her ear to the ground to plot my movements from above.

'Excuse me a moment, my dears. I just need to go fetch something.'

I help Mrs Temple with her chair as she goes to stand. The last thing I'd want is for her chair to fold in on her as she pushes it back.

'Michelle, would you mind helping me?'

'Not at all.'

Michelle jumps up, nearly knocking the table over in her haste.

She grabs one more mouthful before she goes.

'I'm not finished,' she informs us as she takes Mrs Temple by the arm and walks her to the door.

'So, you never did say how old you were.'

'I'm thirty-three, Joe.'

'Wow!'

I take a swig of champagne to soothe my reaction to his response.

I hiccup as I try to ask, 'what... do you... mean... wow?'

'Just wow. You don't look it.'

The hiccups seem to be getting worse. He gauges the fact that he may have caused offence and backs away from the table slightly, eyeing my fork in case I'm considering a Michelle attack. He stumbles over his attempt to make peace.

'I just thought you were closer to my age.'

'How old are you?'

The door thankfully opens and there are Mrs Temple and Michelle, walking in slowly and carrying between them an impressive, flake-covered chocolate cake. I see Joe out of the corner of my eye looking relieved that our awkward conversation has been interrupted. They have already lit the candles. I assume they did that outside the door because I doubt they would have made it up the stairs with them all still alight.

'Happy birthday to you,' all three of them start to sing.

It's painful to my ears but my heart is warmed by the kindness.

'Happy birthday to you, Happy birthday dear Hayley.'

My cheeks are hurting from smiling so much. These are the best friends and neighbours I could ever wish to have.

'Happy birthday to you.'

'Make a wish, dear.'

Mrs Temple's kind eyes glow with the light of the candles. As I lean in to blow the three candles out, a vision of my Tuscan kitchen flits through my mind and I wish for a birthday celebrated there. It does not escape me that in these visions Andy never features.

'Yay!' Joe shouts.

'Hip-hip, hooray!' Michelle calls.

'Happy birthday, Hayley. I hope your wish comes true.'

It turned out that this wonderful meal was the best way to spend my birthday. The cake is put on the kitchen counter ready for me to cut it. Joe has snuck a fingerful of icing which he's aiming towards his mouth. Mrs Temple slaps the back of his hand just before it reaches.

'Hey!' he says as he watches the blob hit the kitchen floor.

Me and Michelle can't stop laughing but he looks as though he's considering going in for another, possibly risking getting the wrath of Mrs Temple again. She's still giggling but it almost unnerves him more and makes us laugh harder. The cake is beyond delicious and we sat around making yummy noises as we sip our champagne - or what's left of it. Although Mrs Temple asked for just a sliver, we all have a quarter each, and she makes her way through most of it.

'Best birthday ever!' I say to them all. 'Thank you all so much.'

Chapter Seven

My alarm blares at 6am. After snoozing it I'm still not fully coherent when it reminds me it's 6.07. At 6.14 I throw back the duvet in a strop. I haul my tired body and aching head towards the bathroom, sighing deeply and pulling strange faces in the mirror, checking for new wrinkles. Not being able to magic any of them away, I go and switch the shower on instead.

Walking through to the kitchen minutes later, I grab a bin bag. I quickly scoop the empty takeaway tubs into it and pile the plates in the sink for later. Unfortunately it appears that we polished off all the cake. Thankfully there is still a clean cup for my morning pick me up. I'm definitely making headway towards becoming vaguely human. I get dressed, dry my hair and apply my make-up. The final sip of coffee downed, I grab my messenger bag, take one last glance in the hallway mirror and wink.

'Let's do this.'

As I open the main door, I place my sunglasses on, ready to face the day. The spring breeze blowing through the avenue is welcomed. I nip down the front steps and just manage to dodge the elderly man walking his dog. His tiny dog looks at me, offended as I disturbed his rummaging through the bin bags. His lead wraps around my legs. Thankfully the lamppost is there for me to steady myself on. I pull my messenger bag back up onto my shoulder just before it bops the dog on the head.

'Sorry. Is he okay?' I say to his owner.

The man looks back at me with indignation. He simply grunts and pulls the lead away from me

'Come on. Don't worry,' he says reassuringly to his dog as he walks away, ignoring me completely.

I straighten back up from my leaning position against the lamppost before someone thinks I'm touting for business. I hurry down the street, passing the other commuters, children and parents off to start their days.

'Morning Hayley,' calls Pat as I enter the bakery.

Pat's Pastries is my salvation. They sell the best sweet treats around and Pat is as charming as they come - young, vibrant, polite and with a winning smile. Obviously, that he is the person handing me yummy food scores him extra points. The fact that it is just along the road from work makes it even better.

'Morning, Pat.'

'Usual?'

'Yes please.' I slide my sunglasses up on my head.

He kisses his children and wife goodbye as they leave for the school run and takes payment for the order of the man in front of me. He's literally a master at multitasking like this and it never ceases to amaze me.

'Heavy weekend?' he asks.

'Pretty heavy, yea. It was my birthday.'

'Well then, have a birthday pastry on me.'

I thank him, as I take my order and count his kind gesture as a good omen for the day. As I squeeze out of the compact shop, holding the paper bag to my chest. My messenger bag decides to knock each person as I pass them, like a child with a stick along railings. There is nothing I can do but apologise repeatedly as I get out of there as quickly as I can.

I practically fall out of the door onto the street and I pull my sunglasses back down over my eyes. The crowds thin out as I make my way the short distance to work. I'm distractedly replying to a text from Michelle as I round the corner and am about to reach the door to the office. As I'm squinting at the screen with my head down, I walk straight into a guy in front of me.

'What the hell?'

I curse at his back as my bag of pastries squash between us. He obviously doesn't know that the unwritten rule of walking in London is to keep going or move aside. He turns slowly and looks down at me. I lift my sunglasses in an attempt to convey my irritation. He simply turns away again, leaving me standing there with a squashed bag of pastries. Also my phone has turned itself off and only works with my thumb print from my right hand, the one with which I'm holding the damaged goods. I'm just about to walk round this guy and into the office door - which is just the other side of him - when I see Bob, my boss, walking towards me.

'Morning, Hayley,' he says brightly.

'Morning, Bob. Good weekend?'

'Marvellous, thank you.'

I'm now standing with the door open ready for him to follow, but instead I'm surprised to see him carry on past and shake hands with the man who is still standing in the middle of the path. People are having to step off the curb to get around him.

'Great to see you, George. How are you keeping?'

Bemused, I set to carry on up to the office when Bob calls me back.

'Hayley. I'd like you to meet George.'

I step back out onto the path, the door slamming behind me.

'Hi. Nice to meet you,' I say, my tone clipped.

'Likewise, I've heard all good things about you.'

I look back at Bob, who nods emphatically. I scan through my mind for any mention of George from Bob. I pull a blank but try not to let it show on my face. Bob suggests we all go up to the office. It's actually the old storage place of the hardware shop below. The shop's sales had dropped over the years, so Bill had decided to rent out the excess storage space that had once housed his many ongoing projects. We, in return, were chuffed to find an affordable space here in Notting Hill.

Bill is a lovely old guy and very wise, both in his trade and life in general. I have often spent time chatting with him and getting advice on little DIY projects I was undertaking. His speciality is for revamping old pieces of furniture. I've purchased a couple of these pieces for my flat. I've intended to learn how to do it for myself, but I rarely find the time. The closest I get is watching Instagram reels of other people revamping things.

He was such a help when we were setting up the office. He recently built us a Zoom cubby that looks like a phone box - it's awesome. Now that most people order from him online, the shop has become more of a store room. I give Bill a little nod as we open the door which leads upstairs to our office. He waves back with a shining smile.

Bob waves too as he holds the door open for us to enter. George stands back so I can go first. Our eyes meet as I turn to thank him and step in front. I can't tell if he recognises me or not. I reach the top of the stairs and open the door that leads into our office. As I enter Debbie's desk is the one to the left.

'Morning Debbie, your hair looks nice.'

This seems to throw her out slightly, as though she'd forgotten that we'd seen each other in the hairdressers.

'Oh. Hi, Hayley,' she says more pleasantly than usual.

As her cheeks flush, I realise it was purely for the benefit of the two men behind me. It is not to say that Debbie and I don't get on. We are civil to each other, but I find her a tricky person. Just as I think we are gelling, she shifts moods. Her and Bob seem to get along fine, so I tend to leave him to converse with her. She considers herself more of a personal assistant to him anyway, it works well.

I nip to my desk in the far left corner to drop my bag and make my way back to the kitchen area, which is just up between Debbie and Bob's desks. I need to see if I can salvage this squashed breakfast. Thankfully they still look edible. I grab a plate out of the cupboard and empty them onto it.

The door opens and George comes in.

'Hi again.'

'Hi.'

'Would you like a drink?' I ask politely as I'm filling up the coffee machine and kettle.

'Yes please. Bob said you know how he has his too.'

He pulls an apologetic face.

'He's so cheeky.'

'He really is. What can I do to help?'

I take in his black hair and unusually dark eyes. Some men with his features might come across mysterious, but he exudes warmth mixed with a hint of awkwardness. The suggestion of an athletic build through his grey suit is almost enough to raise an appreciative eyebrow, and I turn to finishing the drinks before he might think I've stood appraising him for too long. He jumps in to lend a hand, his height proving useful for reaching the upper shelves, saving me pulling the folding stool over.

'I think doing the tea round is the best way to get to know people,' I say.

'Agreed. Here let me carry the tray.'

'Appreciated. It's a full house this morning.'

I hold the door as he squeezes his way past me.

'Debbie, this is George. A friend of Bob's.'

She shifts in her chair, smoothing out her tweed pencil skirt. Her hand automatically fiddles with the top faux pearl button of her cream blouse. I hold off on pointing out to George that she is at least ten years younger than she dresses.

'Thanks for the introduction. I believe we've met before.'

'Yes, briefly. Lovely to see you again.'

He beams at her and she blushes. I roll my eyes.

'Debbie is our customer service. She is the first point of contact for new enquiries.'

'I do far more than that,' Debbie butts in puffing herself up. 'I'm Bob's personal assistant. I organise his schedule, plan meetings with new clients, send invoices and -'

'Yes, of course,' I say over her. 'the company would crumble without you.'

I usher George away before Debbie can argue her case any further and we cross to Josh's desk. He sits up and removes the hood of his metal band sweatshirt as George places the coffee on his desk. Josh moves it onto his coaster.

'Is that one of those electronic mug warmers?' George asks.

'Sure is. Total gamechanger.'

'Josh, this is George.' I say, 'Josh's main role is photographing our events and making those images look fabulous on our website. He's also a dab hand with sweet talking contractors and getting the best prices.'

Lauren is replacing last week's vase on her desk with a fresh bouquet that is in keeping with her floral shirt dress. She looks like a delicate fairy in a forest clearing. She greets us with a beaming smile and takes her mug from the tray.

'What beautiful... flowers.'

'Yes. Hyacinths and tulips are my favourites. There's a great little stall round the corner that sells them.'

'Lauren this is George. George, this is Lauren, our little ray of sunshine. She's a whizz at all things techy. If she doesn't know how it works we're done for.'

'I just do what I can to help.'

'Well, it sounds like you do a grand job, Lauren,' George says.

Just as we reach Kim's currently empty desk she barges through the front door, hands full, heading straight to the kitchen. Moments later she resurfaces and comes rushing across to us, talking a million miles an hour.

'I'm sorry I'm late! The kids decided at the last minute that they needed stuff for the tombola today and all I managed to find was a couple of old tins of chopped tomatoes and a gift set of old lady soap that my mother-in-law gifted me the other year. I just hope I don't win them back!'

She flops into her chair and attempts to catch her breath. George cautiously places her drink down.

'George, this is Kim.' I say calmly, 'Kim, meet George.'

'Oh, hi. Sorry - Mondays are mayhem. I look forward to coming to work for the rest. Not that I do nothing but...' she rambles as she removes her signature denim jacket. Her black t-shirt is spotted with what appears to be the remains of her children's breakfast.

'Kim is our resident mother hen. She looks after our wellbeing. Ensuring the kitchen and stationery cupboard is stocked, the heating is of optimal temperature and giving out hugs in moments of despair. Her actual job title is bookkeeper, but she's far more than that.'

'If only I was as organised as you make me sound,' she says, brushing off the compliments.

'It sounds like after the morning you've had that you deserve this,' George says as he hands her drink over.

'Thank you, George. Nice to have you here.'

I take George over to Bob, plucking my coffee from the tray as I do so.

'I'll leave you guys to it.'

I almost trip over my bag that I'd dumped next to my desk.

'Don't you start.' I mutter to it.

No one pays any attention to the fact I'm talking to my bag. It is not a new thing - I have a habit of chatting to inanimate objects. I can't explain why. It's just a thing I do. I tuck it further under my desk with my foot.

I'm missioning through my emails, headphones on to help me stay focused. Josh was surprised to realise I was not listening to some cultural classic music but in fact an early 00s rave playlist. Now if he catches my eye while I have my headphones on he starts raving at his desk and doing the old 'whoop whoop'. It never ceases to make me laugh.

A short while later Bob appears next to me.

'Thanks for introducing George to the team, Hayley. Sorry I forgot to mention that he was coming in today.'

'No worries,' I reply with my best smile.

'Are you free for a quick chat after the morning meeting?'

'Sure,' I reply absently as my eyes are flicking over the emails awaiting my response.

He turns to the rest of the room and calls them over for our morning catch up. We head to the meeting corner to the right of the door, behind Josh's desk. It's a bit like carpet time for adults. We have an array of beanbags and floor cushions. I opt for the cushions as me and beanbags don't get along. Basically, once I'm in I can't get out again. Well, not without a lot of unnecessary effort.

In the beginning, when we were first launching, we borrowed odd bits of furniture that Bill had, plus a mix match of other bits picked up from the second hand place up the road. We believed this had given us that edgy look Notting Hill was renowned for. This somehow spurred us on to strive and enjoy the small wins before we landed our first big accounts and traded the make-do furniture with 'cool' stuff.

We run a corporate events business. An idea stumbled upon by Bob, who then roped me in. He heard that there was money to be made in throwing parties. Our clients invite the clientele and we provide the glamour. At the time, Bob had just sold his old business and fancied having a go at it. Having worked with him as his assistant on a couple of previous projects throughout the years, I was excited by the prospect of a new job that literally had more sparkle.

I was easily wooed away from my job two years ago. I'd found myself holed up in a temp job that pretty much involved spending my days staring at screens. I missed the face-to-face client interaction so was delighted at the idea of a new project. The added bonuses were the decent wage and that it was located within walking distance of my flat. It was slightly away from my expertise in sales but the same basic concepts applied. We were selling the chance to inject fun and bring new business to our clients. Seeing the smiles, hearing the laughter and watching everyone dancing the Time Warp at the end of the night is a reward in itself.

Occasionally I find myself getting that yearning for change. I know it's silly as Bob is forever open to new ideas or changing direction, but I've had a lifelong dream of moving to Italy, just like in my daydreams. Not totally out of the realms of possibility perhaps. Mostly I'm content in my life; I just get bored sometimes and dream of living in a little cottage in the Tuscan hills. However, I worry what would happen to Michelle and Mrs Temple. Realistically Michelle would be fine, because she travels with her job anyway and would love a new place to visit me. My Mum would think it was awesome and something to gloat to her friends about. Mrs Temple would find a new tenant in a matter of hours. I'm just not quite ready to make the leap. As I list these things off to confirm this to myself that it could work, my ego shouts that the world would still fall apart here without me. Yet the voice of hope whispers 'but would it?'

'Hayley. How is the Hotel al Cioccolato project coming along?'

I hadn't realised I had zoned out until I heard my name. I clear my throat, aware of all the eyes on me.

'Yes, they're going well. We are still on track.'

'When is it you're heading over there?' asks Bob.

'You head out on the 29th,' chips in Debbie.

'So that gives us...'

'Just three weeks,' I say quickly before I can be spoken for again. 'And plenty of time until their relaunch party.'

'Do-able?'

'Always,' is my confident reply.

The team smiles. They know we have pulled off the most spectacular events in much less time. I say they all smile, except Debbie who rolls her eyes at my flippancy and George who is looking at me with interest. I avert my eyes and concentrate on Lauren who always has an encouraging look on her face. In all fairness I am a highly organised solver by nature, which is the reason Bob hired me.

'Hayley, you said the other day that you didn't have someone to fill the plus one on the trip. George, I'd like you to go with her instead then. I think it would be the perfect opportunity for you to see how we work internationally.'

'No problem,' he replies, unfazed.

Bob turns to me.

'Does that work for you?'

'Sure,' I say, shrugging. Even if Andy had agreed to come with me to Florence, that would have changed now.

'George, if you bring me your passport I can sort your tickets,' says Debbie, not missing a beat.

'Excellent, excellent,' says Bob. 'Now Lauren, if you can handle things for Hayley while she's away, that would be awesome.'

'Absolutely.'

'We'll all head out for the actual Ball so that you are on hand,' I add. 'Josh, if you can prepare a list of photos you'd like to get on the night to fully showcase their business, they've asked for copies for their website.'

'Yep, consider it done.'

The meeting continues with everyone else's updates and I wonder what it will be like travelling with George. He seems nice enough so we should get along fine. I look up and he smiles at me from his position next to Bob. I smile back and then down at my notes. He is undeniably handsome. Andy would not like the fact he was joining me.

We conclude our meeting with Kim nipping out quickly and appearing again carrying a birthday cake - bless her heart. As she comes across with her hand sheltering the candles, everybody breaks into song. We all head back to our desks with a chunk of cake.

Shortly after, Bob and I are getting ready to go and scout out a nearby business who have shown interest in using our services. Bob appears by my desk and hands me an A3 canvas with a bow on it. It turns out the team has gotten me a beautiful picture with Italian vineyards on it. I prop the picture up on the windowsill near my desk. It will improve the view which is currently the brick wall of the building across the alley.

'Bob,' calls Debbie from across the office. 'Phone call for you.'

He turns, looking perplexed by the interruption. I sigh. She knows we have a meeting - she was the one who booked it.

'Who is it?'

After she's told him a ridiculously long version of the brief enquiry he tells her to ask them to email him. This is his standard reply. As well she knows. He turns back apologetically and smiles.

'Shall we go?'

I grab my phone and a notepad. I leave my bag - it's normally more trouble than it is worth. We exit the building and both slip our sunglasses on as we walk out onto the street. We walked in the opposite direction from the hardware shop window. I can still hear Bill whistling through the open door and it cheers me slightly. Bob lights a cigarette. He doesn't smoke anywhere near as much as he once used to. Mainly due to the fact that he hates having to come all the way down here every time.

'How was your weekend, Bob?'

I trot slightly to keep up with his long strides.

'It was really good actually.' He takes a long drag on his cigarette, blowing it out away from me. 'I went on a date.'

'That's great. I guess by the fact you're blushing that it went well.'

'You know me far too well.'

'I do indeed. So tell me more.'

'Not much to tell at this point. We just went out for dinner and a couple of drinks. But I thoroughly enjoyed it.'

'That's so nice to hear. It's been a while since you went on a proper date.'

'Yea. I guess it has.'

'Oh, look at your little smirk.'

'Stop it. It was just a date.'

'But who knows? This could be 'the one'.'

'Or just another 'one'.'

'Well, anyway, what do you think of George?'

'Don't change the subject.'

'Too late, the subject has changed.'

'Okay, I'll let you off for now but I want updates and an invite to your wedding.'

'If I must. Now, thoughts on George?'

'He seems nice enough. I don't think he's my 'one' though,' I giggle.

'Enough with the banter already,' he says, but I know he's amused too.

'Tell me more about why you've brought him in.'

'Of course. He was an intern from back when I worked in advertising. He was a sharp young thing even back then.' He pauses to take another drag of his cigarette. 'You know how it goes. You're both in the same circles so bump into each other every now and again. Anyway, a few weeks back we were both at a mutual friend's wedding.'

'The one in Gloucester?'

'Yea, that's the one. So we got to talking and he said he'd gone freelance a while back.'

'In advertising?'

'No, consulting.'

'In what way?'

'Basically he comes into a company and works out how best they can invest or expand, etc., based on the current and predicted market.'

'Sounds like you memorised his elevator pitch.'

'It did, didn't it,' he chuckles. 'Anyway I thought it could be good for us and he's giving us mates rates while he's between gigs.'

'Handy. Sounds more like he's your 'one'.'

'Like fate bringing us together at the point we both needed each other?'

'Exactly. That's so cute.'

Bob stubs out and disposes of his cigarette butt in the nearby bin. We're both still giggling as we arrive at the meeting place a few minutes later.

'Right, now behave,' Bob says in mock seriousness.

'Never.'

Chapter Eight

I'm deep into my work, trying to clear as much as possible before the weekend. Friday has come round so fast this week. A fresh drink appears on my desk, delivered by George. We haven't really had much to do with each other yet. He has held his position as head tea maker, which is greatly appreciated by us all. He certainly knows how to win us over. I've liked watching how he interacts with the others - it's a great way to gauge him. It's not been a difficult pastime between tasks and I've justified it to myself as research.

From my findings, he seems kind, helpful, friendly, interested and his manner is gentle. I passed by the other day as he was explaining to Debbie, not an easy nut to crack, about how to use one of our systems in a more streamlined way. She was hanging on to his every word and looked as though she would agree with anything if it meant that he would stay where he was. From the small amount of the conversation I caught, what he said made a lot of sense and would save her having to use multiple platforms. She could now compile the information and just use one. This, as Bob had hoped, would save money and time. Unfortunately, she would then have less to moan about as it would probably cut out about a third of her workload.

If I remember correctly this is exactly what I suggested to her not so long ago and she went to Bob and told him I'd said she wasn't doing her job properly. Bob hadn't told me off but did pull me aside to ask why I'd say such things. Thankfully, once I'd explained what I'd actually said he then relayed it to her that she had misunderstood me. If we had had a difficult relationship before, Debbie was now even frostier with me, and constantly looked like a hurt kitten every time I was near her and Bob passed by.

I pull out my phone and message Michelle.

You okay to buy wine? I'll order the food xx

She replied instantly with a thumbs up. Sorted. That should set me up to concentrate on packing once I'm home.

Friday has become our work team debriefing session from the events of the week. We don't manage it every week but as many as possible. If it goes too long between them, they are horrendously messy as we both have so much to work through and fill each other in on. It's also the only afternoon that Kim can stay late as her husband works from home on Fridays. If nothing else it's nice for us to gather in a different space where someone else makes the drinks.

'Hi George.'

'Hello.'

He's loitering next to my desk, looking as though there was something he wanted to say. I look at him, inviting him to share what is on his mind. He shifts slightly from foot to foot and then says.

'Are you coming to Gill's café after work?'

This throws me out completely. I was expecting a non-work question by how uncomfortable he looks.

'Yes. I'm planning to.'

'Excellent. Cool. See you in a bit then.'

He wanders back to his makeshift desk next to Bob's and I'm left slightly bemused. Should it not have been me asking him that question? I'm now distracted by thoughts of how cute his smile is and how his eyes could be dangerous to a recently on-a-break lady such as myself. I can't help but feel excited by the prospect of spending time with him. I'm kind of intrigued. Thankfully another email arrives and takes my thoughts back to work before I can dwell on this much longer. The afternoon drags but eventually the clock reaches four.

'Right kids, clear out. We have drinks waiting at Gill's,' announces Bob.

He's already standing by the door with his jacket on and his hand hovering over the light switches. He doesn't have to say it twice, everyone's already closed down their work stations and are filtering out the door within seconds. I follow, holding my messenger bag to stop it taking out the doorframe as it likes to do. I've noticed there is the beginning of a permanent scuff mark from where I sometimes forget to hold it. George is waiting for me outside as I reach the street. I smile widely and pop my sunglasses on.

'This is my favourite part of the week,' Lauren sings out, bouncing up and down.

'Where's Debbie?' asks Kim as we're making our way the short distance to the café.

'She went home to feed her cat,' Josh says with a snigger.

No one replies. We ignore his insinuations most of the time, which doesn't seem to faze him. He still finds it funny and is chuckling away to himself.

'You alright?' Kim appears beside me, linking her arm into mine.

'Yep, I'm fine. Pleased to be out in the fresh air.'

I smile at her and squeeze her arm a tad. She follows my gaze.

'He's quite the specimen, isn't he?'

I try to pretend I don't know who she means. 'Who? Josh?'

She pulls a face that requires no further explanation.

I don't even try to deflect her statement this time.

'He's a welcome addition to the team.'

'And to your trip,' she adds, nudging me playfully.

We arrived at Gill's café. It's the perfect after work hang out. It doesn't get too busy at the time we finish so the wait is minimal. It helps that we order it on our app before we leave the office, which cuts even more time off our wait. This gives us time to chat and round the week off nicely before heading off to have our weekends. Josh and George rearrange some tables while the rest of us just huddle around near the counter to pick up our orders. We each take our drinks as they're served and grab a seat. I choose to sit near the window, next to Kim, opposite Lauren and diagonal to George.

I sit quietly blowing on my cappuccino to cool it. I'm enjoying the conversation and banter between everyone. I find myself smiling, nodding and laughing along as Josh, Kim and Bob pretty much entertain us. The door opens and I turn at the flash of fiery red hair. My mother always said I was nosey. I like to call it observant. I instantly wish that I hadn't looked up. I wish that I was in fact facing the other way. More than that I wish that the ground would swallow me up. I squeeze my eyes closed for just a moment, hoping that it's just my tiredness messing with my eyes - too much screen time maybe.

When I open my eyes, I'm faced with Andy standing at the counter, looking right at me. I guess the laughter coming from our group is hard to ignore. There is a weak smile and a lame wave in my direction. I'm completely caught off guard. I'm not ready to see her. I feel bad I've left it so long to talk to her, but I just don't know what best to say without just agreeing to something that I don't feel is right. I try to pretend I haven't seen her and turn to look out the window. My cheeks are burning. I know she'll still be looking at me, trying to get my attention. I sip my drink and try to concentrate on the story Josh is telling us. He can make the most mundane thing sound exciting. I turn and follow Andy's progress through the tables, hoping with all my will that it's in the direction of the exit. Unfortunately she hasn't got the hint and is headed straight towards our table.

I make everyone jump as I suddenly scrape back my chair, grab my things and run for the door. Poor Kim nearly gets taken out by my bag but having kids means she has honed her skills at avoiding unexpected flying objects. Hooking Andy's arm as I pass, I aim for the door, dragging her with me. She clutches her bag close to her body with her free hand.

'What the hell?' Andy snaps as we make it out onto the street.

'Sorry. I just didn't want to discuss this in front of everyone.'

'Come on, Hayley. They know me well enough.'

'Some of them have met you once or twice.'

'Same thing.'

'Not really.'

She changes tact and gives me one of her winning smiles.

'I tried contacting you,' she says. 'Why didn't you message me back? I was worried.'

'Because I didn't know what to say.'

'Say you'll marry me.' She grins. I can't tell if she's joking or not.

'You know I can't.'

'Won't,' she says, her smile becoming more forced.

'This is why I wasn't ready to talk. You twist everything in the direction you want it to go.'

'I just don't see why you won't even think about it.'

'I have thought about it. It's all I've thought of since the other night.'

'And?'

'My answer is still no.'

As I say the words a wave of emotional exhaustion crashes over me and my shoulders droop.

'So that's it then? We're over?' she asks, the smile vanishing abruptly.

'If it's marriage or nothing, then I guess it is.'

I watch as her face reddens, a storm brewing swiftly behind her eyes.

'Well fuck you, Hayley!' she spits. 'You're a heartless bitch!'

I want to defend myself, to explain further, to still have her in my life in some way. I love her deeply but I can't be tied down because of an ultimatum. She's one of the most amazing people but her jealousy and temper are things I can't handle. Mixed with her lack of public affection, disinterest in travel, and her elusiveness when it suits her, I truly believe that marriage would not be the best move for us. If I was honest, and listened to Michelle, I would have come to this conclusion ages ago, but I like to see the best in people and had hoped it might work. I now see, as we are standing arguing on the street, that it won't. We are not well suited after all. I'm gutted but in some way relieved.

I turn on my heel in the direction of home, pulling out my phone and dropping a quick message to Bob to apologise for my swift exit. I know they will have all seen and will understand, so it's more for my own peace of mind. I don't slow my pace until I turn the first corner. As I pass a shop window I pause to check my reflection. The last thing I want is to be walking through the streets with my make-up smudged down my face from the tears I'm failing to hold back.

'Hayley.'

'No!' I spin round, ready to defend against her fury.

'Woah!'

George is standing with his hands up as though surrendering. Relief flows through me as our eyes meet and I blearily smile up at him.

'Ooft.'

Suddenly he doubles over holding his crown jewels. With wide watery eyes he looks at me.

'Oh god! Sorry!'

I go to place a hand on his back to offer comfort but he flinches. It is at this point I notice my bag hanging triumphantly from my elbow where it has, unbeknown to me, escaped. I obviously forgot to tell it to stand down.

'I'm so sorry. This bloody bag.'

'S'okay.'

He attempts to straighten up, his voice slightly higher than usual. I shift the bag back up onto my shoulder, reprimanding it silently.

'I'm so sorry.'

He's still wary.

'I came to check you were okay.'

His voice is still not at a normal octave. There is some part of me, possibly the one mentally connected to the bag, that starts to laugh. It's more of a giggle at first but then the flood gates open and there is nothing I can do but let it out. Before I can stop myself, I'm now doubled over laughing. The more I try to stop, the harder I laugh. George is standing staring at me as I try to continue apologising but the words won't come. I just look even more crazy as my arm is flailing around instead. I'm holding onto the wall for support and who knows what my bag is doing. I finally stop laughing and take a few deep breaths.

We join the flow of people and are chatting away as we walk. Before long we are turning into my street.

'This is my road. Thanks for walking me back. My friend and I are getting Chinese tonight. Would you like to join us?'

He pulls a quizzical face.

'Oh, not that friend,' I chuckle, realising that he thought I meant Andy. 'I mean, if you need to be somewhere else I understand,' I ramble.

'I'd love to.' He smiles.

'Great.'

I pull out my phone and quickly place mine and Michelle's regular order.

'Here you go. Add anything you'd like.'

He hands me back the phone saying, 'Easy enough. I'm a chicken chow mein kind of guy.'

'That's our go-to as well. They have tons of stuff that's super tasty, but we always end up ordering the same.'

I complete and pay for the order.

'Sorted.'

'You sure you're okay for me to join you?'

'Absolutely. I've just dropped Michelle, my neighbour, a message as we were planning on being at hers tonight. Don't worry, she won't mind one bit.'

Chapter Nine

I pop my bag just inside my door as we pass on our way up to Michelle's. I don't think George will have seen much but I still thank my past self for scooping up most of the debris from last night.

Far from minding, Michelle chimes, 'Come in, come in,' as soon as we reach her door.

'George, Michelle. Michelle, George.'

He goes to shake her hand but she moves in to hug him so they are caught in a momentary bro hug. I notice as she leads us into her apartment that she has 'Evil' written across the butt of her joggers today.

'Lovely to meet you. Sorry to intrude on your evening.'

'It's nice to have someone else for us to spend time with. We know all of each other's stories by now,' she assures him.

'Fair enough,' he says, amused.

As he follows Michelle's gesture to head in, she snags me.

'Have you been crying?' she asks in a low voice.

'I had a bit of a run-in with Andy in the street,' I say by way of explanation.

Michelle raises an eyebrow, inviting me to elaborate, but I tilt my head at George,

'I'll catch you up on it later.

I can tell by the pursing of her lips that she's not happy about it, but she ushers me on in just as George speaks again.

'Have you two lived here long?'

'I've been here a couple of years,' says Michelle, smile at the ready. 'Wine?'

'Yes please,' answers George.

'Absolutely,' I say. 'You know, I spent the day looking forward to this.'

We're standing in her kitchen space. It's all open plan but, unlike mine, she has a breakfast bar that we are congregating around. She hands us both a glass and we cheers.

'How about you, Hayley?' George asks.

'Oh, sorry. Yea, I've been here what... must be three and a half years now.'

'Cool.'

'And George, how do you know this fabulous lady of mine?'

'Through work. I'm doing a bit of work for Bob.'

'What kind of work is it you do?'

'I'm a business consultant. I help companies find ways to streamline their time and money. To make sure both are working as effectively as possible.'

'Sounds good.'

'Yeah, it pays the bills and I meet some great people.'

He looks pointedly at me. I can do nothing else but smile back, trying not to blush. Michelle glances at me, intrigued.

'I love your apartment, Michelle.'

'Cheers. I'd like to take the glory but my decorator did it for me.'

'Your decorator? Fancy.'

'Isn't it,' I chip in.

'Not as fancy as you'd think, to be honest. Apparently it's the 'look'.' She takes a swig of her drink, and answers his unasked question. 'The look people expect you to have.'

'I see,' he says, although he doesn't sound so sure. 'May I ask which people? Are you an influencer?'

'Of sorts, I suppose,' she replies casually.

'Michelle is a YouTuber,' I say to save George having to pry the information out of Michelle.

'For my sins.'

'That's awesome. What kind of videos do you do?'

'Here you go.'

I pull up her channel on my phone and handed it to him.

'Wow! Look at how many subscribers you have. Is that 2.2 million?'

'Yep.'

'Bloody hell. Excuse my French.'

'Excused. It's the only French I speak too.'

'I see what you mean by how good your apartment looks in these videos. And the run-through ones are amazing. You're so fast. I can barely walk in a straight line on Minecraft.'

'Me either,' I concur.

The intercom goes and Michelle buzzes them up, opening the door ready. We arrange ourselves on the light grey corner sofa rather than perching on bar stools. It's set around the glass topped coffee table that has LEDs glowing from beneath it. It shines through the tubs as we empty them onto our plates. Even her plates are classy. Michelle brings the bottle of wine over to us and tops our glasses back up to full.

'George, I have to ask - where have I seen you before?'

'I have no idea, to be honest.'

'Do you go to Frankie's club at all?'

'No, I've not been there before.'

'Hmm, you look vaguely familiar.'

'Maybe I just have one of those faces.'

'George is the guy from outside the hairdresser the other day,' I say, to put them out of their misery.

'Oh, you are! That's it.'

'Were you there as well?'

'Yep.'

'Then I owe you an apology too.'

'No harm done. You seem like a decent enough guy. That is, when you're not knocking helpless ladies into the road.'

'Low blow,' I defend.

'That's a backhanded compliment if ever I heard one.' He's smiling as he says this and is seemingly unfazed.

'I'm really interested in what you do, Michelle. Do you mind me keep asking you questions?'

'Fire away.'

'How did you get started?'

Michelle gives him the quick run-down, missing out the history of excessive drug use, and just keeping in the video game related bits. She's a natural storyteller and gets the appropriate reactions from us. I for one never tire of her story. At one point George nearly choked on his chow mein when she recounted the time when her Mum, not realising she was recording, came in during a live video.

'So there I am and Mum thunders into my room going on about how number 46 parked in her space again and how she'd f'ing kill them. It was hilarious. There I was doing a run-through, I believe that was Fortnite actually, and just as the storm was coming. Tens of thousands of people were in the live chat, watching my playthrough. The comments were hilarious and I decided to keep the recording up on my channel. It became a whole meme thing with a clip of Fortnite and my Mum being the storm.'

'That's hilarious!'

'It really was. The best moment in my career ever!'

'Even better than you getting your golden play button?' I ask.

'I can say with complete honesty that yes, it really was!'

'Oh, I didn't even think of that! You have the button?'

'Yep, it's in my studio. You wanna see.'

We leave our partially eaten meals and make our way through to the furthest door. In my flat, this is a junk room thinly disguised as a guest room. Michelle's is like stepping into another world.

'Oh, wow!' exclaims George.

'I know, it's super messy at the moment. The cleaner's kids are ill and I've been busy preparing for a big meeting.'

'Not that. I mean this room. It's like stepping into a set on your favourite sitcom.'

'I agree. It never ceases to amaze me either.'

'So did your designer do this room too?'

I've become so used to this space that it is cool to see it through the eyes of someone seeing it for the first time. The three screens, light-up keyboard, mic and circular LED lamp. The purple backlights make the space look like something from the 90's films depicting the future. Her gaming chair is super awesome, you could practically live in it, which she often seems to. I've spent many an hour chilling on the sofa to the side, both of us working on our separate projects. When she is on tight deadlines I'm the snack person and takeaway orderer. Even though she is underplaying it I can see that George is impressed.

'Just a few accessories. Most of it's the green screen. Plus I'm normally shown real small in the corner of the stream and the game is the main focus. It is cool though now you just have your head and shoulders and no background. Back in the day it was literally a box in the corner showing you talking and the capture card saved the run-through. It's come so far. It's so much easier than it used to be.'

'But I guess you know more now.'

'Yea, you're probably right. Plus I learned each new piece of technology as it came out rather than like when I first started and knew nothing.'

'Even your chair is awesome.'

'It's so comfy. It's funny actually. In the beginning you yearn and wish for a set up like you saw on other people's videos. Then you start earning the money to gradually upgrade. Then when you're earning the big bucks these companies send you stuff for free! Ironic, isn't it.'

'Oh, for sure.'

'Michelle has a sponsorship program that supports new YouTubers by funding their first proper set up.'

'That's incredible.'

'Yea, I try to be fair and there's an application process obviously, but I think we've supported quite a few now. We run a training program for them to learn the tricks of the trade. I only pop my head in on these a couple of times as we have a team who deals with most of it. They're far better trained than me. I just wanted to give something back, you know.'

'If only more people thought like that.'

'She's a good egg,' I say, wrapping an arm around her and laying my head on her shoulder. 'I love that you didn't go buy some swanky overpriced house.'

'You know my thoughts on that.'

'Michelle doesn't want to be the stereotypical rich bitch. Living in some huge, heartless house that's big enough for multiple families. Instead she's renting here and bought a few places that she rents out through the local authority.'

'It's to help people who are in situations like my Mum was. Everyone deserves an opportunity. Just paying it forward, you know.'

I hug her again. I'm forever honoured to have her in my life.

As we make our way back through to the living area and George is admiring the art and lighting, I'm reminded of when we first became friends and I saw this place. I too was in awe of what she did, how she looked, the fact she had a team of people, including the cleaner. Plus, a stylist for in person events. The way her flat was styled blew my mind. In comparison to mine... well, there was no comparison really. This was the difference between loving revamped bits and playing with fun looks to having an interior designer from Surrey do your place up.

George pokes his head round the bathroom door that is ajar. I remember her first having this installed. We messed about with the speakers and LED lights for hours. She much preferred showers, hence why her designer suggested having the bath removed and the room designed like this. Her wet-room even had a sauna setting. We'd sat on the custom made bench many a night, chatting and drinking, enjoying our toxins being cleansed while we topped them up.

That was how we got talking a couple of weeks after she moved in, actually. I bumped into her one day as I was heading out to work and she was completing her walk of shame back to the building, both of us wearing shades and feeling fragile. She greeted me and apologised for all the noise of the contractors as they were still in the midst of doing her place up. I waved away her concern and assured her that I was out most of the time anyway. I then offered that if she needed anywhere to hide from the plaster dust, she was always welcome. Since then, we have been inseparable and she's at mine most of the time still. As fabulous as her place is, she doesn't feel she can fully relax there.

The only reason we were at hers tonight was because she wanted me to look over her proposal for Netflix. They're wanting to do a rags to riches piece on her that includes the scholarship program. She said she's a tad nervous at the idea of them delving into her past. Even though she's cut ties with most of the friend groups from the old days she worries her past will come back to haunt her eventually.

We make our way back to the sofa and pick absently at the remains of our food while the conversation and wine flow. I believe that something good comes from most bad situations. Such as today. Had I not seen Andy, and George hadn't come to check on my welfare, we wouldn't all be sitting here now enjoying each other's company.

It's not until George leaves around half eight that I realise that he disclosed very little of his own life. To be fair, he probably couldn't get a word in edgeways.

'Fill up my glass again first,' I wink at her.

'Deal.'

Michelle and I settle down on either corner of the sofa, glasses in hand and childish smirks on our faces. I know Michelle as well as I could, yet as much as her tone is upbeat and she sounds her normal self, I can't help feeling that she's not quite as excited by the prospect of George being around as she seems. There are times when she is hard to read and this is one of them.

From all the videos that she does she has learned the skill of appearing happy, excited, motivated and all that jazz even on days when she feels like shit. I remember us talking about this and her telling me that having the videos to do helps snap her out of those dark moments. As though she can switch into her alter ego and trick her brain. I guess it is similar to my baths or talking to myself.

'So...' she prompts.

I slowly take a sip, allowing myself a second to savour it before I start, mainly to annoy her. It works, of course. She jabs me with her foot and I lift my glass up to save spillage. I laugh.

'Okay, okay. No need for violence.'

'Then tell me!'

'Tell you what?'

She growls and goes to kick me again. I hate feet and she's removed her trainers and socks, so I figure I should talk.

'Who is he?'

'He's George.'

She scowls.

'We work together,' I add.

'This I know.' She rolls her eyes. 'But what was he doing joining us for Chinese? Not that it wasn't nice to have him here, of course,' she adds.

'Well, Andy caused a scene outside the coffee shop. George came to see if I was alright,' she nods, not wanting to interrupt. 'We ended up walking back this way together so I offered for him to join us. It seemed rude not to.'

'I see.' She raises a perfectly sculpted eyebrow.

I'm not sure what else to say, if I'm honest. I haven't really had time to process any of it yet and part of me doesn't want to burst the bubble by talking about it. I value Michelle's input; she's good at seeing the side to things that I can't. Many times, the better side. However, on this occasion I feel I must tread carefully.

For example, with Andy she warned me to be careful, and told me that I deserved better. She was right - the whole relationship was a constant drain on my energy. I was always trying to figure out what more I could do to make it work.

'So what did you think?' I ask after I finish my mouthful of wine.

She also takes a drink from and pulls a thoughtful face. She makes me laugh when she does this. I know she already knows what she's going to say, she's just playing me at my own game. I smirk.

'Okay, well the thing is this.' Another sip. 'He's a handsome man, I'd say around your age, possibly single?'

I shrug my shoulders.

'I have no idea.' I bite my lip nervously. 'He didn't seem to contact anyone to say he'd be late. In fact, I don't remember seeing his phone out all night.'

I fear I'm doing that thing where I'm trying to make a person fit into my ideal.

'Hmm. Well, we'll assume for now that he is and that he's available if you fancy.' She shrugs while I'm busy blushing. 'You make me laugh. Anyway, I think he's nice.'

I note again that her eyes are glinting only from the wine, not from the words she's saying. I stay quiet, waiting for her to carry on, but she doesn't.

'That's it? That's all you have? That he's 'nice'.'

'Yep.'

She leans over to fill my glass back up and then hers. I frown at her, confused by this bizarre phenomenon.

'You're kidding, right?' I say, slightly higher pitched than I'd intended. 'You'd give me a better psychological evaluation of a stranger passing us by.'

I believe we're both slightly slurry by this point.

'Oh, you know what I mean. He's just one of those people where there's nothing much to say.' She takes a sip.

I think about this for a second, and realise Michelle's right. She's now giving me the side eye and smirking.

'What?' I demand.

'You.'

'What? I'm not doing anything.'

'You're pouting.'

'I'm not. I was thinking,' I defend.

'You wanted me to hate him,' she states.

'What?' That word is sounding different each time I say it.

'Well if I'd told you he was horrid and to keep away, you would have done.'

I go to argue but have nothing.

'Because you really like him.'

The smugness has turned into gloating. I now start to giggle.

'Yea, he's polite and attractive but I'm still trying to sort my head out about all this Andy stuff. I don't want to go throwing myself straight into another relationship of any sort.' I say the last bit with my mouth resting on the rim of my glass so the words echo, making us both laugh harder.

'Awww, you love him,' she sings mockingly. 'Oh, I wish you still loved me this much.'

She carries on laughing but mine gutters out. Shit. I think this has hit a nerve.

'I'll always love you the mostest,' I say seriously.

Our eyes meet and she gives me a half smile, her laughter having faded too as we hit a sober moment.

'I know, babe,' she says.

She leans in and kisses me on the cheek. I pull her towards me and we half hug, our other arms holding our glasses at arms lengths. She releases first and does a rendition of Whitney Houston's 'I will always love you.' I join in for a verse or too and then down the rest of my wine.

We spend the next hour or so going through her Netflix proposal. Most of the paperwork that she's been sent is painfully overwritten and wordy, so we spend a good chunk of time simply deciphering what they mean. Michelle is determined not to allow all of her hard work so far to be compromised by clauses that hand over her creative rights, and vigorously crosses out the parts that don't sit right with her. We're yawning before the work is finished, and eventually gave in to the tiredness.

'Right, it's getting late, I'd best go.'

'Love you, love you, bye!' I call as the door closes behind me.

'Love you more.'

I laugh as I exit the flat, taking the stairs carefully as the wine catches up with me.

Chapter Ten

With the Florence trip coming up fast, Michelle jumps at the opportunity for another shopping trip. I'm not really up for a trawl around the shops or the market. Today I didn't even want to move out of bed yet. The only reason I ventured out of my cocoon was because I was desperate for a wee and the coffee was enroute. I'm sitting propped up in bed with my duvet snuggled round me, my mug cupped between my hands.

I'm exhausted. There's been more to organise workwise than I'd expected. I'd forgotten just how stressful it all was. I just want to stay here scrolling Instagram whilst kidding myself I'm reading the book that's laid next to me on the bed. Michelle has abandoned our text conversation and has let herself in and appeared at my bedroom door. She tries her hardest to convince me to come but today I'm stubborn. I just can't be bothered to get up, washed and dressed. Finally, after much rib jabbing, tickling and whinging, Michelle gives in. I'd hoped she'd grow bored eventually.

'I'm gonna branch out and become a personal shopper. It's obviously my calling,' she shouts as she leaves the apartment.

She adds something else but I don't hear her - my head is already back under the duvet. I must have fallen back to sleep after Michelle left as I awoke to hear the door to my flat closing and a rustle of bags. I'm disorientated at first, unsure of the time and what the noise is until I hear cursing as Michelle stubs her toe on something. The sound of the coffee machine doing its job works to wake me fully. The curiosity of what Michelle is up to gets me moving towards the living room. I'm greeted by an animated Michelle and a fresh drink.

'What's all this?'

'Well, seeing as you were too lazy,' she says winking.

She's fully aware that I have been burning the candle at both ends and melting it in between.

'I've grabbed you a load of bits from Natalie's for your trip.'

Natalie's is a beautiful boutique between Westbourne Grove and Portobello. She sells the most amazing clothes - a kind of urban chic meets comfy hippy. She had been closed last time we went so I'm excited to see what new stock she had.

'Let's get you ready for your Italian adventure. Go try some on.'

Michelle is so psyched for me. I'm aware that she too is backed up with work, but she's taken the time to do this. Today she has 'Namaste' written across her bottom. I swear she specifically wears them so people look at her arse and it works though.

I go through to the bedroom and step out of my warm pyjamas, my skin instantly breaking out in goose pimples. I quickly chuck on clean underwear and grab for the first item.

'Nat said you can take back anything you don't like,' Michelle calls through.

I can hear her making more drinks. She is my coffee soulmate and my guardian angel, saving me from a shopping trip and keeping a stream of caffeine flowing through my veins. She is perfection personified.

'Remind me to send you the money across,' I called.

'Don't worry, we'll sort it out later.'

Although I can't see her from where I'm standing, I know she's waving her arm in a dismissive action like she always does. With each outfit I strut and swish my way through the living room. Putting on a little fashion show for her.

'Did you just pick one of each thing from the rails?'

'Pretty much.'

'I don't think I can take anywhere near this much. I'm only taking hand luggage.'

'Minor detail, babe.'

'I'm not sure the airport people will see it that way.'

'Stop worrying about that and try them on.'

I take her advice. I'm aware I'm still a bit tired and grumpy. Instead I carry on with the impromptu fashion show. When I'm not worrying about weight limits and suitcase size, I'm enjoying myself. Michelle is lounging on the sofa sipping her drink and making all the right oohs and ahhs like I'm a firework display. I twirl and skip around. I'm feeling better already. Who needs Italy? I could just spend my days doing this instead.

'I'm so envious of you getting to go to Italy.'

'You've been to far more exotic places.'

'Yes, but I chose and booked those. It's not the same as someone else sending you off somewhere.' She grins.

She had taken her channel all over the world, visiting other gamers and calling it cultural research. Truth be told she's prone to suffering from cabin fever if she's stuck in the house all the time. The beauty of her job was that she could do her work from anywhere. These particular videos were done purely from her phone and edited on her laptop. The gaming was done on the guest's equipment. It was so clever really. She had explained that the value of doing these was getting extra reach for the guest but it also introduced their followers to her. Mostly though it pulled her from her funks. Revived her mojo. To see her in these moments you wouldn't believe that she would ever be the kind of person to suffer from such bouts.

After my fashion show I fold everything back up to organise later into what to take, what to keep but not take and what to return to Natalie. Going through them now, I don't think there will be much to return - I love them all.

'Thank you so much. I'd have never got round to sorting it out.'

'No worries. Can't send you off without some glamorous new glad rags.'

'Cheers chick.' I smile wide.

Chapter Eleven

On the Wednesday before I was due to leave for Florence, Kim arrived carrying a couple of tubs of freshly baked goods. This always boosted the morale in the office.

'Afternoon children,' she chimed merrily.

Josh appeared at her side instantaneously, peering over her shoulder trying to work out what she had. Lauren and I watched as he dodged around her. In fact, she dodged around him making him chase her. Bob walked in to see Josh about to rugby tackle Kim as she trotted towards the safety of Debbie's desk. No one messed around near Debbie's desk.

'Hey! Get away,' Debbie scolded from behind her screen.

'It's like watching my little brothers fight,' Lauren chuckles.

'You're worse than my kids,' Kim laughs.

We turned around in our chairs, thoroughly enjoying the show. Bob appeared in the doorway near Debbie whose features quickly shifted to looking amused. George arrived behind Bob and he caught my eye as he scanned the room over Bob's shoulder.

'Josh, Kim, stop that. Hand that over,' Bob demanded jestingly.

Kim apologised as she handed the tubs to him. Then pulled a face at Josh as she walked back past him. He stuck his tongue out and sulked back to his desk, mumbling apologies to Bob also.

'Consider these confiscated.'

There was a groan throughout the office as he walked through to the kitchen.

'George, let's grab a drink so we can dunk these delicious biscuits.'

George smirked and followed. Bob was struggling to keep a straight face. Calm resumed and we all returned to our work. I'd been going through a few bits with Lauren in case anything came up whilst I was away. She had written ample notes and was asking all the right questions.

'I think that's everything for now. Did it make sense?' I ask.

'Yep. I think I got it all down.'

'Brilliant. We're only away a couple of days anyway, so there shouldn't be much.'

'But just in case.'

'Exactly.'

'I'd better find the guys. Thanks Lauren.'

I wander off in the direction of the kitchen. Bob and George are squeezed in the kitchen together making drinks.

'Ah, just the lady,' says Bob.

I bow slightly in response.

'I've just made your drink and snuck these for you,' George smiles as he turns with the tray of three mugs and a heaped plate of delicious smelling biscuits.

'Am I that predictable?' I laugh.

'Yes,' they both say in unison.

I turn and open the door for them and follow through to the beanbag corner. George places the tray on the low table and we all grab a seat. I choose my usual floor cushion. George passes me my drink and as he leans towards me, he smiles. His eyes meet mine and I get a waft of his aftershave. I break eye contact first, turning my attention to my drink.

'I wanted to go through your schedule for while you're away. Make sure everything is covered. I'm also curious to know how things are over there at the Hotel. Did you get a chance to print out the documents I sent you?' asks Bob.

We both nod.

'Excellent. Then we'll begin.'

I update Bob. I'm pleased to see that his list pretty much matches mine. There is very little as it goes over the weekend. It was more of a list of anything that might crop up. This reassures me that Lauren has the full rundown.

The questions in the brief for Hotel al Cioccolato are the ones I'd compiled anyway so I know that is fine.

'Right, that's great,' Bob concludes.

'Excuse me, Bob.' Debbie has appeared beside us. 'Here are your printed out tickets.'

She hands both George and I a wodge of paper.

'Ah fantastic,' George and I both say in unison.

'I've taken the liberty of printing you out a map of Florence and the details of where you're staying.'

'Excellent, thanks.'

I don't want to burst her bubble by informing her that all this is done on apps these days. She's more old school. She still has an old flip phone and refuses to get a smart phone. She once told me how she doesn't trust them. I have no idea how anyone can function without one these days. I don't say any of this though - I simply accept the print outs.

She stays standing there a moment longer as if she has something else to say. George and I are both looking expectantly at her. It is not until Bob realises she's still there and looks up, thanking her too, that she leaves. She huffs as she turns on her heel. Many times I wonder who is actually in charge here. I would never huff or roll my eyes at Bob. I value my job and our friendship far too much. At the end of the day, he's the guy who pays our wages. Debbie, on the other hand, seems to have no such qualms, as though she believes herself to be indispensable.

I'm eating my biscuit when I realise that these are the same as from Pat's Pastries. I glance across at Kim. Her secret is safe with me. I love the fact that she goes through the trouble of bringing empty tubs to fill with these. I have true admiration for the facade.

With the meeting over, I catch George just before he gets back to his temporary desk between mine and Bobs.

'I'm gonna nip and grab some lunch. Would you like to join me?'

'Yes, very much so.'

Delight washes across his face and I smile in response. We hurried towards the bakery. I check the time on my phone - it's already past 2pm. The day has flown by. I'm mentally going through my packing list as I'm crossing the road, lured by the smell of fresh bread. Suddenly George grabs my arm and pulls me towards him. In my slightly absent minded state I'm confused as to what he's doing. It's not until the cyclist swears at me that I realise he had pulled me out of the way of a Lycra-clad, middle-aged cyclist.

'Sorry. Thank you,' I say breathlessly into his chest.

I instantly pull away and check behind me before I step back.

'It's my duty to look after you as we're walking out together,' he states plainly.

'Oh, okay,' I answered distractedly.

I can see them starting to wipe down the bare shelves and I'm not willing to leave here empty handed. I skip through the door, sidestepping a lady who looked as though she might be heading in here too. It turns out that she, in fact, was not. She threw an evil glare in my direction as she passed the window.

'Hiya. Not much left I'm afraid.'

He passes the large tray with a small array of sandwich rolls, a few iced buns, a cinnamon roll, a couple of gingerbread men, and dangerously tempting custard tart.

'Could I have the custard tart please.'

I read the labels of the remaining rolls.

'And this.'

I handed him the chicken salad. We both look to George who points to the tuna one and asks for the gingerbread man and cinnamon roll.

'Good choices,' I compliment George as our things are bagged up.

I hold my phone over the reader. The 'open' sign is turned around to say 'closed' as we leave.

'I'm looking forward to our trip,' I say whilst carefully checking both ways as we cross the road.

'Me too. Hotel al Cioccolato sounds like such an awesome place.'

'It really is. They are definitely my favourite clients.'

'What were their names again?'

'Lorenzo and Juliette. They literally bought this place when it was in total disrepair and have room by room created a haven. I can't wait to see the little chocolate factory in real life.'

'Haven't you seen it yet?'

'No. Last time I was there they were in the early stages of converting the barn ready.'

'It'll be equally as exciting for both of us then.'

'Very much so.'

We both move to the side to save ourselves from being trampled. Josh raced past us just as we were arriving back.

'Is there anything left?' he shouts as he takes the stairs two at a time.

'Not much. They were locking up as we left. You might just catch them.'

I hear him shout sorry to someone just as the outside door slams shut.

George brings me over a fresh drink and hands me the bag with my lunch bits in as I am firing back up my computer.

'Thank you. I was about to come back for it.'

'No problem.' He smiles warmly at me.

I'm deep in work mode as I eat my late lunch. I'm trying to clear as much as possible before we leave. I'm also planning to get a head start on next week's stuff. I glance over at George. He's wiping his hands on his napkin and looks deep in thought. I see him reply to something on his phone. He then huffed and turned it over, looking back at his laptop screen. He looks a bit miffed. My attention is redirected as Josh returns sweaty and out of breath from his run to the bakery. He has a bag of something. I swivel in my chair.

'What did you manage to get?'

'He pulls out a tuna roll and gingerbread man.'

'Aww you and George have matching lunches. You're just missing the cinnamon swirl.'

I light a vanilla scented candle on my desk. The others won't realise that it is to try and mask the smell of their tuna.

'Romantic,' says Kim as she prepares to leave. The kids are about to come out of school.

'Only for you, my love.' I wink at her.

'Sorry I can't stay,' she plays along.

She comes over and kisses me on the cheek. Everyone giggles. I blow her a kiss as she leaves and place my hands over my heart and mouth 'I'll miss you'. As I turn back to face my computer, I see George looking at me over his cup. He's smiling and I raise my mug to him. He returns the gesture and we return to our screens. The scent of the candle has gently replaced the smell of fish. I put my headphones in and listen to Imagine Dragons as I work through the virtual task list.

I walked home that evening feeling chuffed to have covered so much ground at work. It's a lovely evening and

I'm in good spirits. I have Michelle coming over to help me pack, which means she'll be helping me drink the wine while correcting my packing skills.

Later that evening I stand, hands on hips in my bedroom.

'Right!' I announce with certainty.

I survey the space. My holdall is laying open on the bed with a pile of toiletries next to it on one side and one of clothes on the other. The hardest part of packing is always trying to decide what to take, not the actual packing of the stuff. We are discussing all the possible scenarios and what would be the ideal outfit for each. Thankfully an hour or so in Michelle took charge. She is hanging each of the outfits up with corresponding shoes and jewellery laid out beneath them.

My packing pile must have literally halved as she worked her way through. I took photos on my phone as she hung each suggestion out. I write notes on them as she suggests ways to wear my hair for the day or evening. She even lends me her mini straighteners and her plug adapter - two things I'd missed off my extensive list. I should be better at this by now with the amount of travelling I've done with work over the past few years. I'm impressed as the bag was zipped up without either one of us having to sit on it.

The idea of leaving is causing me concern. Michelle has not seemed herself the last few days. She's been busy distracting me from my inner turmoil and organising me. However, something in her seems off. Any query into her wellbeing was brushed aside with claims that she was fine. Instead she just plies me with wine and buys me pretty things. She would make the perfect wife. My mood soothes slightly at just the thought of her and her funny messages of encouragement throughout the day. I'm hoping she's as fine as she claims to be and that I'm worrying about nothing.

She is having a meeting with some investors for her channel on Saturday, while I'm away. This is most probably why she seems distracted. She has had sponsors and such since she was quite new but this is serious money they are talking about. Apparently there is even discussion of a Netflix series on her. Possibly similar to her travel-gaming series she previously did.

We were chatting about it the other evening and she was beside herself with excitement. However, on the other hand, it would take a certain amount of the control out of her hands. She's not quite as bothered as me about being in control per se, but she's run this channel, or business, being the sole decision maker since the start. The idea of having to discuss certain decisions with her investors doesn't sit well with her. She's got suggestions to put forward and knows very clearly what she wants.

She is very much someone who doesn't bow down easily. Although as we had made our way casually down the bottle of wine, she voiced the fact that she might like that the assistance would take some of the weight off her shoulders a bit. Plus, there were zillions of pounds to consider. Now that she's pretty well-known, there are possible future invites to red carpet events. She's promised I can be her date. I'm rooting for this as I very much like the idea of glamming up for such a thing and having people try and guess who I am. She'd have to choose my dress, but I'm sure neither of us would mind that.

Chapter Twelve

'Well, that was close,' I say as I try to get my breath back from our run through the airport.

We'd underestimated how long it would take to get through the Friday early afternoon traffic. Now we shuffle forward up the aisle on the aeroplane, George close behind. As we search for our seats.

'You're there.'

His breath tickles my neck and the warmth of his arm as he points over my shoulder makes my cheeks flush - having him this close is far nicer than it should be. I stretch up to put my bag in the overhead compartment. George helps me to shove my bag the last of the way into space. I look back to George as I climb into my seat. He simply winks and points up the plane to where his seat is. I shift myself as far away from my travel companion as possible, but these seats are not made for space from your fellow passengers.

The man next to me has a full picnic laid out on his tray and a giant newspaper ready to unfold. I drop a quick message to Michelle to let her know I'm on the plane. There is a message from Andy wishing me safe travels. I reply to thank her. Instantly a message comes back from her saying she is looking forward to catching up with me when I return. I sigh. I really don't know if I want to. Do I just want to draw a line under this relationship? Or see if we can still be friends like me and Michelle? Or do I want to keep trying? According to what she said when I last saw her, she is wanting marriage or nothing. To lay her claim on me. To brand me as hers. That is not in alignment with my plans. I take a deep breath, fiddling with the cord of my headphones. I pop my phone on aeroplane mode, stick my earphones in and pick up my book.

The plane finally starts to get moving. The speed increases and I'm pushed back in my seat as we take off. I smile to myself as I look out the window, ready for the next adventure. I close my eyes and see the view from my imaginary Italian villa window. The smell of fresh bread, coffee and apricot jam. As we level out I drift further into my vision. I have an overwhelming feeling of familiar calm. Like coming home. This dream life is becoming more real each time. It is taking my mind completely out of the here and now.

I keep my eyes closed and stay in my dream world. I'm standing in my villa, sounds drifting in from the open door, the sound of friendly banter. The feel of the warm summer breeze on my skin. And then there, standing in the doorway, is the person. The sun is bright behind them so I can't make out their face. I smile as I can sense the same welcoming response from them too. The overwhelming sense of love causes a lump in my throat as the emotion takes me by surprise. They move towards me and...

My eyes snap open as I sense movement, we're preparing to land. I have literally slept the whole way.

*

We arrived in Rome airport and jumped on the shuttle bus to the train station. As it was already past seven in the evening, we decided to grab some food there before the next part of our journey. After a relaxed train ride, our stomachs full of a quick McDonalds, we arrived at Florence station. I'm in a flurry of excitement ready to show George just why I was so pleased to be returning.

It is late and, although there is still bustle, we decide to simply flag a taxi rather than walk. It's been a long day. I give him Debbie's print out with the address. He double-checks that's where we want to be.

'You can walk, no?' he asks, amused.

We shake our heads, confused by his question.

'Okay,' he responds simply, starting up the car.

We turn right, drive 200 yards and then left, and another 50 yards. He stops.

'Here you go.'

We peer out of the window and both chuckle.

I'm tired by this time and grateful to be greeted at our Airbnb by a super smiley Italian man who opens the door. He leads us up the dim corridor and we follow him up the five flights of stairs to my room.

'This is your room. You like? You have everything you need, yes? And a little balcony.'

He walks to the far end of the room and opens the doors. I peer past him and see the rooftops, which make me smile.

'Here is the kitchen and the bathroom.'

He hands me the key and goes to leave.

'Erm, excuse me,' I call after him. 'Where is the other room?'

He turns back, still smiling but confused.

'Other room?'

'Yes. There should be two.'

'No, only one room. You not together?'

'No. We, erm, just work together.'

I realise I'm making lots of hand gestures. He looks amused as he tries to follow them. I'm expecting him to start frantically ringing people, checking email correspondence on his phone and getting all in a tizz. Instead he smiles, walks back past us and points to the sofa that's situated opposite the foot of the bed.

'Here this is - how do you say - sofa bed?'

He's moving the cushions and pulling out the bed. George helps him and they make quick work of it.

I smile and thank our host for solving the sleeping arrangement. He leaves us and is humming a tune to himself which echoes as he descends the stone staircase. George has started unpacking and hanging his few clothes in the wardrobe next to his makeshift bed. I make us both a drink and bring it back through to our room. Walking back through I wonder just how this might work. I'm not great at sharing my space even with people I know well. I even find staying over at my Mum's house weird. I glance in the wardrobe as I pass. I see that he has arranged his clothes on one shelf and only used half the hangers, to the right-hand side of the space, leaving me half the wardrobe and a shelf for my things.

'We made it. Here's to Florence.'

We raise our cups.

'To Florence,' we toast.

We sit silently staring out of the doors and across the rooftops, listening to the sounds of the street below.

'Will you be alright on that sofa bed?'

'Absolutely. Are you alright with me being in the room?'

'Of course.'

We finish our drinks and agree that we're both ready for sleep. As I climb into bed, the sound of the springs pinging and the frame creaking make me giggle. From his position on the makeshift bed George is laughing at my antics. Which makes me laugh harder too.

'I'm so excited to be staying in Florence this time. I'm looking forward to getting to see some of the city while we're here,' I say, trying to compose myself.

I wriggle around slightly trying to get comfy.

'Me too. I Googled the top places to visit. There are so many.'

He's propped up on his elbows looking through the bars at the foot of the bed. I shift up slightly too so we can see each other properly.

'I've been told that the Ponte Vecchio is a must see.'

'Ah, the jewellery shops on the bridge. I saw that on the list.'

'Yeah, I believe it's one of the main tourist places.'

He yawns, which makes me yawn.

'Urgh. I think I'm more tired than I realised,' he says.

'Do you want me to turn the lamp off?'

'Yes please. Night, Hayley.'

'Night, George.'

I reach for the lamp, causing the bed to creak. This gives me the giggles again.

'What?' he asks sleepily.

'Sorry. It's this bed.'

'Is it more comfortable than it sounds?'

'Surprisingly, yes. As long as I position myself so there are no springs digging in.'

'What would the team say if they knew we were sharing a room?' he says in the darkness.

'We'd never hear the last of it.'

The giggles have subsided and I can hear his breathing deepen. I'm finding it comforting, knowing he is close. It jolts me from drifting off as he suddenly speaks again.

'Why do you think Debbie only booked this one room?'

'So she could tell the team we were sharing this creaky old bed.'

The giggles start again. It's as if I'm at a sleepover where I'm too excited to sleep even though I'm tired.

Chapter Thirteen

The next morning we step out into the sunshine and mid-morning warmth of the sun in Florence!

'Our journey seems pretty straight forward on Google maps. We just need to walk back to the station, get a train to the village nearest to Hotel al Cioccolato. Apparently it's only a short distance from there.'

'Fabulous!'

I twirl with my arms in the air, spinning as I look up at the blue skies of Italy.

'Careful,' George warns as he stops my bag from taking down an unsuspecting passer-by.

'It's so beautiful here.'

'Just look at the mix match of architecture.'

'I love how each building is holding its own.'

'Like they all have as much right as each other to be here.'

'Absolutely.'

'I guess it helps that the weather is nice.'

'For sure. Although I think I'd love it in any weather.'

'Even snow?'

'I'd love it more.'

He smiles at my enthusiasm.

'The vibe is just so friendly. I feel safe here,' I added.

'I get what you mean. Perhaps it's just the fact we're not off to work.'

'Ah but we are! In the bestest place ever!'

As though I'd jinxed us, we passed a couple of men who were having what appeared to be a heated conversation. Their voices were loud, arms gesturing wildly as they spoke. I duck to avoid one of their arms, moving closer to George. Instantly he placed a protective arm around me. We carried on walking and kept looking back to watch it play out. Within seconds the two men were laughing and giving each other a farewell hug. I felt my shoulders relax down. We looked at each other and laughed at how the situation had been nothing more than friends talking animatedly.

'Man, they are actually friends,' says George, grinning.

'I'm not gonna lie, I'd have never guessed it,' I chuckle.

I notice that George still has his arm around me and again I wonder if this caring man has a significant other in his life. I'm unsure how to broach the subject without it coming across as me being interested in him in a romantic way. I wonder how I would feel if he did have a partner. He's never mentioned one and isn't wearing a ring, but some people just don't talk about their personal lives at work or like jewellery.

Would I be able to stifle these feelings that were bubbling up in me, even more so now we are here away from everyone and everything we know? What if it turned out that he was just a player and was taking advantage of this situation to just have a fling? I don't believe my currently fragile heart would cope with such a situation. Perhaps a no-strings attached fling is exactly what I need. Michelle would say so. But I've always been more of a relationship type of person.

I sigh deeply at the barrage of 'what ifs' that were racing through my mind. George gave me a reassuring squeeze. I jumped as his hand accidentally tickled my waist, making him jolt too.

'Shit, sorry,' he says, quickly removing his arm and putting his hands in the air by way of declaring his innocence.

'Sorry, sorry! It just made me jump. I'm unbearably ticklish.'

'I thought I'd overstepped the mark.'

'Not at all,' I reassured him.

We entered the station, weaving our way through the bustle of the other commuters.

'That's the one we need,' I say, pointing to the screen.

'Excellent. That gives us time to grab coffee in the café.'

'I like your thinking.'

I follow his lead with a spring in my step. The café smells amazing as we open the door. It is buzzing with late commuters. We stay close so as not to lose our spot in the queue.

'It's strange how everyone is moving fast but seems relaxed,' I say quietly. 'It's a skill I would very much like to learn.'

'Perhaps they run a course we could join. Or an exhibition of relaxation we can visit tomorrow.'

'I'm Googling that,' I chuckle.

'Perhaps we should suggest it to our clients.'

'To be honest I find just being here makes me feel like a more relaxed person.'

'Me too. Seriously, this is your job right now.'

'I know,' I grin. 'This is the way I would love every day to start.'

'You never know. You might be able to talk Bob round.'

'As you're such good friends you could put in a good word for me.'

'I don't think I'd have to. He knows how lucky he is to have you.'

I'm curious to know just what Bob has told him about me. By the seems of it, all good things. We shuffled along until it was our turn at the counter. We both order cappuccinos and brioches. The woman smiles at us, obviously having many tourists through here on a daily basis.

I'm enjoying listening to the locals chatting amongst themselves. There is something about this language that makes me smile. I just can't get over how expressive they are - it's fantastic to watch. George carries our tray over to a table which two smartly dressed men have just vacated. We still have half an hour before our train leaves so I'm pleased to have a chance to savour my proper Italian cappuccino. These tables are small and I'm aware that our knees must be practically touching under the table. I turn in my seat and cross my legs so mine are at a safe distance.

'Isn't this exciting? Drinking proper cappuccinos in Italy!'

'It really is,' he smiles.

'I'm loving just listening to the chatter,' I say quietly, leaning into the table so as not to sound like a complete imbecile.

Being surrounded by the culture, it feels like we've been invited into someone else's world to glimpse at how others live. I'm such a curious person by nature about other people's lives. I like to know the hows and whys. To know how they arrived at the place they were in, the decisions they made to get there and generally how that was working out for them. I guess the fact that I used to watch a lot of old 'Miss Marple' episodes as a kid made it part of my conditioning to ask lots of questions and observe. I like to think it makes me appear interested in people, and we all know that people like nothing more than to talk about themselves. I know, I'm no exception to that rule.

'Have you been to Italy before?' I ask George, just as he bites into his brioche.

He covers his mouth with his hand as he finishes his mouthful.

'No. I'm so chuffed to have finally got here. It's been on my list for years.'

That last point catches my attention - the guy makes lists, and by the seems of it, he actually refers back to it and ticks things off it, such as coming here. I realise that my hand has actually rested on my chest, possibly to hold my heart in from just handing itself over to him without my full permission. This whole thing with Andy must have left me weak. Perhaps it's just a test of resilience. Maybe my heart is searching for answers to what or who it is I actually want. If not Andy, then who? George? I think it's probably more likely that he just happens to be here.

It occurs to me that I've drifted into my own thoughts again when I feel his hand touch mine to get my attention. It felt as though electricity suddenly jolted me back to the here and now and his smile is the thing that greets me. Could it actually be that all the other things that exist around us both on a daily basis have been stripped away to leave just the two of us, thrown together in Florence? I'm not sure either that if we were in, say Sheffield, the same effect would be being experienced right now. But I might be wrong. Without doing a 'Sliding Doors' moment and seeing how it would have played out if we had in fact got on a different train, I cannot be sure.

'Sorry, I was miles away.'

'You're okay. Worrying about things back home?' he asks gently.

'No, no. I was thinking about Sheffield.'

That was the best I could think of as a response at that point.

'Now, Sheffield I have been to. I went to uni there. However, Italy I have not. I'm a Florentine virgin.' He winks.

I sip my coffee and tear off a piece of my pastry to cover my blushing.

'What did you study there?'

'Civil engineering.' He pulls a strained face,

'I'm impressed.'

'Don't be. It was the course my father wanted me to take. I worked in it for a while but it's just not my thing,' he says, putting the last of his brioche in his mouth.

'So many people I knew did exactly that. They followed the path that their parents laid down for them and then later in life they branched out into something that is more them.'

'Exactly that.'

'How did you go from that to being a business consultant?'

'Good question. I'm not sure whether it was a moment of clarity or my calling. It was more a case that I'd been advising friends on their businesses for years. I loved nothing more than catching up with friends of mine who ran their own businesses or worked for start-ups and I found it so interesting. They would discuss how it was going and I'd find myself just offering simple pieces of advice that would solve a problem they'd struggled with for a while.'

'Interesting. How did that turn into what you do now?' I asked as I drained my drink.

'Well, the job I was in came to an end and I was bouncing ideas around with these friends over a few drinks and they suggested it. I thought they were winding me up at first but the more I thought about it the more it seemed like a good idea. I figured it was worth a try, so I went home and researched it. I ended up on WikiHow with a ten-step plan of how to start up my own business consultancy and that's how the story began.'

He sits back smiling, holding his cup.

'That's awesome. I'm always intrigued by how people get to where they are,' I say with genuine interest.

'It's never a simple story though, is it? That's what makes it even more fun and interesting. It's never just one decision. It's lots of little things coming together over time.'

The way his eyes light up as he talks about it makes him literally glow. All I want to do is go round the table and hug him and not let go. I resist the urge though and instead send him a beaming smile across the table and finish my breakfast.

'Ready?' he asks.

'Yep.'

We collect our items together and head off to find our platform. Somehow in the twenty minutes we've been in the café the entire population of Florence seem to have made their way into the train station. We weave our way through the crowd to try to see the screen informing us of our platform. According to the screen, it still hasn't been decided. It's like King's Cross - everyone is staring at the screen ready to run the second the number pops up.

'I feel as though we should be prepping ourselves, warming up, jogging on the spot, stretching out those tight calf muscles,' I say.

'Luckily the platforms are literally all in one row and visible from here so we should be okay.'

'Not like King's Cross where it's more of a marathon and god forbid you slow or take a wrong turn.'

'Exactly.'

'Can you see the numbers?' I ask George.

'Correre!' someone shouts.

All of a sudden the mass moves, filtering through to the gates. The poor ticket guy is nearly swept along with them. I feel George take my hand and we laugh as we follow the crowd towards platform five. Strangely I feel elated by this -

his palm in mine, our glances at each other as we run. My satchel clears a few of the stragglers from around us and for once I'm pleased to have such a violent natured bag on my side. I certainly wouldn't want to be on the receiving end of it.

We get through the gate safely and it's not so crowded now as three of the other platforms have trains arriving soon too. Everyone looks flushed and accomplished at being positioned ready to be some of the first on.

'This must be how tourists feel in London.'

'Yea. I guess it is,' he agrees, looking around at the other passengers.

'I hadn't ever thought of how intimidating it might be for people who aren't used to it.'

'Me neither to be honest, we just take it all in our stride as Londoners, don't we? I know when I first came to London it was a huge culture shock. I was used to a much slower pace,' he says reflectively.

'When you'd been in Sheffield?'

The train pulls into the station.

'No. I'd returned home for a few years after uni.'

We shuffle forward but try to stay far enough away from the edge. The doors open and George takes me by the hand and guides me straight into an empty window seat and sits himself next to me.

'Nicely done.'

He winks in response. After what feels like an age, people stop getting into our carriage and the doors on the platform slide shut. We are off and moving. Somehow at this point everyone seems to collectively breathe a sigh of relief at having made it onto the train and space miraculously becomes available.

I stare out of the window and relax into my seat. We are soon travelling through the Tuscan countryside that is far more beautiful than any photos I've ever seen. The cypress trees stand proudly throughout the landscape. I have an urge to capture it on my phone but I know I could never do it justice. Instead, I allow them to imprint in my mind, so that in quiet moments I can imagine being back here in even sharper detail.

There are random houses dotted about, all of which are the beautiful sandy stone colour that seems to glow in the sunlight. I love how they seem imperfectly made. As though someone just needed a house and started building it until it became what we see now. The roofs never seem symmetrical and the walls are sometimes leaning in towards each other rather than standing alone. They appeared as though they got tired and took a moment to rest. Somehow this makes them far more beautiful than the houses I'm used to seeing. They have real character, as though they have many stories to tell.

Everything seems so lush. As spring makes way for summer I can almost feel the rebirth of the land. That sounds weird, I know, but I can feel myself being energised by it all. I take more deep breaths and turn slightly so I can get the best view of it all.

There are vineyards and olive groves along the way. It would be amazing to come back during harvest season. To see the transformation from this mirage of green with all the colours of the grapes, olives and apple orchards with everyone out getting the crops in. It must be amazing to live in such a place where the produce is grown and transformed into something even more incredible.

I wonder if these small villages still have the old community spirit of coming together with their neighbours to bring in their harvests and celebrate with dinners and parties. My mind flashes up scenes from my daydreams of the kitchen with friends around a chunky wooden table, all chatting and preparing a meal while conversation flows with the wine. It must be a real sense of achievement and relief that the weather has been kind that year, that the harvest is good. I know I have a certain waiting period to see if my work has paid off but I'm in a situation where I'm paid a wage no matter the outcome.

I can see why many places, like Hotel al Cioccolato, have had to branch out into other venue streams. They have the main hotel but have expanded the chocolate production to have factory tours and chocolate making courses as well. This is why they have been busy renovating. They have cleverly gotten their own wholesale chocolate business and send it all around the world.

I think they have done well to keep the friendly, rural, quirky side of things whilst branching out. It would have been so much easier for them to have moved the production and distribution to somewhere else. Yet I remember speaking to Juliette about this and she didn't want to lose the core of their inspiration. She'd said something about the fact that she would feel like a fraud if the only connection to the place that the chocolate had was the picture on the wrapper. She believed it would be bad energetically. I love the fact she thinks like this.

Here on this train, the beauty and possibilities through the window have got the rusty old cogs in my mind turning. The thoughts about the people who live here mixed with the visit to see all the exciting new things at Hotel al Cioccolato have got me thinking.

Do I really want to stay in my current job and home? Michelle and I have often fallen into these conversations, the idea of doing something different, getting out there in the world. She makes a difference to other people's lives as well as her own. I guess I do to a point. But some days it doesn't feel enough. Yet, every time, the wine bottle empties, the moment passes and the alarm clock is set for the next day of work and I forget I ever wanted anything different.

Something inside me is burning for change, new experiences. But I'm a creature of habit, someone who likes structure and to feel in control. I don't believe I'm brave enough to make these kinds of changes. Yet here in Italy I feel as though anything is possible for me.

We arrive at our destination and make our way to the door. George looks back at me to check I'm following. I give him a reassuring smile. He smiles back and helps me from the train. The gap that we are famous for announcing in England is actually about a foot wide. I have to leap slightly to get past it and I'm grateful he is there to steady me.

Chapter Fourteen

After a fun and exhilarating drive from the train station through the winding hills of Tuscany in a hired Fiat 500 we pull into the freshly gravel driveway of Hotel al Cioccolato. The tiny car skims across it and I have to turn it slightly to stop it skidding into the oversized, decorative stone urns, guarding the front steps.

'I don't think doing donuts in their drive is the most professional way to arrive.'

'You're no fun,' I chuckle. 'Bob said to show you how I do business. First impressions count.'

'But you've been here before.'

'You haven't. I'll tell them it was your idea.'

As the dust settles in the driveway, I pull on the handbrake, grab my bag and step out of the car, still chuckling.

'Welcome to Hotel al Cioccolato!'

I swoop my arms wide, presenting it to him. The fresh cream render made the four-storey building glow warmly in the sunshine. New caramel-coloured shutters graced the windows - the ultimate accessory for a villa of this age. As though it had its eyelashes on. The dark frames of the front doors and windows made it the perfect chocolate box image. The time and cost they had put into this was well spent and perfectly executed.

'It's even more impressive than I imagined,' he says, while craning his neck to see the full height of the majestic structure.

'Isn't it just. It's changed so much since I was here last. I can't wait to see inside.'

As if on cue, the dark oak doors open and Juliette trots elegantly down the set of steps closest to us. Her red lipstick smile is as wide as her outstretched arms. My smile matches hers as we connect at the base of the stairs. From this angle I see the urns are bigger than the car. The opulent blooms overflowing from them are the perfect cheerful greeting. Lorenzo descends the stairs more carefully but with an equally welcoming smile.

'George, let me introduce you to the wonderful Juliette and Lorenzo. The proud owners of Hotel al Cioccolato. Juliette, Lorenzo, this is George. He's the friend of Bob's who is joining me on my visit.'

They shake hands.

'It is lovely to welcome you here, George.' Juliette says. 'And Hayley, it's so good to see you again!'

She hugs me tight after kissing my cheeks and holds me at arm's length like she's my Italian mother.

'You are looking well, Hayley,' she manages to make my name sound so exotic. 'Although you've lost weight,' she observes as she pulls a face of disapproval. 'No matter. We'll feed you.'

Juliette is an elegant lady and Lorenzo is equally dapper. They are around Bob's age, in their mid-fifties. Juliette is one of those people who always looks immaculately put together. More importantly, she is as beautiful in personality as in her appearance. Her kind and friendly soul shines through. Lorenzo and her are perfectly suited. He is as charming as they come.

'Lorenzo, how are you?'

He kisses me on both cheeks as well.

'Very good. And you?'

'Yes, thank you. I'm so chuffed to be here and excited to see all the work you've been doing.'

Lorenzo has walked over to where the car is, windows and roof still down, looking as though it wants to go on another adventure.

'Wherever did you find this car?'

'We hired it from the station master,' answers George.

'This is just like our first car, it's a classic,' Lorenzo chuckles.

'Really?'

'It was the most fun car we had.'

Lorenzo and Juliette are stroking the car as though it was a lost pet that had returned home.

'It's getting warm out, you must be thirsty. Let us find drinks,' Juliette says to me, then calls across to the guys, 'We're off inside.'

I look back to where Lorenzo is still leaning with one hand on the bonnet of the Fiat talking cars with George. Juliette and I link arms and walk up the left side of the double stone steps.

'How is Bob? Is he well?'

'He's doing great, thanks. Busy as ever. He went on a date the other night.'

'How wonderful. I've been telling him for years that he needs to settle down.'

'Me too. Perhaps he will one day.'

'Not until he stops wearing those ridiculous trainer boot things.'

'Converse,' I chuckle. 'That's his signature piece.'

'My point exactly.'

We both giggle. Bob and Juliette worked together back in their twenties. I always thought they had a bit of a soft spot for each other, but Lorenzo scooped her up and they moved out here about twenty years ago.

'These doors are fabulous,' I say, running my fingers over the ornate iron work. 'Such craftsmanship.'

'We had them made specifically by a carpenter and ironmonger in Lucca. They are as close to the originals as we could get them.'

'These new frames and the shutters make the frontage so welcoming.'

'We decided to get them done while the scaffolding for the rendering was up. I had no idea just how expensive scaffolding was.'

'I can't even imagine!'

'But we are lucky to have had a mild winter so we could get the work done before the wedding season.'

'How are the weddings going?'

'Really well. Last year was our best yet and that paid for most of these exterior renovations.'

'That's great. I'm so chuffed things are picking up.'

'Thank you. We already have bookings for the chocolate making courses.'

'See, and you thought no one would want to come all the way out here just for chocolate.' I playfully touched her arm.

'I admit I was wrong. Lots of visitors said that it was a welcome change to the olive groves or vineyard tours offered locally.'

'It's good that you found a niche that people love.'

The men have caught up with us now and Lorenzo is finishing telling George all about the landscaping. The smell of freshly waxed wood and the ticking of a grandfather clock greeted us as we stepped onto the polished terracotta tiles of the entrance hall.

'I'm genuinely gobsmacked by the transformation.'

'Thank you. It looks exactly as we imagined it to all those years ago when we first saw it.'

'Look,' Lorenzo says as he moves to a wall beside a couple of red Chesterfield sofas. 'We've taken photos throughout the years and chose the best ones to display. This was how the outside looked - just bare stone and rotten shutters and doors. This is the hallway here.'

'It's like looking at a different building,' says George.

We look from the pictures to the space we're occupying. They have opened it up so the sweeping staircase stands proud, with the reception desk to the right. The space is immense. The walls are painted in a light orange at the bottom and a delicate yellow at the top, with an elaborate floral border separating the two. The classic framed paintings adorn the space. I'm like a child in church, my eyes intrigued by every detail. The array of wildflowers with sunflowers in a mixture of vessels adds to the overall effect.

'Come and see the new garden room. We felt it would be nice to have a light and airy room where people could eat and enjoy the views without having to be outside on the terrace.'

It hugged this corner of the building and had tables positioned throughout, looking out over the Tuscan countryside. I drift towards the open doors, as though something outside is involuntarily drawing me towards it. I can hear the others chatting about the finer details of the building works behind me. I stopped by the railings on the terrace which wrapped round the back of the villa. The scenery is breathtaking. I could stand here forever, with the clear blue skies illuminating the rolling hills. Juliette appears beside me and I follow her back to join the guys, past the outside kitchen, which now has a wood-burning pizza oven.

'It looks like a good party space too,' says George.

'Oh, you wait. There is a party room,' I say.

'We've done a lot there too,' says Lorenzo.

We all follow him back across the room as he opens the double doors to the left of the space.

'This is our favourite room,' Juliette says.

'Okay, I see what you meant - this is a true party room in every sense of the word.'

I stay back as they venture further in, just taking in the sight of the upgraded ballroom. The gold gilding on the architrave and ceiling rose has been freshened up. As Lorenzo is opening and folding back each of the huge shutters the sun illuminates more of the decoration. The tatty wallpaper that was here previously has now been replaced with tasteful muted shades of cream causing the gilding and magnificent chandelier to fully embody the grandeur it depicted without distraction.

I walk slowly through the now aptly named 'Grand Ballroom'. The original parquet flooring has been revived and the glinting of the chandelier is reflected in it, with tiny rainbows as the sun beams hit the crystals.

'This is going to be utterly enchanting for your summer Ball.'

'That was all I could think of as we were working on this room.'

'You've done the villa proud.' It's giving me chills just saying it. 'You've literally breathed life back into it. It feels as though you've got its heart beating again.'

'That means a lot to us. Thank you,' Juliette says, taking Lorenzo's hand. He lifts hers to his smiling lips and kisses it gently.

George and I smile shyly at each other, Lorenzo's gesture is so endearing.

Walking straight through the expansive room we make our way out of the adjacent doors that lead through to the dining room. It has all been decorated in stunning shades of green, from the rich, dark emeralds of the curtains to the rustic olive of the tablecloths. It complimented the view from the terrace perfectly.

George and Lorenzo were still deep in conversation about the building works. George was explaining that he had renovated a house in Lancashire a few years ago. It somehow makes me sad when I see houses standing derelict and neglected. That's another reason I'm so pleased to see this place having been brought back to life one room at a time.

The kitchen backs onto the dining room. They had needed to invest in a proper commercial kitchen to bring it up to legislation. They were catering for large amounts of guests now they had more accommodation and regular events. The steel worktops, large oven and fridges made it look slick.

'I see you've invested in copper saucepans, Lorenzo.'

'I got my giant urns and he got the pots,' Juliette chuckles. 'Although, his cost more than mine.'

They now had four toilets down here which made a lot of sense. Juliette was also pleased to have a larger utility space for all the linen and bedding.

'When we forecasted how much outsourcing the laundry would cost us a year, it worked out cheaper long term to renovate this room and buy larger machines.'

'And this wonderful flat iron press saves even more time. I think it's the only time I've enjoyed ironing. Come and see the bedrooms.'

Juliette leads us up the stairs that stretch up and over the reception area. There were eight modest sized rooms, all with beautiful ensuites.

'I love how you've designed each room with a theme from the painting over the bed. How ingenious,' I say.

The colours from the paintings had been used throughout the rooms and made it feel luxurious yet homely. At the end of the corridor was a door which led up a slightly thinner set of stairs. Being taller Lorenzo and George had to duck slightly as we reached the top but it was worth it. There were four more rooms up here that were individual suites, housing little seating areas. The views were astounding, from this vantage point I had a clearer view of the woods and hills again. I break myself away and catch back up with our hosts.

'Thank you so much for the tour. It's been wonderful to see all the work you've done. I can't believe the transformation.'

'To see it through your eyes makes it all worthwhile,' says Juliette.

'We've been working on it so long it is hard to see the difference sometimes. That's why we took all the photos,' says Lorenzo.

'How long have you been here?' asks George as we make our way back down the stairs and out onto the terrace.

'We found this little gem back in 2002,' says Lorenzo.

'We moved back to Italy in 1999, just after we were married. We figured that if the Millennium bug was going to wipe out the world we may as well end our days somewhere beautiful,' Juliette chuckles.

'Yes. But thankfully it didn't and we came across this place on a day out. It was sitting here abandoned.'

'We instantly fell in love with it and could see how it could look, with just a bit of work. Bless our naive young hearts.'

'If only we'd known,' Lorenzo laughs.

'If you knew what you know now, would you have still bought it?'

'Yes,' they say in unison and laugh again.

'In fact,' Juliette says. 'We'd have bought it twice.'

Chapter Fifteen

I was keen to see the renovated out-buildings, but we all decided that we had best discuss the Ball since that was our reason for being here. As we sat in this beautiful setting, delicious food was served to us with gratefully received coffee. Lunch is divine. I sit back, trying to make my stomach comfortable without tipping the chair. I reach down to retrieve my notebook from my bag and clear a space in front of me. We start discussing the party and as Juliette explains her plans I get a vision in my mind of just how magical the place is going to look.

'Am I on the right track, envisioning fairy lights hanging from every possible place and soft jazz escaping from the main rooms out into the garden here?'

'That is exactly how I see it too. We have a band who will be set up in the ballroom.'

'Will their music reach the garden room and terrace?' I ask, resting my pen on my lip.

'Yes. There are speakers that we had installed so people can enjoy the music in their chosen spot,' says Lorenzo.

'Perfect. Good thinking.'

'Are you catering yourself or do you need me to organise a company?'

'We have a team coming in and using our kitchen. We've used them a few times now and they are great. If you could liaise with them that would be helpful.'

'No problem.' I scribble down notes as we go.

'What were your thoughts on the invitations and social media package?'

'We love the idea of the golden tickets being sent to people already subscribed or who have been here before. If you could tell us more detail about how the social media package works though, that would be great,' says Juliette.

'Yes. We are worried that if we send out too much on social media that we will be inundated - like an illegal rave.'

'Totally understandable,' I chuckle. 'But most of it will just be images of the Hotel and chocolate factory. People will have to subscribe to find out more details and book tickets.'

'That makes more sense,' Lorenzo says, and Juliette smiles with relief.

'Sorry. I should have been clearer. I can see your concerns.'

'Just to clarify, this event is to bring in more bookings for the accommodation and weddings, etc.?'

'Yes. We like your idea of using the images Josh will take on the night to bring in sales for the chocolate. To be honest, although the factory is a bit bigger now, we still can't produce huge amounts. It's more of a gimmick at this point,' explains Juliette.

'After all this work it would be a shame not to capitalise on it, but the hotel part is the most important,' I agree.

'Exactly,' says Lorenzo. 'Plus we'd have to change the name if we didn't keep the chocolate production.'

'I hadn't thought of that,' Juliette says.

'Would you like to state a theme or dress code?'

'It would be nice to have suits and ballgowns. But we think that going too far with the Willy Wonka theme and installing chocolate fountains isn't necessary,' says Juliette.

'Understandable. So we can just state that it's a black tie. Obviously you may still get the odd crazy outfits arrive.'

George picks up his phone, looking concerned.

'Everything alright?' Lorenzo asks.

'Yes. I'm just cancelling my purple velvet suit and top hat.'

We all dissolve into laughter.

*

The largest of the barns houses the chocolate factory. I can now see how a whole book was so famously written based on such a place. The smell of the rich chocolate reaches us as we are approaching the door. I'm tingling with excitement at the idea that there might be a chocolate river and edible trees inside. I'm like a child, jiggling with excitement, George places a hand on my back as we filter through the big heavy doors. The tingling travelled through me from the warmth of his hand. I turn and smile.

'This is even better than I expected. A real live chocolate factory!'

He chuckles and puts a slight amount of pressure to move me forward so we aren't blocking the doorway. A flashback of being on a school field trip and constantly being told to behave flickers across my mind. I giggle at the thought. The guide to the factory, who introduces herself as Helena, is standing with arms open, welcoming us in. She's just about ready to show us the little chocolate factory. Juliette is here but Lorenzo has excused himself to go and deal with something important. I guess he's seen this enough times that he doesn't feel the need to stay with us at this point. I'm not sure if the novelty would ever wear off for me, and by the look on Juliette's face she still finds it uber cool too.

I love that about her - she is so modest. They have achieved so much in just a few years. I guess that's the thing; she is doing what she loves, what they both love. I've found over the years that these are the epitome of successful people. They might not make the most money but they have the loyalty of their customers and guests. Their love for what they do shines through. Which means that people, such as me, consider them friends and want to keep returning not just for the product or stay, but also for the contact with Juliette and Lorenzo.

The intoxicating smell of chocolate is thick in the air. My mouth is watering and I'm hoping we get to test it. I know I was full from lunch but chocolate doesn't really count, does it? Especially if we are just getting little test bits. Helena is explaining about the process the chocolate goes through and I'm trying with all my might to concentrate. I'm honestly just thinking about how if Michelle was here she'd be in there tasting all the chocolate by now. I inwardly smile at the thought.

Once Helena is in full flow explaining the process her smile lights up her whole face. Her enthusiasm is infectious. My phone rings, momentarily breaking us all out of chocolate experience. It's Michelle. I no longer find it freaky that when I think of her she appears in one form or another. In fact, I'm more weirded out these days if she doesn't. I'm pleased to hear from her but her timing could have been better.

'Sorry,' I say to the room, and nip out and answer it. 'I'll be back in a jiffy.'

'Hi. Sorry - it's me. I hadn't heard from you and just wanted to check you arrived safely,' Michelle's panicky voice drifts down the phone.

'I'm so sorry honey. I meant to text but yes, I'm safe. Thank you for checking.'

'Thank goodness. I was just Googling who to ring if your friend is lost in Italy.'

'Did you find out?'

'I did and you don't deserve to know.' She's trying to sound grumpy but I know she'll have been beside herself with worry.

'I really am sorry. I promise to keep you posted from now on. By the way, I'm currently in a chocolate factory.'

'Are there Oompa Loompas?' Her tone is lighter now.

'Not so far. I'll keep you posted. Right, I'd best dash, sorry. Love ya.'

'Have fun. Love you too. Stay safe.'

'You too. Bye.'

I sneak back into the barn to re-join the tour. I'm a bit put out by the fact that Andy hasn't sent messages, even though we had agreed to just be in touch upon my return. To give each other both time. Yet I'd hoped she might fight harder for me. It makes no sense as I don't think 'us' is what I want, but still. I push the thoughts away as I turn my phone to silent. At least I have put Michelle's mind at rest, I can't wait to tell her of the fun I had driving the car. I'm still smiling as I pull the incredibly heavy door open. Everyone smiles back at me as I arrive back alongside them. I'm pleased that they waited for me to continue.

'Unfortunately, we are not able to actually grow cocoa here but we ensure that our beans are sourced from ethical, sustainable sources. These fifty-pound sacks are emptied onto these trays and roasted. The husks are then removed and they go into this refiner for around three days. It is kept moving throughout this process, as the friction helps it along. It's left to rest for two months before it's tempered and cast into these moulds. We do this over this grate so any excess is caught. They are moved over here to cool and set. Once ready it's demoulded by hand.' She gestures at a smiling young man at a long table. 'At this point they are wrapped for sale. We have a small team of four who see this process through from start to finish. We train everyone so they can help wherever they're needed.'

'I never realised how long it takes. I thought you just melt it and let it set in moulds,' I say.

'That's what makes our little factory extra interesting - that we produce from beans,' she says. 'Do you have any questions?'

'Where do you sell your chocolate?' asks George.

'Good question. We mainly sell here at the hotel. You may have seen the little stand in reception. A few of the local shops stock them too.'

'We are planning on selling them through the website and putting hampers together,' adds Juliette.

'I love that idea,' I say. 'Speaking of which, would you like to put a chocolate filled gift bag together for each of our guests at the Ball?'

'Oh yes, that would be wonderful.'

'Is there much wastage?' I ask the lady.

'There can be and we use this in our special chocolate mousse in the restaurant.'

'What a clever way to reduce waste,' says George.

'Any other questions?'

'Are we allowed to test it?' asks George with a cheeky grin.

'It would be cruel to bring you in here and not let you try some,' she says, smiling back at him.

One of her team collects a tray that's been specially arranged and offers them round. They explain what flavour each one is and we thoroughly enjoy testing them all.

'They are incredible,' I say once I've tried three different flavours.

'Yes. I have to be very strict with myself,' Juliette giggles, patting her flat stomach.

'I'm not sure I'd be able to resist,' George says, while helping himself to another one.

After thanking Helena profusely we make our way across to a row of smaller buildings.

'This used to be the stable block,' explains Juliette. 'We now have three chalets being renovated that can accommodate families or small groups.'

We carefully make our way into the first chalets. There are workmen still coming and going and they move aside to let us through.

'These are beautiful. I'm surprised how light it is in here.'

'We have knocked out space for doors at the back there and extra windows upstairs. This will have a living room to one side, a kitchen in the middle and upstairs a bathroom and two bedrooms.'

'Wonderful.'

'There will be a little outside seating area with a perfect view of the countryside beyond.'

I walk across the space to take a quick look in the direction of the woods. This place makes me want to do something wild, adventurous, and experience new and exciting things. I'm loving the feeling. I've been living a sensible, mostly predictable life for far too long. It's possibly the air, the nature, the chocolate I have consumed, or the company, the view or most probably all of the above. I know that I am smiling from the pure joy of being here and I can see without a doubt just how their venture is going so well. There is something magical and fantastical about this whole experience. I'm even more excited now by the concept of the party, it is the perfect setting.

'These will be finished by July and I'll save one for you to stay for the Ball.'

'Wow, that would be incredible. Thank you. I might be the first guest in the chalet, how cool is that?'

There is no doubt that from the moment they are finished they will be booked up.

'As much as I'd love to stay longer, we need to head back now. Thank you again for the tour and it's been great to chat in person about the Ball.'

'You're always very welcome.'

'Yes, thank you so much,' says George as we are all bidding each other goodbye.

'It has been wonderful to see you both.' Juliette hugs us goodbye. 'I'm even more excited about the Ball now too.'

Lorenzo appears round the side of the villa just in time to see us off.

'I'm glad I didn't miss you.'

We all say our goodbyes and wave as we drive off.

Chapter Sixteen

Once we were back in our room we took turns to freshen up and get dressed ready to go and explore. We chatted away as we worked around each other. It was amazing how well we flowed together. Even Michelle and I couldn't have managed so well at not getting under each other's feet. I'd completely forgotten to ring Michelle back. I haven't got time now so I drop her a quick message to let her know I'm still okay and will catch up later or tomorrow morning. I feel it would be rude at this point to chat on the phone while George is here. I'm sure he wouldn't mind but I would. There used to be nothing worse than waiting all week to see Andy only to have them on the phone the whole time we were together.

I've taken the time to pop some evening make-up on. I want to introduce myself to Florence whilst looking my best. I'm dressed in my favourite floaty dress that Michelle had chosen for me. It should keep me cool with it being so lovely and warm here in the evenings. I bring along my purple pashmina to pop over my shoulders if it gets colder later. I'm wearing my flat pumps, aware that I still have to make it down and back up those stairs.

I'm filled with glee at the prospect of heading out into the city and George seems equally excited. In a smog of aftershave, perfume and wide smiles we lock our door behind us and venture out into the city. In no time at all we are greeted with glittering lights hung from every possible place and the sound of the city coming alive after the late afternoon lull. As we make our way further towards the centre we are absorbed by the chatter, laughter and general upbeat atmosphere.

Interestingly on the corners are these pop-up bars. Back home where you get the ice cream sellers and street foods, here they have that for alcohol as well. I find this intriguing and grab us both a drink. Him a Budweiser and me a Bacardi Breezer. My choice was based on the pure nostalgia that they still sold those. I'd not seen them in years. They remind me of youthful, carefree days.

We walk along sipping our drinks. I link arms with him automatically so we don't get separated in the busier parts of the city. He smiles at me and the lights of the bar we are passing glint in his eyes, making them look even more alive. I'm glad I've worn my flats as these cobbles are not the easiest to master. Even with all the shops closed and just the backlights of them on it gives off a friendly and welcoming glow. With each restaurant we pass we are greeted with the delicious aroma of world-renowned Italian food. By the montage of differing accents and languages being spoken around us, others have come in search of tasting the fabulous cuisine too. If the smell is anything to go by they will not be disappointed. It's funny how the voices of English and American tourists stand out to us as English speakers. They sound out of place somehow amongst such cultural diversity.

I wish more than ever at this point that I had stuck to my vow of learning Italian. Maybe this is the time I finally stick to it and maybe by the time we return for the Ball I will be able to converse in basic Italian. I'm relieved that most of the Italians here are fluent in English and as we pause to read the menus outside they have English translations on them too. I imagine this is purely because we are in the tourist area and I yearn to be back out in the more rural part of Italy with the locals chatting away so I can learn the language in the best way, from the people who speak it.

As we wander through the streets I imagine us being locals who have nipped into town for our regular date night. There is a spring in my step as the hustle and bustle, food aromas and mixtures of slow jazz and upbeat music flow around me. I feel exuberant and I give George's arm a little squeeze. He returns the gesture and smiles at me. My senses are heightened and George looks even more attractive in this setting. His cheeks are rosy, his eyes bright.

'How about this place?' I ask.

We pause outside a little restaurant tucked away round a corner just off the main street. The outside is painted in a deep blue. As we peer in the windows we are met with smiles from the bubbly lady making her way out to greet us. I consider whispering 'run' and hot footing it away but there is something in her manner that makes me stop. I want to meet her. I want her to hug us and pull us into her magical world of food. This is so strange to us as I find back home people just don't do this. They wait until you walk in and then crack a smile. Here in Florence they stand in the doorways welcomingly. Whether you enter or not they happily wish you good evening.

'Buonasera, welcome,' the lady says as she's giving us welcoming hugs.

We hug her back - we can't help ourselves, she's adorable, like a friendly Nan. We are laughing and smiling and happy to have her guide us into her restaurant. Inside the place envelops us like her hug. You could tell she has put her heart and soul into making this place and she has done an amazing job. By the look of it, her and her family had made it an extension of their home, as though we're being invited into their kitchen. With the pasta and sauce bubbling away on the stove, the pizza crafted on the wooden worktop that was possibly crafted by her great grandfather. Men, who might have been her husband and sons, busied themselves to cook enough to serve the many customers.

We were served limoncello almost as soon as our bottoms had reached the seats. The place is busy but not crowded and I can't stop scanning the place for more fabulous trinkets, from statues of the Virgin Mary to beaming sunflowers jammed into huge jugs. There are photos on the walls which appear to be the generations that came before. My cheeks are hurting from all the smiling. You can't help but smile in here - it is contagious, compulsory. In fact I can't imagine anyone would manage to stay grumpy here.

'Cheers.'

We clink our tiny glasses together and take a sip of the sweet lemony liquid.

'Wow that has quite a kick to it,' I say as my eyes start to water and then, embarrassingly, I hiccup. I cover my mouth and start to giggle. He laughs too and I take another sip hoping it might stop them but instead I give out an even louder one and a couple of the other customers turn and smile. I've suddenly gone very hot and I can imagine my face is the colour of the poppies on the wallpaper.

The lady has returned with our menus and the tallest of the girls. She gives us each another pat on the back before handing us over to the young lady. Her English is much better and she is less huggy, yet equally as friendly. You can tell she is related. She has the same friendly eyes that are looking out from the photos and from our hostess. She explains the menu to us and answers our many questions with the manner of someone who really has nothing else to do but ensure that we are happy with our choices. It must be lovely to work in a place like this with your family. I don't think I know many people who could work alongside their family like this. Perhaps this friendliness and warmth is part of their genetic make-up.

We can hear the shouts from the kitchen area. I guess it is the Dad or Grandad who is the chef. I love how you can see them preparing the foods as the kitchen has a half wall rather than being closed off. It must be nicer for them too as they get to be part of the experience. The pizza guy spins the dough, then expertly ladles the sauce on, sprinkles on cheese and places the toppings so fast I want to applaud him. At home I struggle to get a pizza out of the packaging in one piece, let alone make one from scratch easily. The next guy scoops the peel under it and slides it into the giant dome oven in one swift movement. Another man is lifting pasta out of giant vats of boiling water. For them it is all a show they are putting on, not just a job they are doing. I'm mesmerised, enchanted.

I can't stop hiccupping, causing us to both giggle as we watch our dinner being prepared. There is a real atmosphere here. The heat from the kitchen mixed with the warm breeze from the doors is so encapsulating. I sip from a second small glass of limoncello they've just brought me. I'm only willing to risk more hiccups because it tastes divine. Plus it's making us laugh which can only be a good thing. Before we know it our lovely smiley waitress makes her way through the tables and presents us with our meal.

'Wow! Grazie,' I say as my mouth starts to water in anticipation.

'Thank you,' says George and I've never heard him sound so formal. I smile at him and we tuck into our meals.

We both chose pizzas, side salads and polenta chips. I love a good Italian meal back home, but none of the restaurants can compare to this. Technically it's the same but there is something also very different about it, like a secret ingredient. Maybe the secret family recipes do exist. If so, they certainly had a very talented family. Each mouthful is like a different experience, as though I'd never truly tasted food until now. I now understand what people mean when they tell you to try in its country of origin.

I've managed to get halfway through my pizza, had a handful of polenta chips and I'm struggling. I don't want to leave anything on the plate, not so much because it would be rude to but because I'll regret it for the rest of my life for sure. George admits defeat not long after me and we both sit back and allow our bellies to rest. Moments later our waitress arrives next to us smiling kindly.

She removes our plates and a few minutes later she returns with the dessert menus. We decide to skip dessert as I quite fancy getting gelato from one of the street food stalls I'd seen on the way through. I look outside and wonder what time they stay open till. I guess until the tourists all head home for the night which, by the look of things outside, is no time soon.

We probably overdo it on the gratitude for the meal and the size of the tip we leave but it's well deserved. I've already found them online and I've bookmarked it to leave them a review. I use this excuse to take a photo of the place that just happens to have George in it. I like to have photographs that remind me of places I've been and people I like, in this case - me, George, Italy.

We step out into the dark street that is still busy with tourists and locals alike. I put my pashmina around my shoulders and George's arm seems to follow it. At first I thought he was simply just helping me with it, as I had got a bit caught up in it. You know how you see these glamorous ladies swoop them around and they land perfectly in place and with one last swing of the corner it looks elegant. Well that was not quite how it looked when I did it, quite the opposite. I look more like a person fighting off a bird that has decided to dive bomb them. But all that aside George has his arm around me.

I feel as though I'm going to burst with bliss. I know there is a cheesy grin on my face and I'm putting that down to the limoncello. The hiccups have thankfully passed and hopefully they stay gone. I try to walk taller, with poise, but with each step on these cobbles I'm flinching. The soles of these shoes are so thin that every lump, bump and sharp stone feels as though it is embedding itself in my sole.

I'm having the most amazing time. Here, in Florence, surrounded by culture, in the glow of the street lights and in the relaxed state of a person who has enjoyed a delicious meal and a couple of drinks, I feel as though maybe, possibly our friendship is creeping towards a tentative line.

We're walking at a slow pace, looking in the shop windows when one in particular catches my eye. I pause and move closer. The window is spotlighted making the bottles of oils and packets of pasta appear like pieces of art, something luxurious. George points and there in the centre of the display is a bowl of uncooked pasta, set out to look as though it is being served. The serving spoon nestled into it and the half empty packet beside it so you know which one it is. As I look closer I see they are shaped like penises. We burst out laughing like a couple of teenagers. I love how we can be so relaxed around each other.

We carry on walking, hopefully to find more funny items for sale. We've not gone much further when his hand gently touches my arm. I turn to look at him. There is a half-smile on his lips and a question in his eyes that I'm afraid he might voice out loud.

'Hayley,' he whispers.

'Yes,' I stage-whisper back.

'Have you noticed what I have noticed?'

'What do you mean?'

In one swift movement he is turning me round to face away from him and pointing upwards. My eyes follow the direction he is pointing. The moon is looming large in the sky. It looks as though it is balancing on top of a giant dome, the closest I can compare it to is that of St Paul's Cathedral. We both stand still, his hand still on my arm and the other gently sitting in the base of my back.

There, commanding our attention, as it rightly should, is the Duomo. I saw it appear in pretty much every search I did in preparation of this trip. It is one of the most famous buildings in Italy. I am literally pinned to the spot in awe. I feel utterly mesmerised by its grandeur.

It has such a presence. Not taking my eyes away from it for more than a second to find a seat, I slowly walk over and sit on a stone bench. The building is lit by lights strategically placed around the perimeter pointing upwards. George arrives next to me and we both sit in silence, drinking in this view. It is so intricately designed, the white, green and pink of the marble is a clear statement of grandeur. As I always do with these historic buildings I wonder how on earth they managed to build such an incredible structure with the limited resources they would have had back when it was built. It truly is a masterpiece, in every sense of the word. The tower next to it stands proud as though it is protecting it. My neck is aching from craning up to see the detailed architecture of the red tiled domed roof, yet I can't stop looking. It's as though I'm scared that if I look away it will disappear.

My bottom is going numb with the coldness of the stone and I shiver. George wraps his jacket around my shoulders, his fingertips brushing my bare skin as I remove my pashmina. We look into each other's eyes as we execute the exchange. The Duomo watches over us and the moon illuminates our sacred spot.

We stay on the bench, him holding my purple pashmina and me tucked into his jacket. We aren't touching, no hand holding or shoulder hugging. We are both just sitting next to each other, content just watching other people walking past, just enjoying the view before us. There may never be another time for us to experience this. This won't be my last trip here. I know I'll be back - the magic of this place will be too strong for me to stay away.

That is exactly how churches have always made me feel. My Grandad and I used to visit little churches around the country. It seems like a strange place to visit and enjoy as a child but I absolutely loved it. The emotions, even when I was young, were always intriguing to me. They felt like mystical places that had magical powers that flowed through them, thus making me feel like I had magic flowing through me.

I don't know how long we stayed like this. I wanted to stay until I'd seen every inch of it, each brick and tile. I can smell his aftershave on his jacket.

'Shall we go?'

My voice sounds loud after not having spoken for so long.

'Yes, let's.'

He stands up first and offers me his hand. Holding my pashmina in the other. I take it and allow him to help me up.

'Would you like your jacket back?' I ask.

'No, I'm fine. Plus, it kind of suits you.'

'Let me take your photo,' I say, fetching my phone out of my bag.

I take back the pashmina and I tie it to my bag handle. We laugh as he poses, one hand behind his head, the other on his hip, pouting his lips and fluttering his eyes. The photo is shaky at best because I just can't stop laughing. A friendly lady from a group of tourists approaches us.

'Would you like me to take a photo of you both?' she asks.

'Thank you so much.'

I hand her the phone.

George and I stand together. I join in his posing and then we go from trying to look like models to him with his arm around me. Which means I have to put my arm around his waist too. I know I must look ridiculous in the jacket so I move away from him slightly to remove it. I lay it on my messenger bag that I had put down beside me. As we go back to how we were standing, his bare arm on my naked shoulders ignites something in me. I looked at him to see if he felt it too. He smiles down at me and I take that as a maybe.

'Kiss,' someone in the group shouts.

We laugh and he leans his head and tightens his grip on my waist, pulling me in close. Our lips gently brush over each other's. I open my eyes and he stays close, looking deep into my soul. Did he feel what I felt? Could he have felt the electricity that sparked between us? Could the camera have captured such an intimate thing? Did the tourist taking the photo notice that they had just snapped our first kiss? Our first kiss - that assumes that there will be more after this. With all my body and soul I hope there is. Yet a voice inside, that very much sounds like Michelle, warns me to beware. This is how it starts, the voice whispers, all happy, all sunshine and roses and then, it brutally reminds me, they leave.

We separate, shyly smirking. I casually hand him his jacket and pick up my bag. Thanking the lady, I retrieve my phone from her. She comments about how lovely we are - a beautiful couple. I nod and smile and offer to take a group photo of them. As I'm taking it on her phone I feel George standing behind me, just close enough so he can see the photo on the screen.

'That's a good one,' he says.

I smile again as the lady takes her phone and we bid them all goodbye. It is just the two of us left standing under the watchful eye of the Cathedral. I untie my pashmina and drape it around me. I'm not aiming to look fancy this time but now that I have taken off George's jacket and moved away from him I feel cold. I notice that he is still holding his jacket and hasn't put it back on as I'd have expected him to. I glance at him from under my eyelashes while I pretend to look for something in my bag. There was definitely a moment between us.

We automatically continue our walk back in the direction of our Airbnb. I'd momentarily forgotten that we would be heading back to share the same room. I blush at the thought in my mind. It would be fine. That brief kiss in the place I'd dreamed of, with the kind of person I had always considered out of my league, has to have meant something. Something worth pursuing perhaps.

I want to look back through the photos to see if the moment was captured in the way I'd want to remember it. Would he expect me to send the photos to him? Would he pine over them at some point in the future?

An image of myself flashes across my mind. I see an imaginary me snuggling with him as we fall asleep. In my thoughts I imagine him bringing me breakfast and opening the shutters on our house. The view from the window is of the Tuscan hills in all their glory. Shit, maybe Andy was right. Perhaps she wasn't enough for me.

Chapter Seventeen

We stopped at a little stall on the corner selling alcopops and gelato. I'm chuffed to find another Breezer so I grab a couple. I go for a classic double chocolate gelato. It has chunks of proper chocolate and I wonder if this might be something else that Juliette and Lorenzo might consider offering to their visitors. In fact, I pull out my phone and write a note to myself, balancing the bottles on the river wall. I realise there are a bunch of messages and quite a few missed calls. Shit. Michelle's picture flashes up as she calls again. Her smile disappears as my phone dies.

'Bloody hell!'

'Everything okay?' George asks, licking the cone of his ice cream in an attempt to stop it dripping.

'It was just Michelle.'

'Everything okay?' He looks up, the sound of scooters passing fades.

'I missed a load of calls from her and now my phone's dead.'

'We'll be back soon.'

'True. I'll ring her when we get back,' I say absently as I'm wedging it back in my bag.

I relieve him of my ice cream and quickly lick the melted outer layer. Surrounding us are strings of lights between the lampposts, illuminating the river wall. From the bridge we're currently on I can see the Ponte Vecchio. I get George to take a photo of me with my ice cream held up and the backdrop of the many lights glinting. From what I know there are amazingly over forty stores squeezed onto that bridge. I find myself already satisfied to have seen it and don't feel the need to actually walk along it. I certainly don't get paid enough to be able to buy anything from there. Perhaps I could bring Michelle back here, she'd have a field day.

George has opened the first bottle with his handy keyring bottle opener. He hands it to me, not quite meeting my eye. I pop the other unopened bottle in my bag and take the open one from him. The mixture of the warm evening, George's company, the stunning view, this delicious ice cream and the fizziness of the Breezer I'm in heaven. I lick my ice cream and take a mouthful of drink. The mixture is like the floaties I used to make as a kid with ice cream and fizzy cola.

We start moving again and I'm so elated that I start to skip and do a little twirl as I carry on licking my ice cream. A hazardous combination, but thankfully the weight of my bag helps me spin and George's quick reflexes stop me overbalancing. With both of us holding bottles in one hand and gelato in the other he kind of uses himself as a human shield to stop me toppling. There is something so innocently fun about twirling. Even as I nearly fell I was laughing, like genuinely laughing from my soul. I can't stop giggling as George is still propping me up with his sturdy body. This place and this guy are risky for me. Florence seems to break down my inhibitions and George brings about so much in me that I'd long forgotten I could feel.

'I can't work out if you're backing away because I'm laughing like a crazy person?'

'I'm testing your balancing skills,' he chuckles, moving slightly further back.

Pausing for a moment to calm the spinning in my head, I look around.

'I think we're going the wrong way.'

'Looks like you're right.'

He looks up at the signpost and it's pointing us back towards where we have just come from, which apparently leads us to the train station. We both laugh and link arms now we have finished our ice creams. I start skipping again and he joins in. We merrily skip along and I begin to sing, 'We're off to see the wizard.' We must be a sight as we both skip and sing our way back to where there are now more people. Some smiled and I think a couple of tourists took our photo on their phones. I'd love to see those photos and to have had this moment captured. However, we are both having fun and my messenger bag is enjoying swinging precariously with the movement. It's lucky we are skipping down the middle of the street or else I'm sure it would have enjoyed bashing a few passers-by on the way through.

Pausing by a bin I take the last swig of my Breezer and pop my empty bottle in it.

'I don't know if I've ever skipped that far in my life,' says George.

We're both laughing and breathing heavily.

'How can kids do that for hours?' I ask.

'Lord knows.'

Over the other side of the street I spot a young busker playing the guitar.

'I love the guitar, there is something so soothing about it,' I say.

'I agree. Do you play?'

'No. You?'

'Afraid not. I always meant to learn but never got the time.'

'Too busy being grown up.'

'Exactly that.'

He smiles but in the streetlight I see that it doesn't reach his eyes. I feel a sombreness wash over me. As though the playing of the guitar has brought us back to reality somehow. We settle at a table outside of a riverside bar so we can carry on listening to the busker. With the lights suspended above the river wall reflecting off the gentle flow of the water below, I feel myself relax further. We both sit enjoying the atmosphere, a smile playing on my lips.

'This is everything I hoped Florence would be,' I say quietly. 'I'm so glad I got to properly see it this time.'

'It really is as magical as the tourist places say.'

A waitress pops over to take our drinks order and is back before the busker finishes his song. With a bottle of wine to share we sit back in our chairs and people-watch for a few moments.

'So this is your job.'

'Yep. It's a hard life,' I chuckle. 'If only every day could be like this.'

'It could be if you wanted.'

'I guess, but it's not that easy, is it? To leave everything and everyone behind.'

'What would be a good enough reason for you to do it, then? Or could you simply never make that move?'

I take a sip of my drink and consider for a moment. My eyes scan the waterway as I think. I imagine leaving my job and colleagues behind and, although it pains me slightly, they wouldn't be what held me back. Andy isn't a factor I could bring into it right now. My flat is lovely but I could easily make a home somewhere new. The answer comes to me and I know it's the truth for me.

'Michelle would have to move with me,' I say, punctuating the point with a nod. 'Life here would lack something for me without her around.'

'What if you met a local who wanted you to move here with them?'

'Ah, well, that's a different thing altogether.'

'How so?'

'Well, I guess either way you're not doing it alone.'

'True. But don't you think you're strong enough without that?'

I pull a strained face.

'I didn't mean you aren't strong, just that...' He stops himself from digging a deeper hole by taking a swig of his drink.

'I know what you mean and you're right.' I lean to elbow him playfully. 'If it went wrong it would be someone else's fault and all that.'

He nods.

'Things are just complicated at the moment.' My smile falters. 'Although, at this point running away or not returning home is tempting.'

'The woman outside Gill's? Andy, was it?'

'Yes, Andy. How did you know?'

'I gathered. Part of my job is reading situations and people.'

'Mine too but I seem to be pretty bad at it lately. Well, in my own life at least.'

'You wanna talk about?' he asks as he tops up my glass.

I take a deep breath.

'Do I want to talk about it? Good question. I'm not sure, to be honest. I was hoping that the time away from home might help me to clear my head and make sense of things but it appears to have confused me further.'

'How so?'

'Oh sod it,' I say as I take a big mouthful of my wine. 'Just before we came away Andy and I had gone out for dinner.'

'For your birthday.'

'Well remembered, yes. It just so happens that she proposed.'

'I see,' he says carefully. 'You don't sound happy about that.'

'It just caught me off guard. I felt we'd been pretty strained lately. Both of us work a lot and not always similar hours so it can be tough to catch up.'

'Unfortunately that's quite common these days.'

'Exactly. We made the best of it but then I found that when we did have those rare occasions together I couldn't fully relax and enjoy it. It felt like we were starting fresh each time.'

He simply nods and takes a sip of his drink. We are both just staring out over the river. The background of the busker and the night sky is the perfect setting for a heart to heart. Like therapy.

'I found myself almost dreading our time together,' I continue, the words coming out in a rush now. 'Hoping she'd be too busy so I could just chill at home on my own or with Michelle. How bad is it when you are looking forward to catching up on your Netflix backlist rather than seeing your partner?'

He chuckles, I think he gets it. I also appreciate the fact that he's just letting me spill my guts.

'So when we went out for my birthday I was desperately hoping that we'd have a lovely time. All I wanted was for us to avoid any petty disagreements and enjoy a romantic evening.'

'And then she pulled out a ring.'

'Exactly. I can only imagine what my face looked like. Then when I couldn't say yes she lost her shit and I ended up suggesting we have a break.'

'Wow.'

'Yep and worse still, just as she stormed out the waiter arrived with my birthday cake.'

'Shit. What did you do?'

'I ended up drinking a bottle of wine to myself while devouring most of the cake.'

'Good girl!'

'That's what Michelle said,' I chuckle.

'So are you broken up now? You two didn't seem to be getting along outside Gill's.'

'Sort of. I think so?' I shrug. 'We said we'd talk about it more when I get back to London. She's of the mindset that we either get engaged or separate. I don't see it so black and white. Our relationship has its positive qualities but there's so much that needs working on before we consider a big next step.' I sigh heavily and shake my head, trying to force a smile onto my face. 'But I guess every relationship has its problems. And it was really, really good.'

'The relationship?'

'The birthday cake.'

George bursts out laughing, the tension broken.

'What kind of cake was it?'

'The best - double chocolate. Maybe even triple.'

'Nice. All this talk of food is making me hungry again. Shall I see if they have any desserts here?'

'Sure.'

He disappears inside. I finish my glass of wine and top it up again. When in Rome and all that. It feels good to say some of what's plaguing me out loud to someone, even if it's a person I barely know. I feel warm inside now, although that's probably a combination of the chat and the wine.

'No desserts,' he says as he returns. 'Do you fancy a wander to find gelato?'

'Absolutely.'

He holds the bottle as I get up.

'Oh no, my glass.'

'Down it, down it,' he chants.

I can't help but laugh and then oblige. Arms linked, we pass the busker. I pause to throw some coins into his guitar case. He nods in appreciation. We make our way back through the square which is still lit up with strings of lights and I spot a gelato shop that is still open on the corner.

'Yay! Let's go.'

Within minutes we're sitting on the steps of a nearby building enjoying our gelato.

'Not to scare you but I think perhaps I...' I pipe up after a moment.

I daren't turn to look at him yet at the same time I want to see into his eyes. See if he might be feeling the same. Watching the people wandering around is soothing and this wine is helping me open up.

'You're very lovely you know,' I finish lamely.

'I see,' he says noncommittally.

I feel the blush reaching up to my cheeks. It's probably nothing. Maybe just rebound stuff and being somewhere different. I know it's the wine talking. I look at him and he's looking back at me with those gorgeous eyes. I turn away and carry on licking my gelato.

'Hayley.'

'Yes.'

'I'm flattered, I really am -'

'Sorry, I've made it weird now, haven't I?'

'Not at all. It's just...' He runs his fingers through his hair. 'I like you too but things are complicated. Sorry, stealing your line.'

'When aren't they?'

'Who knows? You rarely hear anyone say things are easy.'

'True that.'

He passes me the wine and I take a swig. The taste of the wine washing down the gelato is delicious. This is perfect. Us sat here just enjoying the city and each other's company. I watch as an elderly couple made their way slowly across the square, arms linked and chatting quietly to each other, smiles playing on their lips. For all my independent talk and pushing partners away anytime they get too close, I know that in my heart that is what I want. Someone to love, to grow old with, to share these experiences. Someone to join me on the sofa as I work my way through that Netflix backlist.

'Penny for them?' he asks.

'I don't believe that to be a good investment of your money,' I chuckle, brushing away his request to share my thoughts.

'Fair play. Shall we finish this bottle and head back? We've got a long journey home tomorrow.'

'Absolutely.'

As he lifts the bottle we laugh as we realise we've already drained it. He puts our now empty wine bottle in the bin across from us. As he walks back in my direction there is something about the quick glance he gives me that I find difficult to read. He comes towards me and I brace myself, unsure of his next move. He offers me his hand to help me up. Once I'm up he wraps my pashmina around my shoulders and we start our short walk towards our Airbnb. He slips his hand into mine. We walk along taking in the buildings around us. There is still something he wants to say, I can feel it. He seems in deep thought. But then I'm a bit past tipsy so it's hard to work out my own thoughts, let alone his.

*

All I want to do is lay down. I perch on the edge of the bed and slip my shoes off. I thanked them for being kind to my feet, once I had gotten used to the cobbles. I sit cross legged on the bed, cupping my mug and taking the odd sip. I need to speak to Michelle. I lean over to fetch my phone from my bag, nearly toppling off the bed as I do so. I have to get off the bed to reach the plug to charge it. I stay on the floor and sip my drink as I wait for it to charge enough to switch on.

It's taking longer than I'd hoped so I take the opportunity to nip in the shower now George is out. My bare feet are soothed by the cool of the stone tiles which feels lovely as I make my way to the bathroom. I sing Dido's 'Thank You' song in the shower. It's always a good shower song and, as with my bathroom at home, this has a high ceiling which means I sound much better than in any other setting.

It has been the most amazing trip to Florence. Not only was our visit to Hotel al Cioccolato great fun but this evening has topped it all. I check my phone, but it's still only at nine percent - I don't bother to turn it on. I'll leave it to fully charge. I'm pleased to finally crawl into bed. George has been sitting up in his bed for a while now, just chatting away to me and scrolling through his phone. It is strangely comforting to have him here with me.

'Night, Hayley,' he says from across the room.

'Night, George,' I say as I turn over to switch off the lamp, my bed making every noise possible.

Chapter Eighteen

'Shit, fuck, crap,' I mumble as I turn over, the brightness of the room blinding. I hit my phone to see the time. 'Bollocks.' My mobile is still switched off.

I see George's shocked face leap up over the foot of my bed.

'What?'

'We've overslept.'

'Shit!'

'Yep.'

My phone is taking far too long to load up. 'What time is it exactly?' I ask.

'Late.'

I leap out of bed a tad too fast and have to stand still for a second to stop the spinning. I'd momentarily forgotten about our antics last night and hadn't expected this dull ache in my brain. But then I'd not expected to sleep in so late either. Our train leaves - I try to work it out in my mind as I walk towards the bathroom - in less than an hour is the best maths I can do at this point.

I go for a quick wee, wash my hands, and splash tepid water on my face. I clean my teeth and hope that George is on it with the coffee again this morning. There is no sign of it as I walk back through so I nip into the kitchen and get them started.

'Sorry. I was just about to do that,' he says as he looks up from his phone.

'No problem. I'll sort it,' I say lightly.

He stands there running his hand through his bed hair. How the hell does he manage to look this attractive having literally just woken up?

'The bathroom is free if you need it.'

I set the cups down on the table. As I walk through I see that George has already cleared all his side of the room. He's folded the sofa bed up and placed the bedding up neatly on top. His side of the wardrobe is already packed and his luggage sat by the door with his documents placed on top. Lord, I really need to up my game.

I quickly change into my comfy jeans and a t-shirt. I sit on the edge of my unmade bed to put my shoes on. My feet are actually a bit tender and my calves are achy as I lift my foot up onto the bed. I guess we did a lot of walking yesterday, rounding the whole night off with the accomplishment of making it up the three billion flights of stairs.

'Cheers for the drink,' George's voice breaks through my busy mind.

'You're welcome.'

Right, I'm ready to start by making my bed. Without a word George is the other side mirroring my actions. In seconds the bed is made, I give him a smile and a thank you. He smiles back and walks back round the bed to start passing me my things from the wardrobe. I appreciate these simple, calm gestures. Michelle or Andy would have been panicking, throwing items onto the bed for me to pack quickly. Yet George is just doing each thing silently and methodically. No rush, just getting the job done. The same way he approaches most things. He has the sense of urgency relevant to each job but there is no unnecessary stressing about it.

Ten minutes later we are doing one last look round to check that we haven't forgotten anything. Luckily we did as my charger is still plugged in next to the bed. He takes the cups to the kitchen and I hear him washing them up. Then he comes back with my toiletry bag thankfully, as I'd completely forgotten about those. He simply smiles and waits patiently as I try to wedge it into my case.

A few minutes later we're making our way down the stairs. I'm a tad sad to be leaving Florence and our lovely little place behind. George is kindly carrying both our bags. We somehow make it to the train station in good time and I'm pleased that it is not as busy as before. George nips off to grab us both a drink while I watch the bags and the screen for our platform number. I say goodbye to Florence in my mind as I stare out of the opening to the city centre.

I wish we could have stayed longer. It has been such a fleeting visit but I guess that is business for you. We get to go to these amazing places and people we know are in awe of our supposedly glamorous lifestyle. But the reality is that we rarely get to see much outside of the meeting and hotel rooms. This time I was lucky. To have a meeting in such a gorgeous setting and an Airbnb in the centre of Florence which meant we got to see quite a lot of it. Maybe next time I'll see even more. Perhaps my relationship with Italy is supposed to be a slow and gentle one. Like falling in love slowly. And Florence has very much mesmerised me and won a piece of my heart.

George appears next to me and hands me my coffee.

'Thank you so much. This is very much appreciated.' I smile.

'You're very welcome.'

'It's a shame we're leaving so soon, isn't it?'

'It certainly is,' I say, as a lump appears in my throat.

A few more people are filtering into the station and I'm pleased for the distraction.

'I wish we'd managed to spend a bit more time here,' he says. 'Maybe next time.'

I simply nod. This is something I've come to like about George - we very much seem on the same wavelength. I have this strange, overwhelming urge to snuggle into his shoulder. To have him wrap his arm around me. He steps towards me, our eyes meeting and his arm outstretched. I hold my breath in anticipation and then realise he's handing me my case.

'We are platform three,' he says.

I watched through the train window as we made our way out of the city towards Rome. I have the sudden unexpected urge to jump up, demand it stops and just get off. My chest is tight. I want out. Of this vehicle. Of a life that has me going to the same office, returning home to an empty flat with nothing more to look forward to than a bubbly bath and a glass of wine.

There is nothing in my life that I couldn't just take elsewhere. Even my job could be done remotely. There is nowhere higher to go in the company and my flat is lovely but by no means a place that I would want to spend the rest of my life. It hasn't got the same holding over me as it has for Mrs Temple. It is to me just a for-now place.

I consider my life one section at a time and consider whether there is anything I would be truly gutted to leave behind if I was to just stay here in Florence. Sadly, there is nothing. I love Michelle and my colleagues but with things these days, everyone is just so busy and only a video-call away. Plus, Michelle has her big contract coming up and will probably be all over the place with it. Perhaps me having a place in Italy is exactly what needs to lure her back from her fame, somewhere she can go and relax. Also, with travel being so accessible there would be nothing stopping my other friends and family. In fact, if I was to live in Italy they would probably visit more.

As we reach the rural outskirts I see a small villa tucked into the hillside and visions of the house of my dreams run through my mind like a film reel. I see my reflection in a mirror as I walk through my imaginary home and I look happy, healthy and have the biggest, most content smile on my face. In the background the oranges and yellows on the walls make my reflection appear framed in a Tuscan glow.

A figure appears behind me and my smile reaches my eyes and pure love filters out as this person wraps their arms around me and moves my hair away from my shoulder so they can snuggle into my neck, dropping soft kisses up my bare skin. Desire runs through me and I shiver.

I must have shivered in real life as George has turned in my direction. I'm miffed to have been removed from my dream but I know that one day it will be reality. The image is so strong and embedded in my heart. This is no longer a dream but more a premonition. A glimpse into my future.

I'm no longer upset at leaving Italy as I know in my soul I'll be back. Tuscany has worked its magic on me without me even realising it, hence the power of its magic. I smile to myself and turn to George.

'Thank you for the most wonderful time.'

'Right back at you.' He smiles widely.

Chapter Nineteen

London seems darker and more dreary than usual. I pull my jacket in tight around me as we wait for a taxi outside the station. I'm tired. Not necessarily energy wise, but in spirit, as though I've left a part of myself in Italy. George is quiet too. He doesn't seem pleased to be home either. Not for the first time I wonder whether he has anyone waiting for him, someone who has missed him like I would have done. Like I've missed Michelle. I can't wait to get back and hug her so hard she'll never want to let me go. Now I'm back to reality I see that George was merely a crush. It's been like a dream to have spent this short time with him, but he wasn't even on my list of reasons to stay here in Notting Hill. As the rain starts to fall, I don't pull out my umbrella. I just look up to the sky and I know that change is coming.

A taxi pulls up and we clamber in.

George is staring out of the window when I glance at him.

'Good to be back?' I ask with a tone that is heavily laden with my own unhappiness.

'Not at all,' he replies, a smile forced on his lips as he turns.

'Me neither. Do you think they would notice if we turned around and went back?'

'Probably not.'

I give him a weak smile. This was one of the traits I liked most about him - he is great at lifting the mood in one perfectly timed sentence. I think that's what it is about George. He is one of the few people to have entered my life who actually make my world feel better just by being a part of it.

Sighing deeply, I look past the driver, watching the busyness of London through the rhythmic swishing of the windscreen wipers. It's strange that Florence was just as busy yet had such a very different vibe to it. The sunshine definitely helped. These thoughts and feelings could of course just be the business trip version of the holiday blues, but it felt like so much more than that. Like having woken from a dream you didn't realise you were in. You spend the rest of your day grumpy and missing this perfect world you had created in your mind. You wish to return to sleep to experience it again but no matter how hard or how many times you try you can never go back to the same place. It feels unfair, as though you've been cheated out of something that should have and did belong to you for a moment. I'm not upset to be coming home as much as sad to have left Italy. My spirits lift slightly as we turn the corner of my road.

'Right, see you bright and early tomorrow morning,' I say as we pull up outside my place.

I'm eager to race inside and see Michelle. George jumps out of the cab to help me carry my holdall up the stairs.

'Thank you.'

'No problem, Hayley.'

We hold eye contact for a second and I know that the spell has been broken. He is not my prince. In fact, he's not mine at all and I am not his. And that is okay. We have had our moment and that, I believe, is all we were ever meant to have. He breaks away, our hands touching on the handle of the bag. My messenger bag slips off my shoulder and gives him one last thump. He laughs and jogs off down the stairs to the waiting taxi, the driver of which is tapping the steering wheel impatiently.

I give a quick wave as they drive off. I make my way up the stairs as quickly as I can, calling a greeting to Mrs Temple as I pass her open door and smile as I hear her cheery, 'Welcome home'. I can't wait to tell Michelle all about Italy and hear how her weekend was. Unlocking my door I kick my shoes off, dump my bags and jacket. I head straight for the coffee maker. I grab two cups and nip to the bathroom while it does its magic. As the second cup fills I change out of my jeans and into a pair of old pyjama trousers. I swap my socks for fluffy ones for no other reason than comfort. Lastly I throw on a tatty old hoodie and collect the coffees. Holding the door open with my elbow as I slip through, I try not to spill the coffees. At the last second, just before the door closes, I stop it with my foot. Placing the cups on the floor while I grab my keys. That was close.

Making my way up the stairs, I'm careful not to spill a drop. I'm smiling wide, my belly bubbling with anticipation, excited to see her. To some it might seem ridiculous but I've missed her so much, even though it was only a couple of nights. The coffee is not just a necessity, it is also a peace offering for not ringing her back. I think it's the longest we've gone without talking. She'll make me feel guilty for a while but only because she loves to wind me up.

I knock on her door with my sock clad toes and wait impatiently. There's no answer so I try again, slightly harder. That hurt my toes so instead I put the coffees down on the worn carpet and knock properly this time. Still no answer. She must be in her studio. My phone is still in my bag downstairs, so without it to ring her I use my spare key. It's these moments that warranted us swapping keys back in the early days.

Using similar contortionism I worm my way through the door, drinks in hand. One of Michelle's favourite rave playlists is blasting out on the surround sound, no wonder she didn't hear me knock. The stench of old take away, stale marijuana smoke and alcohol hit me. I tut. Honestly, she really needs to get that cleaner in more often, or clear up herself. I call out, even though I know she won't hear me. Once she's in her studio she's literally in another world. We're both messy in our own ways but I at least pile things ready to deal with. Michelle allows it to just take over. The coffee table is still lit up and the debris appears to be moving as the LED light rhythmically changes colour. The VR headsets and controllers are strewn amongst everything.

Clearing space to put the cups on the breakfast bar, I accidentally knock a couple of bottles off the end. One smashes to the floor and another wobbles on the edge, threatening to jump. I habitually swear and apologise as I stand the bottle back up and find the dustpan to clear up the broken one. I'm surprised to see it was whiskey. Bemused, I stand back up to look over the breakfast bar. I can see at least three vodka bottles and by the looks of it there are more over by the sofa. It looks like Michelle has had quite a little party while I was away. There are beer cans and a couple more whiskey bottles too. Not Michelle's usual style. The vodka perhaps but whiskey? Not unless it was in coffee.

I walk through to the studio room to find her before the coffee goes cold. Passing the bathroom I hear the shower. I knock on the door to let her know I'm back and announce that I have coffee. Between the music playing throughout the apartment and the shower running she'll never hear me. I walk back through to the lounge. I get my coffee and clear a space to sit on the sofa. I pick up the remote that I think controls the music but I have no idea which button it is. I try just turning the volume down. It seems to make no difference. Michelle has it all set up to voice activation but I can't remember which one she's using these days. I decide to just leave it, putting the remote down so I can enjoy my coffee.

The smells are making me feel sick. I can't sit here amongst it any longer. I finish my drink and grab a bin bag from under the sink. I clear up to the rhythm of the music, bopping about as I separate the recycling into one bag by the door. By the time I've collected all the other rubbish she's still not out. Honestly, I've never known anyone to take as long as she does in the bathroom. I clear the sink and refill it with hot soapy water. There's no point loading the dishwasher for these few glasses and a bit of cutlery. Plus my running water should let her know I'm here. I wipe down the surfaces and the coffee table.

Holding the bin bag open, I empty the ashtray of butt ends and cardboard roaches. I tip the dusty white remnants from the chocolate box lid, throwing the paper fiver in too. As I do so I realise it's the lid from the box I brought her back from Hotel al Cioccolato on my previous trip. Bloody cheek using it to snort their crap. The handful of resealable pill bags are scooped into the bin bag. Tying it up I place it with the recycling by the door. A quick spritz of air freshener and it's as best as it can be. I stand, hands on hips, smile on my face, feeling achieved.

I go back to the bathroom door and call through. No answer. Just the sounds of the water running and the music playing.

'Come on, I thought you'd have missed me.'

I smile, leaning my ear against the door covering the other to try and hear her sarcastic response. I stay listening for a couple of moments. I knock again. My hand momentarily rests on the handle. My stomach flips. Something inside me is urging me to go in.

'Right, I'm coming in,' I shout.

I pause, allowing her time to cover herself. I push the door open enough to poke my head round, calling through, diverting my gaze.

'Michelle?'

The steam escapes in a purple haze from where the LED lights are fading in and out. The music is playing louder in here. There is nothing she enjoys more than a disco shower.

'Hey lady. I'm back.'

My voice echoes in the space. The lights are now blue.

'Michelle?' I raise my voice. 'You in here?'

Maybe she left the shower on and went to bed or is in her studio. I consider going to check but something makes me turn back as I go to leave. I open the door to the wetroom further, stepping in, the dampness soaking into my socks. 'Oceans' by Taya blasts out from the speakers. The bile rises in my throat. The lights are now yellow. I run across to her slumped figure lying motionless on the porcelain tiles.

'MICHELLE!'

The lights change to green. I fall to my knees next to her. The shower is still washing over her, the water on the floor soaking into my pyjama bottoms. I lift a shaky hand to move her hair from where it's stuck to her face. I'm avoiding touching the gash on her forehead. As I do so, she rolls into me. I reach behind me to grab a towel, covering her naked body. Only Michelle could time her playlist to fit me finding her.

I don't check her pulse. There isn't one. Or see if she's breathing. She's not. Her skin is beyond pale, waxen. Her body is rigid. Her eyes are shut as though as she fell she automatically closed them. I keep trying to brush her hair from her face but the water keeps moving it back. I feel myself start to rock as I lift her in my arms, her head in my lap. The water is pooling around us. The lights continue to change with the rhythm of the music. The song changes and I realise I've been sat with her for a while, stroking her hair, talking softly to her. Waiting for her to realise I was there. Any second now she'll open her eyes and laugh. I gently lay her back on the tiles, placing another towel under her head.

'I'll be back in a sec sweetheart.'

I brush her cheek one more time before slowly rising, not taking my eyes off her until I've left the room. As I exit I take a gulp of breath and on autopilot aim for the door. I scoop my keys from the breakfast bar and as I'm leaving I pick up the bin bags, juggling them as I gently close the door behind me. My socks squelch and my wet trousers make a weird flapping sound as I make my way down to the main door on wobbly legs. The cuffs of my hoodie soaked through and are dripping onto the bags. I nip down the outside steps. The coldness makes my feet ache. I place the bin bags amongst the others at the curb. The sound of the door opening behind me makes me jump.

'Hayley, dear. Have you locked yourself out?' Mrs Temple calls down to me from the top of the steps.

She arrives next to me, touches my arm and it's as though I'm seeing her for the first time.

'You're wet. You look frozen. Come on inside.'

I look her straight in the eye. I look at her furrowed brow.

'Michelle,' I whisper, but no sound escapes.

'Sorry, love. What did you say?'

The panic is rising in me now.

'Come inside,' she tries again. 'Whatever's happened?'

It is at this point I turn, realising once again that Mrs Temple has been talking to me. I strain my ears, attempting to block all noises from the street around us. All I can hear is rushing water. I look at her, trying to make out what she's saying. I use all my strength to say the words.

'It's okay, dear. Take your time.'

'Michelle's dead. We need to call someone.'

The shock hits me again as I hear my own words spoken aloud. She holds eye contact with my wild eyes. I watch as she pulls a quizzical look. Then as the words sink in and register somewhere in an incomprehensible way her face contorts. Upon seeing her reaction, the reality of my words hit me. My blood turned cold, my limbs turned to liquid. The scene seems to be playing out in slow motion yet speedily, as though I'm merely observing it rather than part of it. I'm paralysed to the spot.

I can see Mrs Temple's mouth and arms moving as she's talking animatedly on her mobile. Yet all I hear is white noise. It looks as though Mrs Temple's pale silhouette is fading off into the distance. I want to catch her before she falls but my arms are still not responding and my brain feels weirdly hazy. As I call out to her no sound escapes my dry mouth. I can't reach her, like in dream state I'm frustrated and panicked. As the darkness takes over I realise it is me who is falling. The bile rises again. I step back from Mrs Temple to catch hold of the lamppost to steady myself. My hand misses it and instead I collapse into the pile of black bin bags awaiting tomorrow's collection.

Chapter Twenty

Mrs Temple gently guides me towards her flat door and sits me at her kitchen table, wrapping a blanket around me. It's weird that she seems to have blue lights flashing in her apartment too. I'm watching her methodical movements. I can hear lots of motion in the hall outside her flat. I turn to see what's occurring but her door is pushed to, open enough to allow the noise to enter but not for me to see what's going on. It's strange that she isn't paying any attention to it. In fact, she actually looks like she is deliberately not paying it attention. She just quietly makes a pot of tea and brings it over on a tray with cups, sugar bowl and a little milk jug.

The tea that Mrs Temple has served does little to soothe me, but the shaking has calmed slightly. I guess the tradition for sweet tea in times of unrest works better than I realised. I reckon the process of making it is a great distraction technique. I allow my mind to drift away into a loop of tea facts and thoughts, much better than the movie that had been running through my head of my discovery of Michelle on loop.

I can't escape the guilt. I wonder who discovered tea? I wish there had been something I could have done different to change the events. Is tea actually from China? If I'd stayed home instead of swanning off to Italy would Michelle still be alive? Maybe I could get an old tea chest and make it into a side table - that would look cool. Do I even own a teapot? Was I to blame for Michelle's death?

Mrs Temple interrupts my inner dialogue with a touch of her hand on my forearm. The warmth is comforting and pulls me out of my manic thinking. I feel numb. I pull the blanket tighter around me.

'Hayley, dear. Have a few more sips of your tea before it gets cold.'

I nod and go to lift my delicate teacup. I have to use two hands as it feels like a lead weight. I do as instructed and my shallow breathing slows. Mrs Temple clears her throat gently before she starts to talk. I pop my cup down so I can concentrate fully on what she's trying to tell me.

'Her Mother will be arriving soon.' She pauses and clears her throat again.

I must have pulled a questioning face. For what? Her Mum rarely visited. A bit late to come now. A glimmer of hope bubbles inside me. Perhaps I was wrong and she's okay. But as my hopeful eyes met hers, her returned gaze confirms that no, I had not been wrong.

I stay quiet and lift my cup to my mouth again. It is tepid now. Tepid, such a strange word. Mrs Temple and I sit silently in her apartment intermittently sipping our tea. Tiddles jumps onto her lap. I sit staring at her soothingly, stroking the fluffy cat, the flashing blue lights creating an eerie atmosphere. An image of Michelle's waxen face, the water sticking her darkened blonde tendrils to her beautiful face fills my mind. I leap up, the chair tipping over and Tiddles racing off to hide.

'I told her I wouldn't be long. I have to...'

My legs give way and I grab the corner of the table to stabilise myself. Mrs Temple comes round to me, calmly stands my chair back up and gently guides me back to sitting. She picks up the blanket and gently wraps it back round me.

'It's okay, they are taking care of her.'

'Who?'

She takes a breath, ensuring her voice is calm when she speaks again.

'The ambulance people are here and the police.'

'The police?'

'Yes, it's alright,' she soothes. 'It's protocol.'

'But I -'

Michelle's Mum is going to be mad that Michelle has the police here. Her days of that were long gone. She'd kept her promise to stay out of trouble like a decade ago. My thoughts drift to the fact there was so much mess in her flat, all those little bags and bottles. I'm pleased I'd cleaned up while I waited for her to finish in the shower. Michelle would be in so much trouble with not just her Mum, but the police. I then remember that she was still in the shower.

The hard knock on the door jolts me. Mrs Temple gives me a weak, reassuring smile and makes her way over to answer it. I turn to see who it is but she has gone out and pulled the door to behind her. I can hear muffled voices but as much as I strain, I can't make out what is being said. I turn back round and draw my legs up and wrap the blanket around them. The coldness of my wet trousers sends shivers through my body. I remove my soggy socks and roll my trousers up above my knees in the hope that it will be more comfortable. I rub my hands up and down my legs in an attempt to warm them. It doesn't. I turn up the cuffs of my hoodie as they too are making my wrists cold and achy.

I hear Mrs Temple walk back into the room and she's accompanied by a policewoman who is around my age. She smiles kindly at me and Mrs Temple pulls out a chair for her next to mine, before going and putting the kettle on again. The lady pulls out a small notepad and pen and introduces herself to me. I nod my acknowledgement.

'They just need to ask you a couple of questions,' Mrs Temple says as she lowers herself back down in her chair.

The policewoman began to speak with me. I appreciated the fact that she had a gentle voice. She asked what I imagined were the standard questions. I tried to tell her in a concise way what had happened since I arrived home from Italy. I tune in and out. It's hard to concentrate fully right now. When she starts asking questions about how I found her and why it took me so long after I arrived to tell anyone, I start shaking uncontrollably, my voice wobbly as the shock hits me once more. Mrs Temple comes round and puts her comforting hand on my upper arms, rubbing them. I hear her say something and the lady nods. She stops asking me anything else at this point. My teeth are chattering too much to be able to speak properly now.

A policeman joins us, introducing himself. I hear something about bin bags. I have a vague recollection of me standing next to bin bags in the street when Mrs Temple found me. Then I remember the ones I brought down from Michelle's flat. The worry bubbles up inside me again. The fear that Michelle will be in trouble. Her Mum won't be happy to see what's in there. Hopefully they won't show her.

The policewoman then spoke with Mrs Temple.

'Three people arrived around six pm Saturday evening. I remember as they rang every bell, including mine, trying to get Michelle, so I looked out the window.'

'Have you seen them before?'

'Not for many years.'

'Can you elaborate please?'

'They were friends of hers when she first moved in but soon stopped coming after they started causing trouble. That's why we had the cameras installed.'

I know exactly who she is referring to, even though they were a thing of the past by the time I moved in. These were the 'friends' from Michelle's late teenage years, who had risen from the gutter when they got wind that she had money now.

'We'll need access to that footage from Saturday through to Sunday,' the female officer says to the other colleague. He notes it down.

'Can you give us a description of them?'

'I couldn't make out much, but there were two women and a man. They were scruffy and edgy - like they couldn't stand still as they waited.'

'How was Michelle when she greeted them?'

'Well, she came down rather than buzzed then in. She sounded excited to see them - like she'd called them to come.'

'What makes you think that?'

'I heard her say, 'Yay, I'm so pleased you could come. Did you bring the stuff?', they said yes.'

'Did you see what 'stuff' they had?'

'No but one of the girls had a rucksack and the bloke had a carrier bag of what looked like bottles of alcohol.'

'The bin bags had the takeaway cartons, empty bottles and leftover bits,' the male officer added.

'Yes. They had a takeaway delivered not long after they arrived.'

'Do you remember what time they left?'

'I do. It was late, around 12.30pm. I remember because I was watching 'Going in Style' on BBC1. It didn't end until just gone one. I'd nearly dozed off on the sofa watching it when I heard them leaving. Michelle came down to see them out.'

'You're sure they all left?'

'Yes. They made so much noise that I looked out and saw them heading up the road.'

'And can you tell me how Michelle was or sounded?'

'I'd say happy, cheerful. She kept saying it was great to see them. However I did hear her stumble slightly as she made her way back up the stairs. She just swore and carried on back up to her apartment.'

'Are there any other residents?'

'Yes, Joe Barnes. He lives on the top floor.'

'Thank you. We'll need to speak to him too.'

'Of course. He should be back soon. This is his weekend with his children.'

'Well, thank you. We'll be in touch if there's anything else. If you think of anything please don't hesitate to contact us, even if it's something you're not sure is important. You never know.'

She hands us both a card and stands to leave. Mrs Temple walks them out. Just as they reach the door, the female officer turns.

'We have a counselling service that might be of help to you at this time.'

She reaches into her pocket and pulls out a leaflet and hands it to Mrs Temple but nods at me where I'm sitting at the table. We all turn as there is a bustle coming from the hallway. The police leave and as they do the door swings open. I can hear a lady shouting and then as a black bag moves past on a trolley I hear a keening scream. It goes straight through me. I close my eyes in an attempt to block it out. Michelle's Mum has arrived.

Mrs Temple guides me over to the sofa.

'It's okay, dear. I'll go and see what's going on.'

I'm still wearing the blanket as a cape and my trousers are bulky and uncomfortable as I try to walk. I'm momentarily grateful for the softness of her Persian rug under foot.

'You rest here for a moment. I'm just going to go and speak with Michelle's Mum.'

I nod and she walks away, a concerned look breaking through under her forced smile. I'm unsure if it is concern about leaving me or having to go and face Michelle's Mum. Who, from the sounds drifting in from the hallway, is inconsolable. I sat for a moment staring at the blank television screen. The blue lights are making my eyes ache.

I close them for a moment and snuggle down into the comfort of the sofa cushions. I curl my legs up and rearrange the blanket to cover them. They are like ice.

The noises have quietened. Mrs Temple had pulled the door to again as she left. I shuffle down further, laying my head on the cushion beside me. My eyes are so heavy and my head is pounding. Tiddles jumps up onto my hip and curls into a ball with me. Their warmth and rhythmic breathing was soothing. I feel myself drifting away.

Chapter Twenty-One

I awaken in the soft white glow from the streetlight. I'm relieved that the blue flashing lights have stopped - they were hurting my head. I lay still for a moment, trying to get my bearings. I feel a weight on my hip and see that Tiddles is fast asleep, not having moved an inch. I settle back down, no inclination to move from this spot.

The next time I wake it is to the sound of the bin men on the street outside. Tiddles is no longer with me and there is now daylight filtering through the net curtains. I push myself to sit upright with my forearm, then walk back through to the uninhabited kitchen. I unfurl the blanket from me and lay it over the back of the chair. I pick up my damp socks and tip toe out of Mrs Temple's apartment.

I head back upstairs towards my flat. Just as I'm arriving at my door Joe came down the stairs, presumably on his way out. Had he not been so heavy footed his appearance from the direction of Michelle's flat would have made me jump. I unlock my door and place the balled up socks inside. I'm in my doorway, my back holding the door ajar as I pop my feet into my slipper boots and roll my still damp trousers back down to their full length. I tune into what he is saying and when his words finally reach my foggy brain I spin round with such speed that he steps back.

'You absolute fuckwit!' I yell in his face. 'You thought you heard something but you did nothing about it? Are you fucking kidding me?'

'I told the police that I just thought it was odd her music stayed on all night even after I heard her friends leave. It's not like her.'

I've balled my fists. My blood is literally boiling and I know that I am seconds away from kicking off and doing damage to him, to something, to someone, anyone. I'm infuriated. All the trauma of yesterday is coming out now and Joe is its target. I back away with a look that could have killed. I turn and march straight down the stairs, past Mrs Temple's and out onto the street. I have no idea where I'm going but I need to get away. Now.

Once I'm a few streets away I slow to a stop. Where shall I go? What should I do? Michelle and I were so close that we were always each other's go-to people. At this moment I can't think of anyone I could visit. No one likes to have to deal with grieving people. It's awkward and uncomfortable for all involved. Yet I feel the yearning for human interaction. Just a friendly face, a cup of tea or brandy.

I put my keys in the pocket of my creased, pyjama trousers and wrap my arms around me. I'm freezing. Thankfully it's not raining anymore. I'm glad to still be wearing my hoodie but it's of little consolation. I'm cold inside as much as outside. My steps are making a scuffling sound and I look down to realise I'm wearing my slipper boots. Oh for fuck's sake. What the hell is happening? Who have I become? I inwardly start to laugh at myself as I think about how Michelle would have mocked me forever for this. The internal giggling becomes outward tears as I take a side path into the park. I can hardly tell the difference between reality or the made up crap in my head. I wipe my nose on the cuff of my hoodie.

It's early on Monday morning so the park is a bit busier than I'd expected. Morning joggers, dog walkers and commuters using it as a nip through. I wipe my face as the tears slow and try to work out which route is the least busy. It appears that none of them are so I just walk, head down, arms crossed, slipper boots scuffling along as I try to dodge the puddles from yesterday's rainfall. I hot foot it around the fountain, and then my pace starts to slow.

I can feel the anger ebbing away with every step I take. This might not have been a planned excursion or one I did very often. In fact, I think perhaps twice when Michelle and I decided to take up jogging. I smile inwardly at the recollection. We bought all the leggings, trainers, sports bras and brightly coloured tops to only end up doing half a lap of the exercise park before giving up. Then we'd bought ice creams and sat mulling over how the outdoor gym equipment actually worked. We moved once the fit mums started lapping around us with the buggy fitness group. We decided that this was not our thing and headed to the nearest café to recover. I think I still have those clothes shoved in the back of the wardrobe - just in case.

There are a couple of pre-school age children with their Grandad floating wooden sail boots along the edge of the pond. Their Grandad is using his walking cane to guide them back in when the sticks the children are holding don't work properly and they start to drift. I perch on the edge of a bench and watch the people going about their lives. Part of me wants to stand on the bench and shout, tell them the news, that my best friend has died. Demand that they pause their lives and pay some respect to the wonderful human being who can no longer join me in the park. I want them to stop, yet at the same time I want normality to continue. I'm finding it weird, just sitting here, just watching. Having no part to play other than the observer.

A dog jumps in the water, playfully bouncing around, having the time of his life, but his antics disturb the water and cause the wooden boats to catch inland. The girl starts to cry while the boy is jumping around encouraging the dog by throwing his twig into the water and shouting, 'fetch.' The dog obliges and chases after it and swims excitedly back to his newfound friend. See, that's the thing with animals and children. They make friends so easily. Just the slightest interaction and they are the best of friends, even if for just a few moments. They don't think it through any further than that. Interestingly both dog and boy will remember each other when they come here, perhaps hoping to meet again. If only it were that easy as an adult. I sink back into my grief at the idea that I may never find another friend, let alone one who I was so deeply connected with as Michelle, when I hear a commotion. I lift my head back up from where my gaze had found the stony path more interesting.

The dog has the stick in his mouth and is back on land, shaking himself off. The boy is laughing and skipping about in the droplets, the sun is making little rainbows appear through them which has the girl now entertained too. Their Grandad is taking a moment to light his pipe whilst they are occupied safe enough away from the water. The boats lay at his feet drying off after their voyage. A jogger swerves around them, smiling at the antics. I wish I'd ever looked that happy as I'd jogged. Perhaps they had a kale smoothie before they left the house. Maybe this was where we went wrong, two espressos were possibly not the recommended pre-workout beverages.

A shriek steers my attention away from the jogger, back in the direction of the new friends circle. A couple had been so occupied by each other that they had walked straight towards the rainbow shower but unlike the children the lady was not best pleased. She pats her blonde bob back in place and mutters something to her companion who is more concerned that his Converse are getting specs of muddy water on them.

'Never mind your shoes. What about me?' she says loud enough for all to hear.

They are too far away still for me to hear what he whispers in her ear but by her body language I can guess it to be rude. She giggles and snuggles into his shoulder like a teenager. It is not until he laughs that I realise it's Bob. My guardian angel has appeared. I thank Michelle for her input as I go to call after him, but I stop, half lifted from my seat as the lady turns back to scowl at the soggy group and I realise it is Debbie. I flump back down on the bench. If ever I needed Michelle it was now. She'd love this. She'd be off buying ice creams again and popcorn so we could observe this strange mating ritual of the cat lady and her 'cool' boss from the comfort of our bench.

Yet instead I'm sitting here alone in my slippers. The only saving grace is that they are walking away in the other direction. I can't take my eyes off them. I'm glued to the spot, mesmerised by the vision before me. I rub my eyes, wondering if the trauma has made me delusional. I like to hope that if ever I was actually delusional that I would manifest something much more pleasing to the eye and entertaining to my mind than Bob and Debbie as a couple. I'm staring in their direction long after they've walked out of sight. I'm only now becoming aware of the dampness soaking through my clothes from the bench but it's not enough to make me move.

The sound of someone slowing as they approach me makes me turn. Expecting it to be just another dog walker pausing to rest, I'm surprised to see George. He stops and gestures at the empty space next to me. I nod and shift slightly even though I'm not taking up much space. We both sit together in companionable silence for a few moments, our attention instead on the Grandad and his grandchildren. He taps his pipe out on the edge of a wall and pops it in his pocket. The children collect up the now dried off boats and he's herding them off toward the play park, his stick rhythmically marching them along.

'You picked a good spot,' George says conversationally.

'Absolutely. The best seat in the park.' I give a half smile. 'I didn't know you came here?'

I don't know why I say this as it's not as though this is my regular hang out spot.

'I use it as a nip through to work,' he chuckles.

His look falters as he takes in my appearance. I appreciate the fact that he doesn't comment.

'Work,' I repeat, almost a whisper.

Of course, that must be where Bob and Debbie are off to. Yet I've never seen them arrive together. So many strange things are going on.

We observe the comings and goings around us and I'm transported back to our time in Florence when we sat staring at the Duomo. It feels like a million years ago since we were. It's amazing how so many weeks pass, just blending into each other, nothing much to report and then there are days like yesterday where literal life changing events can happen. Making it a day you'll never forget, no matter how much you wish you could.

George lays his hand on top of mine. He was just about to say something when his phone rings.

'Excuse me,' he says, standing and walking a few steps away from the bench.

He talks quietly into the phone, laughs and then his conversation is over.

'Right, I have to go. I've got an errand to run before work. See you there?'

I nod. I want to tell him but I don't know how to. I want him to take me in his arms and comfort me. But he couldn't. No amount of hugs can take away this pain and warm the iciness that has claimed my body. I feel myself start to shake slightly. My bottom lip wobbles. I tightened my mouth into a smile so he doesn't pause to ask the obvious question. Instead I stand up too and go back in the direction of home while he carries on towards work.

I pause just round the corner and remember that I don't have my phone on me to let Bob know I won't be in. He probably won't question my absence. Perhaps he'll assume

I'm just tired from our travels. George might say he saw me but still, I'll update them when I'm ready. I wouldn't even know to start putting the words together to explain what's happened.

The last place I want to be is at home but it appears that there is far too much drama playing out in the park today for my liking. I was searching for solitude and instead... well. I slowly make my way back towards home. I'm dragging my feet and trying to make the walk take as long as possible but before I know it I've arrived at the steps to my building.

I let myself in and up to my apartment, thankfully without bumping into anyone else. It feels cold and empty in the flat. I switch on the kettle and grab my chunky cardigan from where I'd left it on the back of the sofa. I slip it on and wrap it round me. I crave comfort. The kettle clicks and I make a strong cup of sweet tea. I curl into the corner of the sofa, pulling my blanket over me, cradling my tea and stare at the fireplace. I can't be bothered to light it, as much as I wish for its warmth. I'm drained on every level, too tired to actually feel much.

What must have been hours later, I awaken in the dark. There is a glow from the windows of the houses that back onto ours. I uncurl myself slightly. I ache and am in need of a wee. It appears I must have placed my cup from my tea safely on the table before I drifted off. It's nice to know that even though I've felt so out of it that I still function on a basic level.

I nervously edge my way round my bathroom door, scared of what I might find. Even though it looks exactly as I had left it, I use the toilet and get out of there as quickly as possible. I don't even flush the toilet as I daren't make so much noise. I run to my warm spot and wrap the blanket back around me, warming me slightly. The silence is deafening. Tears escape me as the realisation that the lack of noise in the building is mostly due to Michelle's absence.

When her Mum had come I had stayed in Mrs Temple's. I hadn't felt ready to face her. My mind walks through her apartment. As much as the police had seemed suspicious at first about my cleaning and taking out of the bins, I'm pleased I did. Michelle wouldn't have liked people, especially her Mum, in her apartment in the state it was in. I wonder whether the shower is still running or if the plugs are still switched on, if her desktop set-up is still sat on standby. I'm curious to know if her Mum saw her still in the bathroom. I then have a vague recognition of the trolley and Michelle's Mum's scream. Did they let her see her before they took her away? Did she want to? Had she taken anything of importance with her? Was she alone or did she have people looking after her? I hope she has.

I had many questions, but none that I was ready to ask or hear the answers to. They could wait. I shiver. The idea that Michelle is laid all alone in a mortuary upsets me -

she'd be so cold and bored. Then the realisation hits me again that she will not be feeling either of these things. She'll be feeling nothing. This thought does nothing to soothe my raw emotions. I sink deeper into the sofa and wrap the blanket tighter around myself, the sobs wracking my body.

Chapter Twenty-Two

I've been drifting in and out of sleep here on my sofa. My eyes are sore and my throat is dry. At times I've been woken by noises in the hallway, footsteps and muffled voices. Each time I've held my breath, hoping they don't disturb me. I want to be left alone here under my blanket. The bottom of my trousers feel crispy from having dried out. I can't bring myself to move and get changed, despite feeling the need to rip these clothes off. The ones that had Michelle laid across them, dampened from the bathroom floor and her wet hair. I'm glued to the spot, my mind spinning out of control one minute, followed by nothing, just darkness. If I move, take these clothes off, it will change everything. Whilst I'm still here unmoving, changing nothing, I'm pausing time. I'm holding on to the now. If I alter anything, the spot I'm cocooned in or the clothes I'm wearing, everything will change. Time will start ticking again. Propelling me forward into the future. One that I don't want to be a part of. The future without Michelle in it.

This undesirable future holds nothing for me. Without Michelle, what is the point? What am I supposed to do? Carry on as though nothing has changed? To let time heal, as they say. Well, what is it healing? What difference is that going to make to me? Healing might be great but healing won't bring back my best friend, my ex-lover, my soulmate.

Perhaps, I ponder, if I stay here long enough time will start to fall backwards. To a time with Michelle still alive in it. Laughing, gaming, breathing. The image of her stiff body, cold and wet, unmoving in the shower keeps flashing in my mind. The expressionlessness of her pale features. The remains of mascara around her closed eyes, the lipstick in the corners of her mouth. The gash on her head. There was no pain showing on her face. No signs of distress. Just nothing. Each time the image appears I try to change the outcome. To have her open her eyes. To giggle. Or to have her wake up, disorientated from having hit her head on the porcelain tiles, only injured.

Perhaps if I'd called her back or arrived home earlier or not gone at all, she would still be alive. If I'd gone straight to the bathroom and not cleaned the apartment instead, would I have got there in time to catch her? Was I right to not do more to save her? Could I have done something to try to bring her back? No, the voice of her in my head says, you were too late. The tears choke me and I splutter as the deep-rooted sobs consume me once more.

'Fuck's sake!' I shout, as I thump the back of the sofa.

I collapse back down on the sofa, cuddling into the back of it, my back cold where the blanket is no longer covering it. I feel clammy, as though I have the flu. Burning up one minute and freezing cold the next. Maybe staying in those damp clothes made me sick. No, this is not an illness. This is despair in its rawest form. This is the effect from the remnants of my shattered heart attacking my soul. Punishing me for letting my best friend down the one time she needed me most.

She had seen me through so much. Crappy relationships, bad days at work, rainy Sundays, family drama. I had seen her through similar times. We were always there for each other, a consoling hug and a bottle or two of wine. We helped each other to survive this complicated, unexplainable existence. Yet now I'm alone and her journey has come to an end. Why? Why now? Why her?

I've wondered many times since if I was wrong. Was she actually alive? Had I mistaken her for dead? No, her body was stiff and beyond pale. There was no mistaking that. So what now? I pull the blanket over my shoulders and round to cover my back. The cushion soaks up more of my tears, the coldness making my cheek feel cold and sore. I deserve more than just a cold back and sore cheek. I should be punished for letting Michelle die. Her Mum will hate me, blame me. I hope she does. I deserve it. It should have been me lying there, not her. She had so much more to offer the world than I could ever deign to. She was making other people's lives better. Not just mine. Millions around the world. What of that now?

'Shit!'

I haul myself up, tripping over my tangled blanket as I scuttle across to find my phone. I haven't so much as looked at it since I arrived back. No, before that. I put my hand to my aching head as I sit next to my bag in my hallway. I have no idea when I last looked at it. Everything before feels lost in a vortex of jumbled thoughts. Like a drama I once watched but played no part in. I dig into my bag to retrieve my phone. It's dead. Is everything around me dead? Am I dead? Did the world come to an end and I'm the sole survivor? If so I may as well give up now. I'd never make it. Even if it's not the end of the world as a whole, it is the end of mine as I knew it. I fish my charger out and make my way through to the kitchen to charge it. I put the coffee maker on. Placing the cup on it I lean against the worktop. I feel so weak. I have no idea of the time. The sun is shining through the back window but that gives me no indication of the time of day. Or which day it even is. How long have I been here like this? Drifting in and out of sleep? A few hours? Days? Weeks?

I take my coffee back to the sofa and pull my legs up, covering my bare feet with the warm blanket. Resting my cup on my knees, I sip it slowly. My throat hurts too much to manage it any faster. Halfway down I remember I left my phone. I don't care, the moment has passed. It needs more time to charge anyway. I finish my drink, place the cup on the coaster and lay back, one arm behind my head, and stare at the ceiling. The distance between me and it feels never ending. It makes me feel small. Tiny. Insignificant even just in my own space. A space that once made me feel safe and comforted now feels empty, lonely.

The ceiling rose is beautifully decorative with budding flowers and I follow the swirls with the eyes. Drawing over them with my mind. The lampshade was here when I moved in. I never bothered to change it. It's a simple beige shade. The only interesting thing about it are the cobwebs that have gathered in the time since I last remembered its existence. I can't see any spiders. It's weird how they create such intricate, delicate webs and then hide away, not knowing if it will be there on their return. Will there be a juicy fly or nothing at all, not even their web? Yet they mission on. No emotional attachment to their creation, no matter how long it took them. They just simply weave another one, just as beautiful, not choosing a lesser version just because the old one was destroyed.

As I lay here I wonder if I could learn from this. To be more like the spiders, to rebuild a beautiful life even after it's been destroyed. I avert my gaze. No. I roll back to face the back of the sofa. I'm not that strong or resilient. I'm just a broken mess of a person. I could rebuild everything yet the pinnacle thing, person, would still no longer exist in it, leaving it just as empty as it is right now.

Just as I'm drifting off I hear footsteps again. I hold my breath. This time they pause. I sit up, peeking over the back of the sofa. Shit. I gulp. The sound filling my head. I listen intently, hoping they carry on walking. Silence. Then I hear movement again and the sound of descending footsteps. I let out a sigh. I hear the front door close. They've gone. I go to the door and look out the peephole. The distorted space is empty. I open the door an inch. No one to be seen. Then I look down to see a bunch of flowers. I clutch my heart. What? Why? I crouch down to pick it up. They are beautiful. Pinks and blues. I close the door and sit cross legged on the floor. I place them down carefully, the bubble of water in the box balancing it. There is a card. I slide it out of its miniature envelope.

> I'm here if you need me
> Look after yourself
> Andy xxxx

I crumble. The kindness in her gesture hits me. I wrap my arms around myself and draw my knees up. Laying there in the foetal position as the tears rise up and drown me in their intensity once more. I squeeze my eyes closed and allow my emotions to flow through me.

Chapter Twenty-Three

The sound of my phone ringing wakes me, yet when I open my eyes my apartment is silent and shrouded in darkness. The ringtone must have been in whatever dream I was having. I smell the sweetness of flowers and as I try to find my bearings, my eyes adjust and I can see the bouquet. I lift my stiff body from the coldness of the floor, using the wall to stand. I switch on the light, its brightness stinging my eyes. I slowly make my way to the kitchen, switching on the lights as I go. They are too bright, my head is thudding. My own footsteps echoing through the dullness in my mind.

I retrieve my phone, the screen blank apart from showing that it's now fully charged as I unplug the charger. I turn it on. As the notifications land I switch it to silent, the noise is too much. I place it down again while I grab a glass of water. My throat is ridiculously sore, my mouth dry. The phone now seems to have finished updating me on the virtual life I've been missing out on. I couldn't care less.

There is nothing in that matrix that holds any importance, except one thing.

I walk back to my spot on the sofa, phone in hand, and pull the blanket back over me. There is little solace in it now that it has lost its warmth. I hold my phone under the blanket, having made a tent with my knees. I ignore the notification bubbles on the corner of my app boxes and go straight to YouTube. Accessing Michelle's channel, I choke on my tears as her smiling face appears, stunningly beautiful, perfect make-up and her long blonde hair glossy. I take a deep breath. My hands are shaking as I hit the play button on the top video. I need to see her as she was alive to push this other vision of her from my mind.

I may not have been able to revive her in the shower but I yearn to see her full of life, instead of the waxen shell I held in my arms. Her voice singing out from behind the tiny screen in my hands makes me smile whilst simultaneously sending pain through my body. I slide down, laying my head on the arm of the sofa. The hardness digs in but I don't shift. Instead I pull the blanket up over my head so Michelle and I are here in our own world. Both of us together. Her voice fills the space and my vision blurs as the tears cascade. The sleeve of my cardigan is wet from mopping my tears, and even my hoodie cuff is damp now I'm crying so hard. She's so animated, smiling and chatting as she missions her way past skeletons riding spiders. I cough out a chuckle as she shrieks when a witch appears and starts throwing potions at her.

This is exactly what I needed right now. To see her personified. Eternally young and happy. I'm warmer now. As she had in real life she makes me feel better. I find it ironic that it is her who is helping me through this. I can't imagine anyone else being able to get through the fogginess in the way that her videos are now. How could she have survived so much in her virtual life only to be taken out by a shower in the real world? It was just wrong. She'd have been disappointed in herself for not having had a more dramatic ending.

We'd gone through lists of ways that were worthy of writing on our gravestones. Her favourite was death by llama. Not falling off it - she said that was too cliche - but being accidentally sat on by one or spat on and falling back into a ravine. I'd never known anyone so overjoyed when Minecraft had llamas added. We'd agreed that my death of choice had to be in Italy, of course. She knew I was as obsessed with the country as she was with video games. I believe we finally decided on my death being by one of the statues falling on me in a museum. Preferably, she'd said, whilst being in a compromising position with an attractive Florentine. Perhaps in ode to her I could have this arranged on my next visit.

As I shift my position slightly, the screen rotates so I can see the chat box beneath the video. Shit! My hands fly to my mouth as I drop my phone. They know. Her fans have infiltrated our private space. My blanket tent is no longer a safe space for just the two of us. Word must have gotten out. Fuck! The couple I'd seen said 'RIP', 'you'll be missed', 'too young to die'.

I flee from under the blanket, jumping off the sofa so fast I hit my shin on the corner of the coffee table. My head spins, my phone landing face up on the carpet, Michelle chatting away as though nothing has happened. But even in this virtual world they are killing her off, one comment at a time, rippling across the world as each person hears my earth-shattering news. I feel protective of her now more than ever. Even though no words can ever hurt her again, they have the power to sully everything she had worked hard to achieve. Everything she, as a brand, stood for. All the people she helped in many different ways. From the ones who watched her videos for entertainment, to those who learned new skills to her scholarship members who found a new lease of life from her funding.

I feel a whole new level of sadness. Michelle wouldn't want this. Me literally hiding under a blanket feeling sorry for myself. She'd hate that my finding her had caused me suffering. I need to do something. To find out what people know, what's being said online. Has there been a press release already? Do they do that stuff straightaway? I guess they must. I pick my phone up. I need to contact someone. I try to focus through my scrambled thoughts. I can't just ring her Mum and ask. I can't even imagine what she's going through right now.

I check the time on my phone - only just gone six in the evening - swooping the notifications off the screen. I have no interest in any of my messages, calls or emails right now. And I sure as hell don't care about my social medias. The only person I can think of is George. He was the last person I saw before... when the world was as it should be.

Chapter Twenty-Four

George arrives what seems like only moments later. I'm standing holding the door open with my shoulder, hugging my cardigan tightly around me, as he makes his way up the stairs. Our weak smiles say so much more than words could at this point. I'd not said much on the phone, only that I needed his help. I was spared from having to tell him the news. He must already be aware - I guess the whole world knows by now. I close the door behind him and pad my way through the kitchen. He removes his shoes and neatly places them next to mine. He follows as I automatically make my way to the kitchen, switching on the coffee maker. I lift up a cup to signal coffee. He nods.

We settle in. I'm curled back in my corner of the sofa and he is sitting across from me on the high back chair. We both sit holding our cups. So that he doesn't feel the need to say the standard words I tell him why I've called him here.

'I need your help to find out what the media is saying about Michelle. Moreso, I'd like to contact someone who can explain how this works now...' I can't finish my sentence. Instead I take a sip of my drink.

'Probably the best place to start is her Mum,' he says, but upon seeing me frown he changes tact. 'Or did she have an agent? A media team?'

'I'm not sure about that but she definitely had an agent. I can't remember who though.'

'Right. I'm not gonna lie but this isn't something I know much about. Let's have a quick search and I'll see what I can find.'

'Thank you. I couldn't bring myself to Google her yet.'

'Understandable.'

He smiles reassuringly. As much as I thought I wasn't ready to face anyone, I think my decision to call him was right. He's busy searching on his phone as I sit quietly drinking my coffee.

'Can I ask you another favour?'

'Of course,' he says, not taking his eyes off his phone.

I chew my lip before speaking, even in my head the words seem silly.

'I'm skanky.' I try to sound light-hearted about this. 'But I didn't dare take a shower.'

He looks up at me now. I look away, I can't say it with him watching me.

'Would you sit outside the door while I go in? Just in case. I don't wanna... slip.'

The words choke me, I take a shaky breath. He moves to sit on the sofa next to my feet. He puts one hand on my arm and one on my face.

'I wouldn't ask but...'

'It's okay,' he reassures me quietly.

He pulls me close as I start to cry. This was not what I had planned. I had hoped to have him simply help me with Michelle's stuff, to find out what people knew. Instead, here I am crying into George's shoulder.

'Sorry.' I pull away. 'I'm making you all soggy.'

'No apology needed. These shoulders were made broad for a reason. Come on, let's get you de-skanked.'

I smile through my tears. We get up from the sofa. I fetch my dressing gown while he patiently waits in the hallway. He has a cushion in his hand. I frown slightly as I see it.

'I don't want to get a cold bottom.'

I giggle, wiping at my tear-stained face.

'I really appreciate this.'

'Honestly, it's no problem.'

He settles himself against the wall, his phone in hand.

'Take your time. This might take a while anyway,' he says, as he holds up his phone. 'Sing as loud as you like.' He winks.

I wish I'd had either the inclination or energy to sing but I don't. I set the shower to run and clean my teeth as it heats up. As the mirror starts to steam up I move away from it. I'm edgy. Nervous of drifting in my mind for even the slightest second. I need to keep my mind in the here and now. One lapse in concentration could bring back the flashbacks. I talk my way through the process shaky under my breath. I know it is partly from the coldness now I've removed my clothes for what I now know I've been wearing for two days.

I wash my hair, keeping my eyes open, risking the shampoo stinging rather than closing them. Once the conditioner is out I can concentrate on keeping my balance while I wash my body. I carry on my dialogue. By the time I turn off the shower and am safely back on the bathmat I sigh with relief. I braved it. At this point I finally flush the toilet - the noise doesn't seem as loud now George is here.

Feeling fresher and wrapped in my dressing gown I nip across to my room to dress. George is looking quite content perched on the cushion. I throw on a pair of joggers and a hoodie. I need comfort, not style, right now. I like that I feel so comfortable around George now. Our trip to Italy means that I consider him a friend. By the fact that he is here, I assume he feels the same. I put on a fresh pair of fluffy socks. I'm pleased to be clean and comfy. Strange how even the slightest thing at a time like this can help.

'Fresh drink?' I ask as I pass.

'Please.' He follows me back through, returning his cushion to the sofa as he passes. 'Feel better?'

'Absolutely. I know it was silly but -'

'Not even. It's completely understandable under the circumstances.'

I look at him as if to question how he knows why the bathroom held such unease for me.

'Mrs Temple stopped me as I was coming in,' he says by way of explanation.

'Of course, she doesn't know who you are. I hadn't thought with everything going on just how much that might freak her out.'

'She seemed fine, just curious and checking in on your wellbeing. To be honest she was pleased you had reached out.'

I turn back to make our drinks.

'I hadn't realised that you actually found her,' he says softly.

He steps closer but I move away to get the milk.

'Well, how would you have known.'

'You should have said something when I bumped into you yesterday.'

I chuckle ironically.

'And how do you suggest I'd have started that conversation?'

'Fair play.'

I pass him his drink.

'I found out what the media knows, by the way. Would you like to read it?'

I stand next to him as he tilts his phone to show me. As I glance I see a photo of her and recoil.

'On second thoughts, do you mind reading it out?'

'It reads - YouTube and social media sensation Miss Michelle Jordan (29) was found dead at her home in Notting Hill on Sunday evening. The cause of death is still unknown. Her manager, Mr Grant Warne, has kindly requested that fans respect the family's privacy during this difficult period. A GoFundMe and condolence page have been created so fans can express sympathies to her family. Any money raised will go to a charity yet to be decided. A full statement is expected in the coming days.'

As he finished reading I released the breath I hadn't realised I'd been holding.

'It's weird to hear it stated so bluntly, without emotion,' I say.

'It is.'

'I'm glad they don't seem to have any more details. Do you think that her manager will put something else together? Perhaps with her Mum?'

'I don't know.' He pulls a sympathetic face. 'How about we look again tomorrow. Perhaps we can find a way to speak to him,' he says, glancing back at his phone. 'This Grant fellow.'

'Good idea.'

He checks his phone.

'It's getting late,' he says, finishing his drink. 'I'd best be off.'

My stomach knots up instantly at the thought of being alone again.

'Will you be okay?'

'I want to say yes, but if I'm honest, I'm really not sure.'

He runs his fingers through his hair.

'Would it help if I stayed?'

'I couldn't ask you to do that.'

'You didn't. I'm offering.'

Chapter Twenty-Five

The knock on my door jars me from my fitful sleep. George seems not to have heard it as he's still bundled up under the duvet on the sofa. I uncurl myself from the armchair, wrapping the blanket round my shoulders. I'd like to say that it was my uncomfortable choice of sleeping positions that had stopped me from settling, but it wasn't. Each time I drifted off I'd be jolted awake again by visions or sounds. Each time I woke I'd find it hard to know if I'd seen or heard these things in my dreams or if there was something going on in the real world. However, having George sleeping soundly nearby had helped settle my wrought nerves.

'Good morning, dear. Sorry to disturb you.'

'That's okay. I wasn't really sleeping anyway.'

She nods understandingly. At least, I hope she does, and it's not the fact that she will have clocked the fact that George didn't leave last night. The blush of my cheeks probably doesn't help my case.

'Michelle's Mother is here and wondered if you were free.'

It transpires that I had no reason to worry. There were far more important things on her mind.

'Erm. Of course.'

The words from my mouth are the complete opposite of what I want to say.

'She's in my flat at the moment.'

I'm relieved to hear that. I'm not sure I'd have coped with seeing her at all if it meant going back into Michelle's flat. Yet my helpful nature overrides my selfish thoughts. The ones that are scared to see the grief in her Mum's eyes. I'm struggling to comprehend my own right now. I wonder if maybe it will help us both in some small way. Not forgetting that Mrs Temple will be grieving in her own way too. Communal tea will probably help us all.

'I'll just be a minute.'

'No rush, dear. I've got the kettle on.'

This familiar gesture is appreciated. I clean my teeth and splash water on my face. It's not until I'm drying my face that I realise that autopilot took over and I rushed straight into the bathroom without a second thought. 'Progress', I whisper to my reflection. I scribble a quick note to George on an old envelope I found on the kitchen side to let him know where I am. The poor guy has been kind enough to stay and the last thing I want to do is freak him out if he can't find me when he wakes up.

With trepidation I make my way downstairs. I'm still in the clothes I slept in and have put my slipper boots on. I feel naked without the comfort of my blanket. I considered taking it with me but that seemed weird, even at a time like this. Michelle's Mum is sitting with her back to the door as I enter. Mrs Temple is bringing the teapot over to the table and she acknowledges me with a smile. Michelle's Mum, Paula, turns in her chair and leaps up, embracing me in a tight hug. I hug her solid frame back. Her sadness emulates from her. We stand like this for a moment and as she pulls away I look down. I can't look her in the eye yet. From her embrace I know what I'll see there. She returns to her chair and I sit on the spare one. Tiddles has the other.

We sit silently watching Mrs Temple bring the cups and other bits over to place in the middle of the Formica table. Where this previous brought me solace it now brings back the wrought feelings of the last time I sat here. I wring my hands in my lap. My shoulders are aching from holding the tension and sleeping in the chair. As the tea is served both Paula and I cradle our teacups. I wait for her to speak. I feel on edge. What might it be that she wants from me? Is she angry at me for not keeping her daughter safe? I'm miles away in my mind, staring aimlessly into my tea as the bubbles in the centre are still slowly spinning. I feel Paula's eyes on me and she clears her throat.

'I wondered if you'd be able to help me with something.'

I looked at her properly for the first time, as though by her speaking to me she had given me permission to do so. It's the only time I've ever seen her without make-up. Her eyes look bruised and puffy, her nose red raw, her cheeks sunken. Her lipstick-free lips appear to blend with her pale skin, as though the life has been drained from them.

'I can certainly try.'

My shoulders drop an inch or two.

'The police say that they have all the evidence they need from...' She gulps, then shakes her head slightly to right herself. 'The apartment.'

I nod in acknowledgement. I feel my own throat tighten at this point as I pre-empt her next question.

'I don't want to go in there alone. Would you...'

Her eyes meet mine at this point. The depth of her sadness is far greater than I had imagined. Shivers run down my spine, making me spill my tea slightly into the saucer. Mrs Temple fetches a square of fruit patterned paper towel and hands it to me. As I take it from her, her kind eyes meet mine. I mop up the liquid, relieved to have something else to focus on.

'I completely understand if you'd rather not,' she continues without waiting for my answer. 'The police said it was you who...'

She doesn't finish her sentence. Instead, she sips her tea, giving a little cough to clear her throat, as though the drink had got caught up with the words she was trying to say. I simply nod, my head still lowered. I'm concentrating on the pattern on the soggy paper towel.

'It doesn't have to be right now if you'd rather.'

I consider this for a few moments.

'Now is fine. I don't think they'll ever be a right time.'

Paula gives me a watery but grateful smile. The three of us make our way slowly up the stairs. Mrs Temple leads and I follow. I pass my key to Paula as we reach the door, noting the remnants of police tape on the doorframe. I hadn't considered that they would have cordoned it off. It seems even eerier, like a murder scene from a film rather than real life. I recognise that my current concept of reality is messed up. I wonder whether things will ever feel 'normal' again.

Our footsteps are light as we step into the space. The glow from the coffee table dimly illuminates the room. Paula turns on the main light. Michelle rarely bothered to open the blackout blinds. She didn't spend much time in here during daylight hours. I look to Paula for guidance. I'm not quite sure what she's wanting to do here today. Neither Mrs Temple or I move into the room. We give Paula her space as she wanders around the kitchen and living area.

'Has the cleaner been in since?'

'No, I cleaned up a bit for her.'

She looks at me quizzically. I choose at this point not to elaborate. I'm not sure mentioning just how long I waited to find her would help. It certainly wouldn't make any difference to the outcome, but was possibly something that might upset her further. She runs her hand along the breakfast bar as she walks back across the space.

'I'm not sure what I'm supposed to do,' she voices to no one in particular.

I'm pleased that Mrs Temple is with us as I have no idea either. She steps forward and touches Paula gently on the arm.

'You can just stay here for a bit if you'd like time to yourself.'

'No, I think I'd like you with me.'

Mrs Temple nods in agreement. I'm pinned to the spot. I don't think I'm able to venture any further at this point. As though Mrs Temple has read my mind, she offers to walk through with Paula but doesn't ask me to join them. I gratefully stay standing where they left me. I can hear them talking softly and the sound of crying at points. Then they must have walked further through the apartment, out of ear shot. I take a couple of deep shuddering breaths and the tears start to fall as the chill of the empty place and the silence envelop me. I wrap my arms around myself.

'Oh Michelle,' I say, barely a whisper.

I wish, not for the first time, that I had my blanket with me now. Hopefully they don't take too long because I'm not sure how much longer my wobbly legs can hold me up. I can feel my head starting to spin and the darkness creeping in. The tears are in danger of turning more vigorous any second and I'm feeling as though I might pass out. I have to get it together. I'm supposed to be here as support for Michelle's Mum. The last thing either her or Mrs Temple need is to come back to discover I passed out.

I decide the best course of action is for me to sit down. I carefully make my way across to the breakfast bar, hauling myself up slowly onto a bar stool. I rest my head in my hands, elbows on the worktop. Closing my eyes for a moment I manage to push the dizziness away. I open them and plaster a sympathetic smile on my face as the ladies return. Mrs Temple is supporting Paula with the crook of her arm. I can see they have both, understandingly, been crying.

Michelle's Mum flops down onto the sofa. Mrs Temple sits next to her, putting a comforting arm around her shoulders as Paula releases hard, heavy sobs. I move over to sit on the other side of her but a slight distance away. Both Mrs Temple and I share a look over her slumped body. She starts to talk, unintelligible mumbling into her hands. Then she sits upright and her angry tears turn to furious words.

'Why the hell did she let those fuckers back into her life? Her apartment? Could she not have waited for you to get back?' This is directed at me but she doesn't turn. She stays staring straight ahead. 'Those murdering cunts!'

I see Mrs Temple flinch at the language but she keeps her face neutral. We both do.

'She was so young. She was doing so well. She had this Netflix thing coming up. She had everything she ever wanted and more. So why? Why did she let this happen?'

We both stay quiet. Paula's not looking for answers from us. Her heart has been ripped out. Her only child was taken from her far too early. Her words ring true - Michelle had done everything she ever could to get herself away from the druggies and dregs who had tried to pull her down. And she'd managed it. She'd excelled at it. She'd used her past as a springboard. Her teenage angst and self-hatred had been redirected and ended up helping so many people in a multitude of ways. Paula starts howling and thumping her knees in anger. Then suddenly she stops and looks me in the eye.

'My beautiful baby girl,' she says with such yearning that my heart breaks all over again.

I shift forward and allow her to cry into my shoulder. We are all crying now. Mrs Temple nips to grab a handful of takeaway napkins from the kitchen draw and hands them round.

'Mine smells of kebabs,' I say.

'Mine is Chinese.'

'Mine's cheese on toast. Oh no, actually it's pizza.'

We all dissolve into laughter at the ridiculousness of grieving for Michelle and only having these smelly napkins to mop our tears.

'Oh that girl, honestly. Could she not just have a box of tissues like normal people?' Paula chuckles.

She leans back into the sofa now and we all relax slightly, the tension released.

'Would you like me to make a drink?' They look taken aback, so I quickly explain what I mean. 'In my apartment. I can bring it back.'

'I think that would be lovely,' says Mrs Temple.

I nip out and down the stairs, taking a second halfway down to steady myself. Seeing George in my lounge folding the duvet makes me start slightly. I'd forgotten he was here. He offers me a smile.

'I'm just nipping back to get drinks. Mrs Temple and Michelle's Mum are up in her apartment.'

He doesn't say anything but comes over with me into the kitchen.

'I'll give you a hand taking these up and then I'd best go.'

I don't have fancy cups or a teapot so I start making three teas in mugs. I make sure they have plenty of sugar in them. I think we all need it.

'Thank you for staying last night. It was very kind of you.'

'Think nothing of it. I was pleased to be able to help in some small way.' He opens the fridge. 'You're out of milk.'

'Shit. I've been using the coffee maker.'

'Have you even eaten?'

'How do you mean?' I reply absently while tipping the dry contents of the cups in the bin, ready to start again.

'When was the last time you ate?'

I pause, pretending to think.

'I have no idea.'

I get the first cup going. Hopefully the ladies won't mind coffee.

'Since we got back?'

'Erm. No, probably not.'

I shrug it off.

'I'm gonna nip to the shop and get you a few bits. You need to eat.'

By his tone this is non-negotiable. I don't argue. Whether I can manage to eat anything or not is a whole other question. We'll see when the time comes. For now it's taking all my mental energy to make these drinks. I'm pleased that he walks up with me - the last time I'd walked up with drinks to Michelle's it didn't end well. I'm aware that had nothing to do with what I was doing but still, I'm not sure I'd have coped with doing this alone. George doesn't come in with me. He simply waits for me to take two of the mugs in and hands me mine as I return to the doorway.

'I'll be back in a bit. I won't disturb you. I'll just drop the bits off.'

'If I give you my spare key I -' My words stop at the realisation that Michelle had my spare key. I'm not ready to hand it over. 'If you just take my key and leave my door on the latch, that'll be fine. Thanks again, George.'

He takes the key and squeezes my hand gently, smiling softly at me and turns to leave. I settle back down on the sofa, apologising for the drinks being coffee. Neither of them mind. The three of us sit for a while and our conversation eventually turns to regaling stories of Michelle. Each of us had very different versions of her that we knew.

'I remember when she first came to look at the flat,' Mrs Temple says.

'Yes, it was the first time we met,' Paula says. 'I knew you'd look after her. You have a kind soul.'

'As did she.'

'Very much so,' I add.

'I couldn't believe the way her designer made this place look. So hip,' Mrs Temple says.

Paula and I both giggle at her use of the word.

'Me too. That's why it was so funny that she spent so much time in my place,' I say, smiling sadly.

'You were the best friend she could ever have had,' Paula says sincerely.

She touches me gently on the arm. The gesture releases more soft tears.

'She'd laugh if she saw us all sitting here crying into our drinks,' Paula chuckles.

'She'd definitely be telling us to get a grip,' I say.

We stayed finding comfort in each other's company until our drinks were finished and our tears had run dry.

'I'd best go feed Tiddles,' says Mrs Temple, looking at her watch.

'Thank you for this, ladies. Strange to say, but this has been nice,' says Paula.

'It has,' we agree.

Making our way towards the door, I carry the cups and slip my key back into my pocket. I'm not ready to offer it over just yet, in the same way I couldn't give George Michelle's key to my place. I follow close behind as they exit the apartment and give the room one last glance and bid Michelle farewell in my mind. After much hugging and well-wishing outside my apartment the two ladies, arms linked, make their way the rest of the way to Mrs Temple's. As I'm pushing open my door with my elbow I hear them chatting away. Paula was right, this was nice, good for all of us.

'I bet Uncle Eric is fast asleep in the car,' Paula chuckles.

'Has he been out there all this time?' Mrs Temple asks.

'No, he nipped off to do some shopping and then was going to wait in the car so as not to disturb us.'

'That's kind of him to bring you.'

As I'm about to go in I see Joe coming up the stairs. He gives me a hesitant smile. I smile back trying to show that he needn't fear me. I wait for him to arrive on the landing.

'Joe, I just want to apologise for the other day. I didn't mean to be so horrid. I was just -'

'It's alright. I totally understand. You said nothing I hadn't thought myself. I guess all of us wish we'd have done something different. To have...'

'Would any of it have made a difference?' I ask, shrugging.

He gives a half smile in return.

'I can't even imagine how difficult this is for you,' he says. 'If there's anything you need, let me know. A cup of sugar. A shoulder to cry on. Somewhere to hide from the bustle.'

'I'll keep that in mind. Thank you.'

I smile genuinely as we part. It was pretty much what I'd said when Michelle and I first made friends. My heart sinks when I remember that George has gone. The door key and a big bar of Dairy Milk is placed on the coffee table with a scribbled note under the one I'd written him, simply saying 'Eat Me!'.

I sit on the sofa, pull the neatly folded duvet over me, and cry big, heaving sobs into it. Fuck, that was hard. Nice to connect but horrid seeing the flat empty. Seeing Michelle's Mum so obviously lost and broken was heart wrenching. I cry for her. I cry for myself. The smell of

George's aftershave on the duvet is vaguely comforting, as though I'm crying into his shoulder once more. Eventually, the persistent flood of tears exhaust me and I sink into yet more fitful sleep.

Chapter Twenty-Six

The day of the funeral comes round far too soon, yet after what feels like such a long wait. It's an aptly dreary Thursday. I dress in all black. I've never felt right doing the colourful dress code thing that some people request. I've done little more than change into clean pyjamas for the last couple of weeks and feel too sombre to consider something vibrant. I stare at my pale, gaunt looking reflection as I button up my simple black shirt. The black against my skin doesn't help add colour to my cheeks. The paleness is emulating from the inside and nothing on the outside of my body will help. I scrape my hair up. I look away from the mirror, no longer wanting to make eye contact with myself. Focusing on anything, including myself, is too much right now. Even showering this morning took every ounce of energy I felt I had. I'm still not comfortable with being in the bathroom. Drying my hair made my arms ache, so it is still damp. Just standing this long to get dressed has made me feel fragile in every way possible, vulnerable somehow.

If this is how I'm feeling I can't even imagine how her family is doing, especially her Mum. I haven't seen anything of Paula since the day we were in the apartment together. On the multiple occasions I heard her rattling around upstairs I just stuck my headphones in or curled further under my duvet. Each time, I'd have a brief moment of hope that I'd awoken from this nightmare and that Michelle was in fact still there, pottering about as she'd always done. I'd half expect the all too familiar knock on the door. Then it would hit me again that she was gone and then the fear would grab hold of me, the dread that her Mum might pop down and ask for help. I know I should have offered but I couldn't. Just the idea of stepping through the door at all was seemingly impossible, let alone speaking to anyone. I'd sunken into a very dark place.

However, today I'll have to step over the threshold and leave my safe place and look her Mum in the eye again. As much as we'd spoken that day, I had not said the words I'd wanted to. Such as telling her just how much I missed Michelle and how I wish I'd held on tighter to her, loved her more deeply, more openly, been less afraid of my feelings for her. Been here for her when she needed me most. How I wish I'd rung her from Italy. How I yearned for her. How I felt so empty. How I'm so very sorry. How can I show my face when I can't even look myself in the eye? Would my declaration have been enough to give her a reason to risk her life with party drugs? Who do I think I am, to have been strong enough to have helped her cheat death?

Technically our friendship should have been enough, but I didn't know all the thoughts that crossed her mind or why she'd risk her life by doing the things she did. From what Paula had said, it was even more heart-breaking for her Mum to find out that her flippancy with partying too hard was her demise. What she considered to be fun, to pep her up when she was down or used to celebrate, was what finally broke her. If I'd been with her she wouldn't have done anything more than drink. She knew my views on these things - we had long before agreed to disagree. I no longer nagged and she no longer tried to justify it. I blame myself more for going away and not being home to distract her.

Perhaps that's the bit that upsets me most of all. I've run through this over and over in my mind. It appeared from what Mrs Temple said that she'd called in her friends from back in the day. The old days, before she'd found a way to tame her demons. Maybe if she'd just waited until I was back. The idea of her being alone after her night of partying far too hard broke my heart over and over again.

The sound of the knock on my door breaks me out of my thoughts.

'Are you ready to go, dear?'

'Yes.' My voice is croaky. 'I'll just grab my bag.'

Mrs Temple, Joe and I travel in silence to the church. I stare out of the window, aware that Mrs Temple is just looking through the windscreen as we make our way through the busy midday traffic. As the taxi approaches the car park I come back to the here and now, scanning the groups of people gathered outside the church. As we exit the car we walk in sync.

It's funny how even approaching the church our pace is slow and respectful. Mrs Temple links her arm through mine, which makes me flinch slightly. I'm so in my head right now, even more than I have been the past couple of weeks. I'm glad of her support, I feel jittery. If I could ever say there was a time I had the urge to run, it is now. An image of me and Michelle trying to jog through the park flashes through my mind and I wish more than ever that we could both do that now. If only. I push the emotions back down.

It's a warm day yet I'm shivering as we sit in the pew. We are a couple of rows back and I'm looking at the gargoyles and stained-glass window. The details of the eagle on the lectern, the verses on the wall. I turn and see the church is packed. There are people standing at the back. It's just a blur of unrecognisable faces. I turn back and sigh deeply and as I breathe out, my teeth are chattering. Mrs Temple takes hold of my hand and gives it a squeeze of reassurance as the music changes, at which we all stand. Michelle is entering the church, her mother and other close family members following. She'd have loved the fact that these black suited men are carrying her as 'All of Me' by John Legend is played by the organist. It sounded so much more haunting than ever.

I'd imagined if she'd ever gotten married, everything about the event would be over the top. This might have even been the church she'd chosen. I'd have been walking behind her as her maid of honour and her Mum would have worn a fabulous hat. It's hard to see Paula looking so broken - she's always been such a bubbly character. I guess that is what these things do to a person. It is so unnatural, so tragic, the most nightmarish scenario of all the scenarios. I'm not even trying to hold back the tears now. If there was any moment to let it all out, this is it.

Mrs Temple hands me a pack of tissues and I silently thank her. I wonder if I can ever portray to her just how much her being here has helped me. I would, of course, have done this alone but I'm not sure how. The vicar does a little speech about death, the 'just in another room', reading and says how she's with God now. The congregation mumbles their way through 'Amazing Grace' as Michelle's Mum makes her way up to the lectern next to her daughter's coffin.

As Paula slowly, shakily makes her way through the eulogy I stare at her hands as she clings to the printed pages in front of her like a life raft. She doesn't place them on the lectern. I watch her mouth, her dry lips moving as she forms the last words she'll say in front of her daughter. A small smile plays on her lips as she tells an anecdote of a time Michelle was learning to roller skate, and of the joy and pride she felt when her first YouTube video went viral and how she didn't even know of such things until that point. The pride, the loss, the love all shine through. The whole congregation is listening intently. There are sniffles and smatterings of giggles at the funny stories. As she thanks us all for being there and goes to step down she turns and says 'I love you my baby girl'. If they hadn't cried up until now, that was the breaking point. I see Mrs Temple pass a tissue to Joe on her other side.

The music starts up as Michelle's Mum makes her way back to her seat, playing 'Spirit Lead Me' by Raspo. The words were too real. I'm sobbing now and Mrs Temple pulls me close to her. The men reappear and the vicar says a quiet prayer as they carry her back out to the hearse. The family follow behind and everyone respectfully filters out, ready to make their way to the cemetery. I slide my sunglasses on. Many of us start the short walk, making a head start while the cars prepare themselves. An elderly gentleman is being told by a middle-aged lady to put his cigarette out so they can get in the car. He holds his ground for a few more puffs until Michelle's Mum comes over. She takes the cigarette from him, takes a long drag of it, winks at him and stamps it out.

'Come on, Uncle Eric,' she urges.

I smile at the minor altercation. I like this man. I can see where Michelle inherited her stubbornness and humorous characteristics. She obviously comes from a long line of them. Although had it been Michelle, she would probably have joined him and lit another one just because she could. I smile at the thought. She was such an awesome person. My throat catches as I notice I'm referring to her in past tense.

I'm glad of the walk. Joe has wandered off ahead with someone he knew so Mrs Temple and I are just slowly making our way along the track. We've linked arms again, this time it was me who instigated it. I know she's a capable lady but the path is uneven. We're both concentrating on our footing. I'm finding the soft chatter of the people in our little walking group somehow soothing. Being here now, nothing else required of me other than to simply put one foot in front of the other, is welcomed. It has been a testing day to say the least, and it's far from over yet.

Standing in the warm sunshine it could be any other day, except it isn't. We are congregated around the currently empty grave. At this stage is it called a grave or just a hole? I busy my mind with this thought as the funeral directors arrange her coffin precariously over the hole. I guess at this point if they do drop it, it doesn't matter. She can't come to any more harm than she already has. It can't get any worse for her. My sick, twisted humour starts running through comedy sketches where the coffin drops, or someone falls in or... well, the possible scenarios are endless. Mrs Temple and I still have our arms locked and I hold back the urge to bring her in on my private thoughts. God forbid I end up in fits of laughter at a time like this, the most serious of serious. I guess that's why they say deadly serious. Honestly my brain is coming into its own today, making all kinds of connections and logic. It's so clever how your mind works to distract and justify what's going on.

The vicar clears his throat and silence drifts across the group. Heads are respectfully bowed and the words drift over us like the breeze. I take a deep breath and smile slightly as I quietly say goodbye to my best friend, my soulmate. I swallow down the lump in my throat and take another breath, standing taller. No one is even trying to hold back the tears now. This is the final goodbye for all of us. The only sound other than the words of the vicar are the sniffles of her nearest and dearest. I can't even look up. I'm not able to invite anyone else into my sorrow at this point. This is my moment, our moment. I hear her voice, her laugh, her whispering to me and I know that she hears my silent conversation too. Wherever she is now she can hear me and I her. I hope this never dulls. Selfishly I'm not sure I can cope without her as my confidant. I've relied on her, possibly far too much. I'm not confident that I can function as the responsible adult I'm supposed to be without her wise guidance. Okay, so yes, sometimes her ideas were far from sensible but at least they were fun. I wish now that I'd allowed her to talk me into that tattoo she'd kept on about. At least that way I would have something physical to remember her by.

I sense movement around me and realise that we are at the 'ashes to ashes' part. I look up at the point her Mum steps forward and takes the offered handful of dirt and throws it down on the coffin holding the body of her beloved daughter. For whatever I'm feeling I know that she'll be feeling it tenfold. Mrs Temple signals that she'd like to throw some down so I guide her safely round and join her as she says a silent prayer, her lips moving but no sound. I take a handful and sprinkle it down, being careful not to step too close to the edge. We step back to our previous space and then drift away from the graveside as the group disperses.

The wake is being held at a pub local to Michelle's Mum's place. Mrs Temple and I have decided not to join them. Joe is heading off somewhere else so we go to say goodbye to Paula before we go. We hug her and offer more condolences. We know we'll see her again soon when she comes to empty the flat. Mrs Temple assures her that there is no rush whatsoever. I smile agreeably as they talk. Seeing the flat emptying will make this real. Selfishly I want to keep the dream of her alive. Today was just part of the process. Up until this point I have been kidding myself that all is well, that she is well and still sitting in her flat recording her next videos and I've just been in my creaky bed in Florence having a bad dream.

As we walk back towards the church, I turn my phone back on. I have a very different relationship with it these days. I'm no longer so obsessed and constantly attached to it. It let me down in the worst way ever. Plus, I hate the fact that I can't just ring Michelle or have her funny messages pop up throughout my day. While Mrs Temple and I wait for our Uber, my phone notifies our driver is on the way. Mrs Temple finds this incredible and talking to her about how it works has been a great distraction - the magic of a change of subject.

Once we've been successfully delivered home I give Mrs Temple a huge hug and thank her for being with me, and I mean it from the bottom of my shattered heart. I head back up to my flat. Kicking off my shoes, I then curl back into bed fully clothed. I wrap the duvet tightly around me. Safely back in my cocoon, I instantly fall asleep. I have nothing more to give.

Chapter Twenty-Seven

I became aware of a voice softly speaking to me. I try to home in on it, to hold on long enough to make sense of the words. I struggle to prise my eyes open. I aimlessly wonder, as my mind drifts off again, if this is how newborn babies feel when they first enter the world. I try to force myself to leave the thoughts of the newborns in the back of my mind. How is it so difficult to just lift my eyelids?

'Focus,' I whisper.

'Hayley.'

The word I hear sounds familiar.

I have a vague recognition of the voice. My eyes are managing to stay open long enough for me to have a blurry image of my surroundings. I strain my eyes, squinting, willing them to work properly. I feel a touch on my hand and I flinch slightly. I return my hand to where it was, reaching out to feel it once more. It was the most 'normal' thing I had experienced thus far. In jolting my arm, my eyes had shot open fully and the images of the space around me filters through like a kaleidoscope forming a picture. The light in here is that of dusk. I think just the lamp must be on and I can see the curtains are closed. There appears to be just a sliver of half-light showing through the gaps. The figure whose touch I feel is silhouetted by the window but their face is illuminated by the lamplight. As the mind fog clears I realise that it is Michelle. She has her make-up on but her face looks more drawn and pale. Perhaps it's the lighting, but to me she looks concerned.

I try to speak but my mouth is dryer than my eyes.

'Hayley, are you awake?'

I feel my head nod slightly in response, a sharp pang in my neck as I do so. She sits on the side of the bed and waits for me to sit up slightly. She passes me a pina colada - exactly what I'd been craving for days. She puts the straw to my lips. I don't remember owning straws and the paper of it sticks to my dry lips. The liquid feels alien yet refreshing as it rushes down my throat. I gag slightly and she giggles and moves the straw away, gently peeling it from my lips. She holds a tissue out for me and I take it to mop my chin. My limbs ache. Everything aches, from my thudding head to the pins and needles in my legs. I want to stretch to bring life back into my body but I don't have the strength.

Thankfully my vision has corrected itself and I see that I'm in my bedroom. Michelle has set up a little cocktail station on the end of the bed with tiny umbrellas and fruit on sticks. I watch her as she threads more on some skewers. Her gaming chair has been squeezed into the room as well and I recognise the dressing gown thrown over it.

I must have fallen back to sleep almost straight away as I awakened to see her back in her chair, leaning forward, eyes glued to the computer, her fingers moving speedily across the keyboard. She's wearing her dressing gown again, her face lit by the three screens in front of her. She's wearing her headphones so I can't hear anything but the tapping of the keys and the odd creak from her weight shifting in the chair.

In the darkness beyond my vision other feelings creep up and start to envelop me and I awaken startled. Deep inside, I know that something is not quite right and the cycle starts again, over and over. The only thing interrupting it is the presence of someone nearby, an unknown presence which is like a beacon of hope in the darkness of my psychosis. However, this circles around with the rest of it and there is nowhere in or out of my mind to hide.

I reach out to touch her, trying not to startle as I know she hasn't noticed that I'm awake again. She gets so absorbed by her gaming that I could jump up and down on the bed and it wouldn't even get her attention. I have to lean quite far as she's further away than it looked, or my arms are shorter than I'd thought. As I stretch out I lose my balance, toppling off the bed, my legs tangled in the duvet, which follows me. I tuck my head in to stop me headbutting anything in my way.

I start flailing my arms and legs, trying to untangle myself from this godforsaken duvet, but the cover is sticking to my feet and it's now wrapping around over my head. I'm feeling suffocated and trapped, and as though I'm still falling, flailing and my head is spinning with confusion. I'm breathing heavily from both the exertion of trying to get free and from the fear that is taking hold of me. What the fuck?

'Michelle!' I yell.

How could she not have seen me fall or heard the thud? Was there a thud?

'Michelle,' I shout again, but realise that the sound is echoing through my head and I can't hear it outside of myself.

Michelle must have noticed me as now she is in the duvet with me, laughing and pretending the duvet is her wings. I try to grab hold of her arm as she starts to fly upwards as I'm now careening at high speed in the opposite direction. I squeeze my eyes shut, bracing myself for impact. I gasp as my eyes spring open from the shock of the water hitting my face. We're back in the shower. I'm panting and wiping the water from my face. I can't breathe. The smell of coffee suddenly fills my nostrils. My eyes focus, and in the dim light, and I see that I'm on the floor in my living room, my blanket twisted round me. I guess I must have knocked my drink over in the commotion because the blanket and I are both soggy. I lay back on the carpet and allow the tears to fall once again.

'Oh my god, Michelle. I miss you so fucking much.'

My voice is raspy and the words voiced out loud cause me to turn on my side, pulling my legs up to cradle.

'I can't do this,' I say through my tears.

Flashbacks of the dream play in the darkness. I cry harder as I think of how close Michelle was in my dream.

'I can't do this anymore,' I repeat with vigour.

I feel the ever-present frustration, anger and upset overwhelm me. They are never too far away these days.

My phone bings and pulls me back to reality. I slowly ease myself up with the help of the edge of the sofa. The cup rolling off the blanket and onto the floor makes me jump far more than the noise warranted. The blanket drops to the floor and I step on it to get my phone that is wedged between the cushions on the sofa. I cringe as the dampness soaks into my sock. I plonk myself down and open my phone. I sigh. It's a work email. Great, is this what my life has become, so that I'm sitting here covered in coffee, puffy from crying and sleeping and out of breath from fighting with an imaginary duvet. Lord.

Having nothing better to do right now other than clear up the mess and myself, I turn on the lamp and open the email instead.

Carissima Hayley
I'm so sorry to hear from Debbie about your friend.
Please accept our heartfelt condolences.
We are here if you need anything.
Prenditi cura di te
Ci vediamo, Juliette & Lorenzo

I burst into tears and hug the phone to my chest. This is now pretty much my response to anything anytime I'm alone. Thankfully I'm able to hold this side off whilst in company - well, so far so good. I understand these reactions. Feelings, emotions, or whatever are normal responses to suddenly losing a loved one, but it doesn't help to know this. There is still a part of me that is scared that this is now my new 'normal'. That I'll be stuck in this depressive state forever. What if the shock has been too much? What if I can't... I start sobbing uncontrollably at the thought of this. I know this will have changed me somehow but how much? Like what, what if... what if... I try to calm my breathing and gradually my sobs turn to just crying.

My throat and eyes are so sore that it just makes me want to curl back up and sleep. Each time I sleep I have the most horrendous dreams. I'm exhausted, my whole body aches. My head is thudding. I need a drink, I need to eat, I need a bath or at least a wash and some clean clothes. I'm still dressed in my funeral attire. The smell of old coffee on me is making me feel sick. I have no inclination to move or do any of those things, even though I know I should. That word, 'should'. I should still have a best friend. I should have been able to hold on to her. I should have kept her safe. I shouldn't have to spend the rest of my life without her. We still had so many things to do together.

The aching in my heart is the worst of all. No amount of food, drink or sleep is going to get rid of that. Logically I know that people lose loved ones all the time and somehow manage to carry on with their lives in one way or another. But what if I'm not that strong? And how long does it take to 'heal'?

I like to have a routine, schedules and deadlines. I require a time scale. A date when I will start to feel better and be able to go an hour on my own without crying. I must look hideous. This is one of those times when Michelle would have helped me recover and given me loads of tips on how to soothe sore, puffy eyes and how to do my make-up afterwards to look 'normal'. Well, better than normal. Because Michelle suffered from bouts of depression as part of her struggle with mental health she had many coping mechanisms. When the darkness caught hold of her she was able to outwardly 'fix herself up', as she termed it, so that when she sat in front of her camera no one could tell that she was struggling. No one saw that at times it took hours for her to even get moving so she could plaster on her make-up ready and they didn't see that the smile shining out from the screen hadn't reached her eyes. Yet, it was doing these videos that kept her going, gave her purpose, a reason to physically and mentally move out from those dark times.

The tears started again. The memory of the sadness in those eyes was painful. All the hugs and wine and time together could do little to ease it. It was internal. It was a hidden demon inside her, ever present, ready to consume her on a whim. Sometimes it crept up on her and she'd know it was coming and be able to warn it off, other times it hit hard and fast, literally knocking the life out of her. It could at times take weeks for her to start to recover, for the angry outbursts and lethargy to subside. It was horrid for her but hard to watch too as there was nothing much I or anyone else could do other than stay and comfort her.

I miss every version of her that I knew and I wonder how it will feel to not have someone in my world who knows every side of me. My phone drops from my grip, snapping me out of my thoughts. I must move. I haul myself up, not an easy feat, I'm so stiff and achy. But I must. If not now, when? I slowly walk towards the bathroom to run a bath. I avoid looking at my reflection in the mirror as I pass it. I don't need to see how I look. The sound of the water filling the bath is deafening in the silence and I want to turn it off but I resist. Instead I go to find a clean towel. I wander back to the bathroom. I glance at the soggy blanket and cup still where they fell. I simply look away. I don't care.

I strip off and step into the bath, every movement taking effort. I sit, my legs hugged to me as I watch the water. I used to love baths. I loved watching the bubbles forming and foaming and gently popping. This has always soothed me. It's no longer soothing. I'm still not comfortable being in here. Because Michelle's wetroom was located above my bathroom, the one time I tried to relax in the bath since, I kept imagining her melting through the ceiling, crying out for help. I shake my head to remove the thought of that horrific vision. I dip in and out quickly. Just long enough for me to wash my hair and body. Once I'm out, my breathing calms. I wrap the towel around me and quickly escape this room. I dry myself and dress in the only comfy clean clothes to hand - an old pair of leggings and a t-shirt that I never normally wear. But I have let myself, the flat and everything else go.

Going to see Michelle in the Chapel of Rest, seeing her looking peaceful, rested, with make-up on again, helped. Her hair brushed beautifully and laid over her shoulders. Her arms crossed over the ends of it. Her Mum had chosen to have her wearing the funeral director's white satin gown. She looked like an angel in every way I'd ever imagined them to be. Yet, on my return home I'd spiralled further into the darkness in my mind.

I decide that now is the time to rip those musty sheets off and clear the bunches of tissues and piles of clothes that have taken over my space. I need comfort, I crave it. I pop my phone on the side and set one of Michelle's videos going. This way it feels as though she is there sitting on the edge of the bed directing my efforts as she'd done for so long. I wonder what will happen to her channel. Will they pull the videos down and close it? Will they keep it going? Can they? I spent the last few weeks watching her videos on loop. I find it reassuring and heart-breaking at the same time. Just hearing her voice and seeing her smile has kept her alive for me, held her place in the world.

We always laughed at how ironic it was that she inspired me to clean when she lived like a messy teenager. I smile at the memory as I release my hair from the damp towel, adding it to the washing pile on the floor. As I'm putting the new sheets on I'm mentally pushing against the overwhelming urge to just curl up in the bed as it is. Who cares if the sheets are fresh? 'You do,' says Michelle's voice. I appreciate the input as she knew that for me there is nothing more comforting than climbing into a freshly made bed. I may not have even bothered to shave my legs but I'm clean, and now my room is fresh and clear. I'm okay.

I leave Michelle's video chatting away as I go and put the washing in the kitchen and pop the bin bag next to the front door. I leave my hair damp and climb into my little slice of heaven. I take a deep breath. So many everyday phrases now conjure up very different images these days. I roll over and say goodnight to Michelle as I plug my phone in to charge. Her voice lulls me to sleep again.

I awaken to the sound of the dawn chorus and lay still for a moment, revelling in the comfort of my cocoon. For a moment all is well in the world. I'm well rested and clear headed. Then the wrecking ball swoops across and reminds me that actually, all is not well. I can no longer hear the birds singing, the darkness within me has returned. I need to get away from this train of thought before it consumes me completely and I don't leave my bed, again. It had taken me long enough to escape it before to go to the funeral.

I'm feeling stronger of mind today, as though moving is better. This is huge progress. Michelle would be proud. I turn and smile at her. Her videos are still playing on the tiny screen. I carry her with me as I go about my morning routine. It's time. Michelle wouldn't have wanted me to wallow like this. Well, for a moment perhaps, I jest with my inner dialogue, but this would have been the last thing she would have wanted. I consider my options.

Bob had said I could take as much time as I needed from work but I can't spend another day here in this space. I guess the fact that there seems to be something going on with Bob and Debbie means they'll be distracted. I'd forgotten about seeing them in the park. It'd be nice to see George. He's kept in touch with the odd daily message to check I'm okay. Obviously, I reassured him that I was. He'd offered to come to the funeral but I'd declined. Hopefully Lauren or Josh have a crazy weekend coming up they can tell us about. If not, I'm sure Kim's weekend will be destined to be full of family drama. She may even have Friday treats for us. These people are friends as much as colleagues and I need that right now.

It is helping to even be thinking about going in. I find myself on auto pilot, getting myself dressed and ready, and packing my bag before I can change my mind. Before I know it, I'm closing the main building door behind me. I take a deep breath, sling my messenger bag across my body and set off to work, sliding my sunglasses on. I breathe in the morning air. It feels good to be out of the house.

I lift my sunglasses up onto my head as I enter the bakery. The smell alone wraps me in a giant hug. I grab a couple of pastries from Pat's and a coffee from Gill's, they will help. This is the most normal thing I've done since my return from Italy. It feels better. I feel better. Just going through the motions seems to be helping. I approach the door to the office, waving to Bill. Then I pause, my hand poised ready to open the door. Something in me flips and pure dread courses through my veins. 'I can't do this.' The voice in my head is truly mine this time.

A lady barges into me with her buggy and it jolts me back to the here and now. The urge to confront her is strong, to ask her how she could be so thoughtless as to just hit someone and keep walking. Thankfully my rational mind takes over and I see she is just a fraught mother taking her children to school. I sigh. I can't face this. I'm not ready to be out in the world again. I'm too raw. I'll end up ripping someone's head off like I did to Joe. The anger is still bubbling inside me and my feet do the sensible thing and start to walk me back in the direction of home.

Once I'm round the corner I send a message to Bob to let him know I still won't be in today. As I place my phone back in my pocket I look at the path ahead of me. I move to the side so as not to get trampled again. I can't do it. I can't return home. I can't go into work. I just can't. The voice in my head asks, 'What can you do?' The lump in my throat returns and I wash it back down with another sip of my drink. 'I don't know,' I whisper back.

Chapter Twenty-Eight

My sudden movement from where I was leaning against the wall makes the couple passing me jump. I step to the curb and flag a taxi.

'Where to, love?'

'Richmond, King's Road, please.'

'No problem.'

He pushes his way back into the stream of traffic and I lay my head back against the headrest, my bag hugged to my chest, my cup still clutched in my hand. I close my eyes momentarily and allow the rhythm of the vehicle to soothe my anxiety. I can think of nothing that puts my mind at ease. I'm just relieved to not be where I was anymore. I feel as though I'm losing my mind. Perhaps I already have. Do crazy people know that they are crazy? Am I?

I hold my position but open my eyes beneath my sunglasses and just stare out of the window. The rain has started again, how fitting. Collars are being pulled up, umbrellas opened and the pace of the people has become more urgent as they try to escape the downpour. That is exactly how I feel, as though I'm trying to escape this downpour of emotions. Yet it seems to be following me like Winnie the Pooh and his fluffy cloud. I wish mine was just a cute fluffy cloud, but it's not. It's a storm cloud, ever present and threatening and when it unleashes its fury there is no dodging it.

In what seems like no time at all we are turning into the top of King's Road. It's been a while since I've been here but nothing seems to change much year on year. The church still looms on the corner and even the disused phone box, untouched for decades, still stands proud.

'Just here on the left, please.'

We pull up just a few houses along. I pay and slowly climb out.

'Thank you.'

The second I close the door he drives off. I stand on the path looking up at the cherry blossom tree as the rain waters it. I step to one side as a lady walks past.

'Good morning,' she chimes from under her clear waterproof headscarf.

I simply smile in response.

It's so quiet here in comparison to my road. Life is a bit slower in this district, and I guess all the school kids and workers are gone for the day. I hear the bus pass the top of the road and it breaks me from my thoughts. I walk a few strides, into the driveway and up the steps. I ring the bell. I love how it's still set to Big Ben tolling. I hear footsteps and automatically move back a tad. The locks and bolts are undone and the heavy Victorian door opens.

My Mum's hand twitches slightly and pats her perfectly coiffed silver hair. She glances down at her perfectly ironed tan trousers and smooths her ivory blouse. Once she's sure she's 'guest ready', she looks back at me and gestures for me to enter. My Mum is not good with surprises. She likes to have a plan, to have her week plotted out way in advance. It took me years to realise that I too have that trait. In fact, we share many characteristics, which I guess explains our sometimes strained relationship. We are possibly too similar.

She moves aside, opening the door further and guiding me through. I allow her to prize off my sopping wet cardigan. After closing the door she takes me and my wet cardigan through to the living room. She has a fire going and lays my cardigan over the airer next to it. I stand glued to the spot in the middle of the room. This house, like the road, never changes much. Perhaps the odd photographs were added but the old ones remain. I scan my eyes along the many frames on the dresser, the faces of generations staring back at me. I catch my reflection in the antique mirror behind them. I look pale, gaunt, tired, and even here in my childhood home I look lost.

I can hear my Mum popping the kettle on the stove and then she passes through the room and returns with a towel.

She automatically reaches up to start drying my hair. I just stay rigid and let her carry on. I slowly drop my messenger bag to the floor but hold on to the handle so as she makes her way around me she doesn't trip on it. Plus I'm not ready to let it go. Mum works around me, no questions, not even curious glances in my direction as she finishes towel drying my hair and then answers the call of the kettle whistling. It is not until she is re-entering the room with the two cups of tea, which she places on floral coasters on the side table where my Dad's empty ashtray still sits, that she speaks.

She offers that I sit and I find myself automatically sitting on the rug in front of the fire. The warmth and soft sound of the flames licking at the coals are familiar and welcomed. She crosses her ankles and I stare absently at her slipper clad feet until she passes me my tea. I take a sip and feel it travel down, warming me. She glances at the bottom of my jeans that, when I followed her gaze, seem to have soaked up a lot more rain than I realised had fallen whilst I'd stood outside. She doesn't comment though. I'm grateful. I carry on sipping my tea and stare into the fire. She does the same. It is not until I've nearly finished mine and relaxed slightly to lean my back against the chair behind me that she clears her throat.

'It's lovely of you to visit. It's lucky you caught me in. It's usually tapestry class this morning but our teacher's car broke down, so it was cancelled.'

'I'd forgotten that you went to that,' I say absently, still facing the fireplace.

'Yes, it's all coming along nicely. We're working on a piece for the Virginia Woolf exhibition. Did you know they are fundraising to put a bench on the terraces in memory of her?' She takes a sip of her tea. I merely nod and she carries on. 'I have no idea why. I read that she didn't much enjoy her time here in Richmond.'

'It's a great place to sit though.'

'It is,' she agrees, placing her cup down carefully on the coaster. 'I'm so very sorry about Michelle. Tragic.' She swallows hard. 'I'm sorry I wasn't able to make it to the funeral. The Peak District holiday was booked months ago.'

'It's okay, I'm...' I start to say but can't find the strength to say the words out loud.

I want to tell her everything, about how I've been feeling. She doesn't even know I found Michelle. Only that she'd died. I'd kept the details to a minimal. I hadn't wanted to upset her or for her to fuss over me. If I was honest with myself I'd say I probably could have used a bit of fussing. I didn't feel I could tell her about how I couldn't face reality or my dreams. How I felt I couldn't escape from my own thoughts. Yet I don't need to. My Mum knows me better than anyone else alive, now. She knows without me having to voice it. She understands grief and all that comes along with it. When my father died eight years ago I moved back home for a few weeks to be there for her. I think back to how she was then, comparing the memory to the image of her sat here. Everything about her is together, from her hair to her nails, to the space around her and her social calendar. It is hard to imagine she was any other way.

I remember it being a long and exhausting journey for us. I had to run her baths and cook her meals. What I could not do was wash and eat for her. She had to find the strength and inclination to do that for herself. Back then I was strong when helping her but shut myself away to grieve on my own. As I run through this in my mind, watching the flames dance amongst the coals, as they glow rhythmically, it occurs to me that it is exactly why I'm here now. Perhaps I should have come sooner. I know that just by being here today I have found hope that one day I will come out the other side of this. Just getting out of my flat was progress.

Mum makes us a fresh cup of tea each. She hands me mine and pops out of the room. I hear the familiar sounds of her climbing the stairs and fetching clean bedding from the airing cupboard in the hallway. Her footsteps fade as she walks towards the spare bedroom and onto the carpet. I sip my tea and wonder if I should go and help her, but I know she'll be humming away as she works, quite content to do this by herself for me. I finish my tea and place my empty cup on the hearth. I rest back again, bending my legs towards me and wrapping my arms around my knees. I rest my head forward onto them and relax further. There is something soothing about hearing the sounds of her moving around while I continue staring into the embers. My eyelids start to feel heavy and I allow myself to be soothed by the sounds and warmth.

What must have only been moments later I felt my Mum touch my shoulder as she tells me that my bed is made up if I'd prefer to sleep there. I'm not sure I want to move. It is the most relaxed I've felt since. Yet I follow her lead, putting most of my weight through the seat of the chair as she helps me up. I'm a bit more with it as we make our way up the stairs. I pop to the bathroom quickly and as I enter the room the bed looks so inviting. Mum has laid a set of my old joggers and a t-shirt on the bed with a pair of her fluffy socks.

'It's a good job I hadn't cleared these out and taken them to the charity shop,' she says.

I smile to acknowledge her words.

'I'll leave you to get settled.'

She backs out of the room and goes to close the door.

I spin round causing her to pause.

'Sorry, it's just... erm... can we leave it ajar?'

'Of course.'

I like the fact that she didn't question it. I don't want to have to explain that I'm scared to be alone. I'm worried I'll have more nightmares that I'll struggle to escape from. Somehow knowing that the door is open a tad and that if I need her she will come feels reassuring.

Having dry, clean clothes and fresh sheets feels better. Being here, in what was once my childhood home, feels odd yet comforting. Knowing my Mum is just down the hall reading her book or downstairs preparing dinner makes me feel safe. Being in bed at this time of the day would have felt strange not so long ago, decadent perhaps. However, my bed has become my safe haven. Well, when there aren't the vivid dreams. I hope that in being here they might ease off or stop altogether.

I know that the grief is within me and no matter where I physically am I can't outrun it, but if I'm at least here I can possibly cope better with it somehow. I'm not sure why I think that. As I drift off to sleep, the duvet wrapped around me and half over my head, I feel like a child again, cocooned in the safety of the bed. For the time being someone else is responsible for my welfare. It feels good. Reassuring. Safe.

Chapter Twenty-Nine

When I awaken from a deep, dreamless sleep, the room is dark. I'm disorientated for a moment until I reach for my phone and see that it is still Friday and 9.12pm. It dawns on me that it was the first time I hadn't had Michelle's videos playing in weeks. As I pull back the duvet to sit up, I switch on the globe lamp that is one of the few remaining items from my childhood still present in the room. I used to spend hours reading all the funny sounding names of countries as I'd spun it slowly, imagining what they all looked like. I wondered if other people around the world were doing the same from their far-off countries, imagining what a funny sounding place England was like. The world seemed so vast back then. Places like Fiji, Turkey, Iceland, Hungary, Greece, Timbuktu - I run my fingers over the globe as I find them again.

My eyes are drawn to the boot-shaped country that intrigued me the most as a child - Italy. It always seemed the most magical of places. It's amazing to think that all these years later it was still one of my favourite places in the world and just as magical in reality as I'd imagined. It seems like forever since our trip to Florence, George and I. In my mind our Italy trip has merged with the weirdness of the reality and dreams that are hard to differentiate from these days.

I think the naive part of me is still holding out hope that the last few weeks have been just a strange dream and that at any moment I might wake up in the safety of my flat and hear Michelle pottering about, trying to find a clean cup for her morning drink. That Mrs Temple is milling around making tea and toast for her breakfast, sitting with Tiddles by the window that looks out over her little garden space. That Joe is chatting to his kids on the phone as he checks the weather to know whether he needs to wear a coat to work. And I'd be hauling myself from my warm bed and replying to emails on my phone as I wait for the coffee maker to fill my cup.

I spin the globe as I sit here willing it to be just a dream, but in my gut I know that it is not. As a child I used to believe this globe was magical. If I squeezed my eyes closed and wished hard enough that I could transport myself to these countries, to anywhere. Perhaps, I consider, watching the world turn, my wishes did come true and my trips to Italy were in fact the wishes of my childhood coming true. Who's to say that wishes happen immediately? I like this idea. I close my eyes, my hand still walking the spinning planet and my cottage in Tuscany appears as though I've turned on a TV in my mind. It's nice to have this daydream back - it has been hard for me to access it as of late with how heavy my thoughts have been.

In my fantasy I hear the familiar sounds of nature, including the birds chirping away to each other. As the kettle boils on the stove in my rustic kitchen, I smell the richness of fresh coffee. The sun warms my back as I stand smiling at the contentment I feel in this space. A warm breeze drifts through from the open back door. I close my eyes as it washes over me and breathe deeply as it nourishes my soul. The sound of jolly banter between my friends in the garden drifts through to me.

'Hayley, are you awake?'

'Yea. You're okay to come in.'

Mum pokes her head round the door and smiles. I know that face. It is the one she uses when she is trying not to look concerned. It is an expression I've been using a lot lately.

'I made you a drink.'

'Thank you.'

'I'll let you sit up properly first.'

'There. Thank you.'

'I thought it best I let you sleep. I've saved you some dinner. Shall I fetch it for you?'

'I was about to say no, but...'

'Your belly is speaking for you,' she chuckles.

Moments later she is back with a tray, the smell of the pasta bake sets my belly into hyper excited mode and it gurgles away loudly. Mum places it on my duvet covered lap and I pop my mug on the coaster next to the globe. It smells divine. I pick at it, taking forkfuls carefully so as not to drop it and make a mess. I don't want to worry her by not eating much but I'm forcing down each mouthful. I've hardly eaten lately. I'm not sure why my grief has stopped me eating. In my limited experience it seems to be a common trait in grieving people. Well, it was for Mum.

She is perched on the end of the bed and is chatting away about the neighbour two doors down and the conflict with the neighbourhood committee over their trees. It is helping to have her there as it's stopping me thinking about eating. It was an old trick she used back when I was a teenager. She would chat away at the dinner table to distract me from the process, hoping I would at least eat something. I remember it annoying me at the time, her incessant chatter about nothing of interest to me. She'd ramble on about work colleagues, distant family members, the cat from number ten. It was years later that I realised it was a distraction technique and appreciated it. I don't manage to eat much of the pasta bake but it is sufficient to stop my belly rumbling and to gain a satisfied smile from Mum. She takes the tray away and pops back with a glass of water.

'I was watching a program the other day on all the benefits of staying hydrated.'

She stands over me to ensure I drink at least half the glass. It is all I can do to stop myself making a contented noise as I do. She walks round the bed and gets the other coaster from the bedside table and passes it to me. A silent gesture to ensure I don't break this rule of the house. I smile inwardly now, seeing myself as so similar to her. Poor Michelle was nagged to high heaven about coasters. I gulp as I think of these words. I hope she's enjoying heaven and I bet she even has white joggers, with 'Angel' written across the butt, to complete her heavenly ensemble. It is not until my Mum hands me a tissue from the pretty box on the dressing table that I realise I'm crying.

'It's only a coaster sweetheart, I wasn't nagging. It's just an irreplaceable piece of furniture, that's all.'

'It's not the coaster,' I chuckle. 'I'm just as obsessed with them. I just can't stop the thoughts of Michelle popping into my head.' I wipe my nose. 'Even if they're happy memories they still make me cry. More, in fact.'

'I know, honey.'

She leans over and tucks the duvet around my waist. It is her way of comforting me. This simple act of kindness makes me cry more. Honestly the water must have rehydrated me enough that I could once again produce tears. I wonder if there will be a time when the tears stop, when the memories no longer blindside me and knock me off balance. I want to ask all these questions yet I know that there is no set timeline for grief. Like with so many things, everyone's experience is different.

*

The next few days are pretty much spent in bed, drifting in and out of dreamless sleep, with Mum bringing me food and drinks. On the third day she runs me a big bubbly bath.

'It will make you feel better to have a lovely soak. I've lit candles and popped my Enya CD on so it's like a spa.'

There is no point in me trying to say no. Mum has this way of making it sound so super exciting and yet I know it is a direct order. I know that I must smell pretty rank and probably look even worse than I smell. She pulls back the duvet as she chats about the fact that she bought the candles at this lovely little shop off the high street that her friend's daughter recently opened. She is telling the story to me as she helps me up. Before I can even register, I know this stranger's life story, full CV and the name of her three children and I'm standing in the warm bathroom staring at the bubbles as they sway slightly from being disturbed by Mum's temperature test. I thought for a second she was going to dip her elbow in as she had when I was young. Thankfully her nurturing did not go as far as this and a simple dip of her manicured hand concluded that it was the perfect temperature.

She leaves the room and without me having to voice it, leaves the door pulled to rather than closed. I strip down, my body breaking out in goose pimples even though the room is being well heated from the towel rail. I hadn't realised how much weight I had lost until I'm now seeing myself fully naked. Under any other circumstances I would be celebrating this loss but now even I'm a tad concerned. I look gaunt, not healthy. I look away, distracting my thoughts. I see Mum has placed two big, fluffy mint green towels on the heated rail for me. As I glance around the space I see that she has gone into overdrive to create this spa for me. I carefully step into the bath. My muscles feel weak from lack of use and even as I lower myself down my arms twinge.

The makeshift spa is wonderful. The water is warming my aching muscles, the music is relaxing, and the candles are creating a lovely ambience. Yet even with the bubbles hiding my body beneath them, I feel vulnerable. I feel exposed emotionally - as though this setting is trying to draw out of me all that I'm trying to keep buried inside. I know, logically, that it needs to come out. I know that the idea of this is to allow it to release but I can feel myself clinging to it as I lay in the bath, my knees up and my arms crossed over my chest. As the bubbles dissipate I pull another clump to cover myself. I'm not ready. I can't do this. I can't let go yet.

I fear that if I let go one of two things might happen. One, I can never switch off those emotions and I'll go crazy, like forever. Two, that by releasing these emotions I will be dishonouring Michelle somehow. The image of her strutting around in her white tracksuit across the cloud floor of heaven pops into my mind again. I imagine her chatting with the other angels, laughing and smiling. I see her literally glowing with contentment. Then she turns and just stares back at me as the observer of her other worldly existence. I snap out of my thoughts and sit up sharply, sloshing the water over the back of the bath.

I stay still, breathing heavily from the bizarreness of having the vision of Michelle and I seeing each other. What the hell was that about? I may not have been having my bad dreams being at Mum's, but this was disconcerting. I quickly wash my hair, leaning back to rinse it off, keeping my eyes wide open. As soon as I've given my body a scrub with the sponge I haul myself up and pull out the plug. A mixture of the exertion of the bath and the vision makes me feel exhausted again. I just want to be back in bed. I wrap my body in the bath sheet and my hair in the smaller towel. No matter how big, fluffy and warm these towels are it is still not creating the desired effect of cocooning that a duvet creates.

I look around for something to mop up the floor and decide that just using my t-shirt will do the job for now. It needs washing anyway. I blow out the candles, switch off Enya and rinse the bath with the shower hose. As I cross the hall with the yearning to crawl back into the bed I'm instantly deflated. Mum has stripped the sheets and all that remains is the pile of coverless pillows and duvet. If I was back home I know I would have just crawled into it as it was but my Mum would not approve of such laziness, no matter how deep into the grieving process I am.

On the dressing table stool are the clothes I arrived in, laundered and neatly folded. I sigh. Hint taken. I finish drying my body and slip into my clothes. They feel uncomfortable. Jeans after wearing joggers for days feel horribly restrictive even though they are looser than usual from the weight loss. I keep the towel on my hair as I wander off to find Mum so I can borrow her hairdryer. I found her in the kitchen. The kettle is on the stove and she is making sandwiches as the washing machine is swirling away under the worktop. She smiles as I enter.

'Feeling better?'

'Much - thank you,' I lie.

'Enya works every time.'

'Absolutely.'

'I'm nipping up to the shops after lunch and thought you might like to join me.'

I glance out of the window, it's still daylight. I look at the clock above the dresser. It's only just gone one. I've lost track of time and days since I've been here. I've kept my phone charged but also on silent most of the time. I'm trying to recuperate and part of that process is to wean myself off watching back-to-back episodes of Michelle. It's been challenging, and I have to admit to a couple of times where I broke my promise to myself. Yet, as the bad dreams have lessened since I've been here, I can only assume that it has played a part in it.

Stepping out into the street once we've had lunch, I put on my sunglasses and take a deep breath. I'm grateful for the push from my Mum to get out of that bed, that headspace. Mum links arms with me and we stroll up the road, cross over and aim towards the shops. Mum greets everyone we pass with a cheerful hello. I start off simply smiling in acknowledgement but soon find myself saying hello too. Having that human interaction, as small a gesture as it is, lifts my spirits.

Mum, as always, bumps into someone she knows and stops to chat while I fuss over their dog. He's a lovely old thing, soft black coat and shiny eyes. I'm not sure who enjoyed the fussing most, me or him. I can see how therapy dogs are so helpful in people's recovery, there is something about it. There's no judgement, no objective, just being together and enjoying the moment. I find myself smiling and softly praising him on what a good boy he is. I nuzzle closer and the lady pauses her chat with my Mum to comment on how he's never this friendly to people he doesn't know. I smile up at her and tell her how lovely he is. She thanks me and they carry on their conversation. I literally feel as though I could just drop my bag here and sit on the floor and wile away the hours cuddled up with this dog. I tear myself away as my Mum and the lady part ways.

The dog and I take a glance back at each other after saying our goodbyes. I thank him in my mind.

The bell rings above the door as we enter the newsagents. Much has changed with the decor and layout but the bell is the same as it's always been. I'm grateful for the familiarity. This is why I had such a strong urge to come home for a bit. I needed reminding that many things change - people and things come and go from our lives, yet some things remain the same, such as my globe lamp and this bell. While Mum goes to pick up her paper and a sneaky Kit-Kat, I aim for the penny sweets. It appears that penny sweets are no longer just a penny, just like a 99 ice cream is no longer just 99p. I dig the scoop in, fill my little candy bag and take it to the counter. Mum moves aside from where she has paid and is chatting to the lady about today's headline. I pay for my sweets and then I tune into their conversation as I glance at the front page of the paper.

'Shit!'

'Hayley,' Mum reprimands me.

I hold out my hand after tucking my sweets into my bag. I stare at the headline and the photo accompanying it. I move aside as another customer joins us. I hadn't considered that this would hit the media. I suppose as much as I knew Michelle was awesome I forgot that she was a celebrity in her own right. They have found an awful photo. It's a close-up of her in a club looking rough, her face clammy and her pupils severely dilated. The headline reads 'YouTuber dies under the influence'. I scan the article. I read that one of her 'friends' has given the story of their drugged up partying with her and told them how she was found in the shower by a neighbour. I'm furious and crushed for her family and real fans. There's no mention of how she'd put all this behind her until that fateful night or how many young lives she'd positively changed through her gaming channel and scholarship program. Classic case of people cashing in on someone who is not here to defend herself. Plus, how dare it say that they were a friend and refer to me as just a neighbour! I slam the paper onto the counter.

'I have to go.'

'Hayley?' she says, concerned. 'Honey, calm down.'

Even the lady behind the counter looks worried. I kiss Mum hastily on the cheek, give her a quick hug and run for the door. I closely avoid colliding with the gentleman coming the other way. Once outside, I race down the street, yanking my phone from my bag.

Chapter Thirty

The grass is muddy from yesterday's rainfall so I tread carefully to avoid slipping. I arrive at the graveside. The footprints from her funeral gatherers are still visible. I crouch down and move some flowers to one side so I can read the little sign displaying Michelle's dates of birth and death. I sigh as I read it. Such a short life, yet she lived it to the full. I wonder, not for the first time, if people only live for as long as they are needed on this planet. Perhaps once they have achieved what they were sent here to do they are off, to dance in the clouds until the next time their soul is needed back here on earth. I like this idea. It feels less harsh, less final and as though my best friend is still alive - just not in the physical form in which I knew her.

'So you're causing quite a stir out there in cyberspace,' I say to the pile of dirt in front of me. 'Apparently your videos are getting loads of views and everyone is sending condolences. You know, we could have just faked your death to get you this kind of coverage.' I go to chuckle but no sound comes out.

I stand silently for a moment, looking at all the bunches of flowers and wreaths that are scattered across the mound of dirt. In some places they are three or four deep. I guess more people than they thought have found out where this is and have added to the ones left on the day of her funeral by the friends and family. Michelle's Mum had put an announcement out to ask people to respect their privacy during this time and Michelle's agent had authorised a GoFundMe and a condolences page so people could pay their respects virtually.

'The story of the old days and how you partied that night is out. I don't know how to fix that, but I'm gonna try.'

A soft breeze blows across and I close my eyes for a moment as it brushes past me. I hug my arms around me and take some deep breaths. I can't hold the crying back any longer. The loss is hitting me again and at such a deeper level. This time I'm allowing it to filter through. Crying is pretty much mandatory in a cemetery. Yet this is a different kind of crying. It truly feels like a proper release.

'I miss you so much. I wish you hadn't rushed off so fast. I can't believe we didn't get to say goodbye. I'm sorry that I wasn't there to celebrate and I'm even more sorry that I wasn't there to stop you being a div. I can't believe you'd allow such a stupid thing to take you away from me. How many times did I warn you? How fun was it really in the end? I'm so angry at you for being so thoughtless. I'm angry at myself for leaving you alone and not being there at the point you needed me most. I'm so annoyed at myself for not getting to you sooner. Perhaps if I hadn't stopped to clean up. I'm pissed off that I didn't ever let you get me that tattoo. I miss you every second of every day. Just so you know, you haunt my dreams, like for real. Please stop that it freaks me out! I know you'd find it funny. It really isn't though. I can't function without you. I'm such a mess. A big crying, blotchy mess. Although, I've lost weight I guess that's one positive. I've been staying at Mum's for this weekend as I couldn't face being in the flat anymore. Without you there it's eerie and quiet. The coffee doesn't even taste the same and there's no wine. I don't know how to sort it out, to get my head straight, to start functioning again. Seriously, you are the person I would have asked but you're not here anymore. If ever I needed you most, it's now but it's because you're not here that I need you. Does that make sense? I'm just so lost. I'm full of regrets and you know I don't do regrets. I regret not telling you how incredible you were or how much I love you. Like, proper love you. I don't think I ever loved anyone as deeply as you and I don't think I ever will. No one will ever know me as you do. Fuck. Move over honey, I'm coming in.'

I could literally lay down on the bed of flowers and stay here with her. I wonder how long it would take someone to find me here if I did. I take another couple of deep breaths and reach into my bag for a tissue. As I'm blowing my nose and wiping my face with the back of my hand I hear Michelle's voice in my head.

'Now who's being the div? Sort it out babe.'

I laugh at the bluntness that I loved about her. She's right though. She always was. It's time to sort it out. To pull myself back together. No one else can do it for me, it's up to me. I stand taller and take a deep breath.

'Right!' I say decisively. 'If you stop haunting me, I'll stop being such a sap. Deal? See you later. I love you.'

I take one last look back and smile through my tears as I lower my sunglasses back down. This moment, just me and Michelle, getting to say goodbye. This was exactly what I needed. I follow the mud path back to the main road. Just as I'm scrolling through the Uber app on my phone it starts to ring. Juliette's name flashes up. I clear my throat and answer.

'Juliette. Hi.'

'Hayley, it's so good to hear your voice,' she sounds flustered, most unlike her. 'I'm sorry to call. I know you are away from work at the moment but I...'

'That's okay. Is something wrong?' I prompt.

'Well, I hate to speak badly of people. I know Lauren is doing her best but it's - it's not you. You see my vision. She just keeps pushing the idea of chocolate fountains. You know how I feel about chocolate fountains.'

I hold in my chuckle. She's not trying to be funny.

'How can I help?'

And just like that my mojo rears its head. I'm a solver and she obviously has a problem.

'Oh, thank you. It's hard to explain. I just need your help to get things back on track with the Ball. She wants *glitter balls*, Hayley!'

'Don't worry. I'll find out what they've organised and get back to you. We can sort it. We've still got time.'

I literally hear her breathe a sigh of relief and her smile return.

'You really are a lifesaver.'

Unfortunately I am not, but I forgive her the choice of words and turn my mind back to sorting out their Ball. 'Nicely done' I say to Michelle in my head. She has sent me exactly what I needed - a purpose. Sitting in the Uber looking out the window I fetch my penny sweets from my bag. I savour the nostalgic taste as I'm filled with a renewed sense of faith.

Chapter Thirty-One

Making my way into work Tuesday morning, I'm thankful that my bag seems to behave when there is no one around to show off in front of. George, it seems, is its number one target. As I walk through the office door, Debbie unexpectedly steps round her desk to hug me. George comes over to welcome me back, just patting my arm and giving me a gentle smile. As soon as his arm reaches me the bag swings for him. He has honed the skill of avoiding it now. His quick dodge makes me chuckle.

It's a bit disconcerting that Josh and Lauren also crowd round as though I've been away for years instead of weeks. I very much appreciate it, along with the distraction of the bag misbehaving as it stopped them going into the classic 'I'm sorry for your loss'. I know that they are. I know they'll have been worried about me the same as I would have them. It's surprisingly nice to be back, even though my plan of slipping in unnoticed didn't quite work. As I'm settling in at my desk Lauren places a coffee and a plate of biscuits next to me.

Before I can start questioning her about the project, she cuts to the chase.

'Have you got time to have a quick chat about the Hotel al Cioccolato Ball?' she asks.

'Yes, of course.'

'Cool, thank you. Is now a good time?'

I nod and she grabs her notepad and pen.

'Ready when you are,' I say, as she pulls her chair over.

'Well, I've set up a Pinterest board so that Juliette and Lorenzo could see what I had in mind. Unfortunately they didn't seem too clear on what look I was trying to achieve. When I asked them what they thought they just said they didn't like it,' she says, looking apologetic. 'I have tried to find out which bits they didn't like or what they would prefer but it's been... tricky.'

'No problem. If you can get me what you have so far, I'll give them a call. See if we can clear this up. We still have time.'

Lauren stands up, thanking me. Her and her chair were back at the desk before I even took a sip of my drink. That was an unexpected turn of events. I'm pleased she broached the subject first. She doesn't need to know that Juliette rang me. I'm happy to pick it up from here. I know from experience that it is not easy to manage someone else's account, especially if it is part way through a project.

I scan through the emails she's zipped across. Straight away I can also see that she is not in line with Juliette's style. I pull up my original files on it and compile a quick email to Juliette reassuring her that everything is in hand. I look at my calendar - we still have about three weeks. Not long but we will manage it. As I'm only just back, the others are still covering my other accounts, so I can pile all my time and attention into this. It's going to need it.

It takes me a couple of cups of coffee and a good playlist to get going, but once I'm searching for the right look I'm straight back in the swing of things. It's not until George gently places his hand on my arm that I realise just how deep in the flow I was. I remove my headphones and look up and smile. It takes a few seconds for my eyes to readjust after staring at the screens for so long.

'Hi. I just wondered if you fancy some lunch?'

'Sure. What time is it?'

'Just gone two.'

'Wow, I hadn't even thought about food.'

'How's it going?' he asks as we make our way to Pat's.

'Good. It's nice to be back, to be honest.'

'It's nice to have you back. Lauren was saying that Juliette was being, how did she put it... tricky.'

'I don't think they gelled too well. I'm surprised as both of them are such lovely people. I thought they'd hit it off.'

'Agreed. It's a shame they don't seem to be on the same page.'

'True,' I say as I place my order and George asks for the same.

As we leave, George turns to me.

'Sorry it all got a bit messed up.'

'Not to worry. Lauren just got the 'look' wrong, having met Juliette and having seen the place you understand that she is very specific in her taste and how she likes it done. It was just bad timing to have to step away from it.' I take a deep breath, as we make our way outside. 'But I'm back now.'

'Good,' he says and bumps me with his hip.

I laugh as I try to rebalance myself on the curb. Luckily I left my bag back at the office or else it would have got retaliation for sure. It's nice to be feeling more human again. Mostly it's nice to be laughing. I appreciate the fact that I have people around me who are still reminding me to do things like eat. It's strange how the basic things drop off your radar at times like this. Yet between a few days at my Mum's and being back in the office I can feel myself chipping away at that cocoon I was hiding in.

I've arranged a Zoom meeting with Juliette and Lorenzo for 3pm so I'm back and re-energised ready. I nip to the toilet and touch up my make-up. As I look at my reflection I see that the circles under my eyes have started to be more visible again. I know I've been rubbing my face a lot today while I was deep in concentration. I could do with a Michelle makeover about now. I smile a watery smile at my reflection as I pop a bit of lippy on and return to the office. I take my laptop into our Zoom phone box.

'Buon pomeriggio, Juliette, Lorenzo.'

'Oh, Hayley. Saluti mio caro amico.'

'It's so lovely to see you both. How are you?'

'Very well. Thank you so much for taking the time.'

'It's fine. Honestly, it's been good for me to come back. I'm especially excited to get back to helping you with the Ball.'

Juliette claps her hands together excitedly and they are both smiling as wide as I am. I go through the ideas I have and they seem to go down well.

'They are wonderful. We're so worried. The Ball is very soon and there is so much to do. Are you sure you can change the things already booked and get them in time?'

'I'll try my best.'

'I know you will but...' Lorenzo says and looks at Juliette.

I've worked with them for a while now and I've not seen either of them look this concerned before. Although, I guess we haven't changed the entire plan at the last minute before. I decide to switch the subject.

'How are the building works coming along?'

Lorenzo pulls a face and Juliette rolls her eyes.

'Not so well?'

'It's all a disaster, Hayley. The builders say it's too hot to work and the process is slow when they are.'

'I'm sorry to hear that.'

I'm thinking on my feet now.

'Well, I know I can't do much to cool the weather or to get your builders to work but I can make sure your Ball is the best event ever,' I declare in the most upbeat tone I can muster.

I was hoping for a cheer or a round of applause but instead they both give forced but grateful smiles. We all bid each other goodbye. I sit for a moment once the call ended to consider how best to tackle this. They really were quite deflated. It's a lot of pressure at these times and I'm usually so good with reassuring clients. This time, however, I dropped the ball, literally. Having a good reason is no excuse in my book. I can't let them down. I sit and stare at the ceiling.

As I'm making my way home a couple of hours later, after a pitstop for coffee from Gill's, my mind is busy mulling over how best to execute these plans for the Ball. Headway has already been made in the sense that Juliette and Lorenzo are happier with the visuals I showed them. All I need to do now is source and book these things. We are going to be cutting it very fine. The distance between us is also a bit tricky.

At least with events nearer I can zip across and arrange things in person if need be. In fact, I'm a bit old school I guess in the fact that I prefer to be there on site as much as possible in the few days running up to it. This way I have found it takes the pressure of the clients as they can see you there and it all coming together. It also means I can run to grab last minute bits that might have been overlooked or not arrived on time. I want it to be as perfect as I expect it to be, or better.

I'm halfway home as I pass the interior shop which sells fabulous items that are mainly upcycled and one-offs. Each time I pass it, it reminds me of Juliette's place. Of each of the rooms kitted out in their own unique way. As I'm standing staring in the window, I see myself looking back from one of the gilded mirrors. That's when it hits me. I know what I need to do. I smile and wink at my reflection.

'Hi Bob,' I greet him as he answers his phone. 'I'm going to head to Hotel al Cioccolato to get this Ball sorted. I think it's the only way we're going to get it ready in time.'

'Sounds good to me. Whatever you need to do. When would you like to go?'

'Sooner the better.'

'Tomorrow too soon?'

'Nope, that's perfect.'

'Excellent. I'll get Debbie to sort the tickets for you. Will you be staying at the Hotel?'

'That's my hope. I'll give them a ring now to check they've got space.'

'Well safe travels and keep in touch. Anything we can do to speed things up, let me know.'

'Thanks.'

'Oh, and Hayley?' He pauses. 'It's good to have you back.'

I smile broadly and hotfoot it the rest of the way home, excited to get going with my plan.

Michelle's Mum meets me on the stairs as I arrive home.

'I'm glad I bumped into you,' I say. She raises a curious eyebrow. 'I guess you've seen the papers or online or whatever. Well, I was thinking we need to do something to turn this around. Show people who Michelle really was.'

'Agreed. What's your thinking?'

'I'm not sure just yet. Perhaps some kind of event?'

'That would be great, but I wouldn't even know where to start.'

'I'm sure we can come up with something spectacular,' I say, smiling to reassure her that she is very much a part of this.

'That would be amazing,' she leans in and hugs me hard.

As we part ways, she turns back.

'Oh, I meant to ask. Would you be free this week to go over a couple of things?'

'I'm so sorry. I'm literally heading back to Italy tomorrow.'

'No problem. Message me when you get back. I'll get them to hold off.'

'It's okay. Don't hold things up just because of me.'

'Out of my hands,' she says, shrugging. 'Michelle insisted in her paperwork that you be there.'

'Well, I can't argue with that.'

Chapter Thirty-Two

I arrive back in my apartment, dump my bag and sip the coffee that I lazily bought from Gill's on the way home. I'm curious as to what it is that Paula needs my help with. I head to my bedroom and open my case out on the end of the bed. I take a deep breath and try to push the thoughts of Michelle from my mind. I don't remember the last time I packed without her help. It seems silly but I guess it is these little things that are going to cause me to stumble as I navigate my life without her. I'm not sure how long I'm going to be away this time, but I'm sure Juliette won't mind me using their washing machine or I can nip and buy anything I forget. I stand cradling my coffee as I stare at the empty suitcase.

'Right. Come on. You can do this.'

I place my coffee on the coaster on the bedside table and haul the pile of folded washing from the chair onto the bed. As I'm scrolling my phone for music to get me moving it starts to ring. Andy's picture flashes up. I'm stumped for a moment but decide I may as well answer it. I've been meaning to contact her.

'Hello,' I say, trying to sound more upbeat than I feel.

'Hi.' Even down the phone her smile sounds false. 'How are you?'

'Good thanks. You?'

'Yea, also good.' She takes a breath. I wait. 'I wondered if you were free to catch up?'

'Erm, I'm afraid not. I'm literally heading off to Italy in the morning. I'm needed at Hotel al Cioccolato.'

'Not to be pushy but are you free now?'

I look at the array of things on the bed and decide that actually, yes, I could do with not doing this right now, no matter how much I know I need to.

'Sure. Where do you want to meet?'

'I'm just round the corner. To be honest I saw you walk out of Gill's.'

'Oh, okay.' I'm not quite sure what to say. All I know is that it is nice to hear from her. 'Right, I'll be down in a minute. We can go for a walk - this place is a state.'

I grab my coffee, jacket and bag. She is waiting at the bottom of the steps as I close the front door. We smile at each other in greeting. As I reach her she pulls me into a hug. I allow it.

'You've lost so much weight. How are you doing?'

'I'm getting there. It's been a difficult road,' I answer honestly. 'Sorry I didn't call when I got back as we'd planned.'

'No, please don't apologise. You had other things to think about. I can't even imagine what you've been through.' She takes a breath. 'I'm sorry I haven't been round. I didn't know if I'd be welcome.'

'I'm not sure I was very welcoming of anyone to be honest.' I swallow the lump rising in my throat. 'I headed to my mum's for a bit.'

I point up the road with my cup as a suggested route to walk.

'How was that?' She knows the situation with my mum.

'It was surprisingly nice actually. It turns out it was exactly what I needed. I was finding it impossible to be here.'

'I wish you'd called. I could have... bought your shopping or something.'

'I know you would have but you know me and asking for help.'

'I do,' she says, a kind smile on her lips.

'Thank you for the flowers by the way.'

'You're welcome. It was the least I could do.'

A moment's silence hangs between us as we both dig for conversation.

'So are you back at work?' she asks.

'I am. Today was my first day.'

'And you're flying out again already?'

'There are a few issues with the upcoming Ball that I figured would be best sorted out in person. Plus it gives me a good excuse to get away for a bit.'

'You can't always run from your problems, Hayley,' she says. I look at her and see it was not meant with malice.

'I know. I never was any good at running,' I jest.

We walk a few more paces, the silence companionable this time.

'It's good to see you by the way,' I say. 'I'm glad you called.'

'How could I not after I saw you?' she smiles. 'I didn't want to freak you out by running up the road after you.'

'You'd have caught me. Like we just said, I'm not very good at running.'

We chuckle and I open the gate to the park for her. I aim us in the opposite direction of the bench I had sat on the other week. I throw my empty coffee cup in the bin. We settle on a picnic bench near the now closed ice cream van. Sitting opposite each other invites us to get to the crux of things.

'I'm truly sorry that I scared you off by proposing.'

'It wasn't the proposing so much as the fact that we seemed to both be coming from completely different viewpoints.' I take a deep breath so as I work out how best to explain. 'There were just so many things that were causing a strain on our relationship and, as you know, public signs of affection was one of them.' She nods, listening. 'So when you produced a ring box in the middle of a crowded restaurant I was flummoxed. Plus we hadn't caught up in ages before that and, in all honesty, I thought it was phasing out.'

'I thought if we committed it would bring us closer.'

Tears are welling up in her eyes and I look away to gather myself.

'I know, and it was a good idea in theory. But with me wanting to travel more and you not wanting to, it was starting to make things harder.'

'I wish I'd have joined you in Florence now.'

'Honestly, I'm not sure at that point it would have made much difference. We had drifted too far apart already.'

'I guess the fact we are both overcommitted to our jobs really doesn't help.'

'I think you're right. I must say, and this is not to hurt you, but I realised that I didn't even contact you to tell you about Michelle. I'd have hoped that with something that drastic that any hostility between us would not have mattered. That I'd have wanted you there with me.'

'But you didn't,' she says, her voice a whisper.

I shake my head and the tears start to escape.

'I'm sorry,' I say.

'Don't be.' She reaches for my hand. I look into her tearful eyes. 'At least we know now,' she adds.

I nod.

'Just know that if ever you do need me, for anything, I'm still here for you.'

'And me for you,' I say as I squeeze her hand.

'Would you like my help to pack?'

'Thank you for the offer, but I couldn't subject you to the state my flat is in right now.'

'Understood. Well, safe travels, Hayley.'

We step away from the picnic bench and give each other a hug.

'Thank you. Take care.'

We part ways and I turn to watch her leave, her hair lit up by the fading sun through the trees.

As I walk back in the direction of home I smile at the thought of Andy. She genuinely looked content, relaxed. It was good to see her. We had definitely done the right thing in calling things off and I'm glad we had a chance to talk things out. It had left a bitter taste to have ended it the way it had. I feel at peace with things now and we may or may not catch up again, who knows. All I know is that it's great to know that I don't have to hide if I see her. I like that.

Chapter Thirty-Three

As I plug in my seatbelt and look out of the plane window, I confirm to myself that this is the right move for me right now. I give a half smile to the lady next to me as we collect our things together and prepare to disembark. It feels better to just be going somewhere else. I'm fully aware that this is a form of escapism for me, my way of finding a place to hide from the pain and the heartache. Well, at least take it somewhere different. It has been all consuming in my real world.

At points I truly feared that I would not bounce back from this at all. I knew if I didn't take hold of it and put it in its place, it would keep hold of me and keep me in a very dark mindset. Juliette will never know just how much her cry for help has been the life raft I needed. Having my mind distracted with work and knowing that I'm needed has thankfully broken me out of my fog.

Mrs Temple was out when I was heading off this morning so I slipped a note under her door. I believe that she'll think this is a good idea. I dropped my Mum a selfie from the airport of me holding up my coffee. She sent back well wishes. I think she'll be relieved. I could tell that she was more worried about me than she let on while I was there for those few days.

Lorenzo and Juliette have kindly come to pick me up from the Florence train station. It's quite a way for them to come, but they insisted. As with most people who live outside of the capitals, they've mentioned that they try to avoid it if they can. However, I think me coming to stay has sent Juliette into natural mothering mode. They hug me tight as I walk off the platform and through the gates. I don't hold back the emotional relief at seeing them, and hug them just as tightly. Juliette thrusts a takeaway coffee into my hand along with a paper bag containing a sandwich and fruit. It was homemade, and as I opened the bag it smelled delicious. I'm grateful and hug her again. This was exactly what I needed. Not just the refreshments but their presence.

We are making our way out of the city, Lorenzo zipping through the traffic at any opportunity but more carefully than I imagine he would usually. Thankfully they came in the Range Rover so it was a comfortable ride. It's strange, I think as we slip on to the faster roads, that I had the yearning to be here rather than at home at a time like this. I would have thought that I'd prefer to be in familiar surroundings - in the office or talking about Michelle over tea with Mrs Temple. Yet neither of those two things seemed to fit. Also Michelle's untimely death had proved just how short life could be and I'm done with playing it safe all the time. Living life as I think others expect me too. I feel the need to break the cycle and this is my first step. To trust my instincts and follow my heart.

I have a bubble of excitement in my belly as we get closer to the hotel. I'm excited to get to work on the preparations.

'After our chat yesterday,' I say to them from the back of the car. 'I booked in and ordered as much as I could online. So far it's looking as though most of it should arrive in time.'

'Hayley, that's wonderful. I'm excited for it to all start arriving. Will we be able to return anything that is no longer needed?'

'Absolutely. I'll do that as soon as I can. I've also dropped emails to the band and catering company to let them know of the changes.'

'Hayley, you really are a blessing.'

'You said you were struggling with the chalets?'

'Oh, we really are. We are so behind. Between the lazy builders and the Hotel being fully booked, it's been mayhem.'

'Well, you have an extra pair of hands now I'm here.'

I see her shoulders lower as I remove some of the weight she's been carrying on them.

'You may wish you hadn't offered,' chuckles Lorenzo as he casually swerves in front of a truck to get to the lane he needs.

We arrive at the Hotel and Juliette opens my door and Lorenzo gets my small suitcase from the boot.

'I've popped you into one of the attic rooms - the one you really liked when you came,' Juliette says as we make our way towards the entrance.

'Oh wow, thank you.'

The room looks even more beautiful than I remember. It literally feels as though it hugs you in welcome. I sit on the edge of the bed. I kick off my shoes and lay on my side, pulling the soft blanket over me and sink into the pillows. The window is ajar and the warm breeze is comforting. Closing my eyes, I let the gentle sounds from the house and the builders outside wash over me. From this position I can see just the tips of the trees, the blue sky. I lay for a while, staring at the clouds as they lazily pass by.

I must have fallen asleep as I'm awoken by a soft knocking on the door. It takes me a second to comprehend what the sound is and another to work out where I am. After having had so many weird dreams lately, everything seems to take an extra moment to register. I call to say they can enter. Juliette appears with a cup of coffee in hand.

'Grazie.'

'I'm pleased you slept. You must be hungry, yes?'

I'm about to say I'm okay but, as it had at Mum's, my stomach answers with a ferocious rumble.

'I take that as yes,' she laughs.

She places the hot drink on the side table as I sit up.

'I slept so deeply,' I laugh.

'Grief can do that.' The seriousness in her tone takes me aback slightly, but she follows it with one of her winning smiles. 'You'll be okay. The air here is healing, it will help mend your broken heart.'

I follow her back downstairs, my cup in hand. I hold the banister as we make our way down the two flights of stairs. My legs are still stiff from the journey. I follow Juliette out to the veranda where there is a lovely spread of breads, cheeses, olives, tomatoes and salad. I feel healthier just looking at it. This, right here, us sat out here overlooking the Tuscan countryside, with the soft breeze, great company and yummy food was what my mind had conjured up is exactly what I needed. To have purpose but also, as Juliette rightly said, to start mending my broken heart.

'Thank you so much for letting me come and stay.'

'It no matter. It's always lovely to see you,' Juliette says.

'We should thank you for coming to help us at such short notice,' Lorenzo confirms.

'I think we all needed each other,' I say softly.

Chapter Thirty-Four

Over the next couple of days we mission on, executing our plans. Juliette and I are in full swing. We work well together, making phone calls at an impressive rate of knots. We made the trip to Florence several times to give ourselves a bit of a break. All in the name of work, of course, since each time we ran a necessary errand. The added bonus was the restaurants she took me to for lunch. I'd have never discovered them if it wasn't for her local knowledge. Being busy is helping. It is not to say that the thoughts of Michelle or the weird dreams have completely evaporated, as if by magic. It's more that they have moved to the background of my mind. At times they catch me off guard, but I feel I'm coping better.

In the privacy of my room at night I watch Michelle's videos. I'm sticking to my personally assigned limit of just one video as I settle down each night. This way I feel her presence, as though she is walking alongside me on this journey. She'd have loved this. I talk to her at times, chatting away like we always did. I find these things help a lot. I guess that's the thing - there's no way to circumvent the grieving process. All you can do is find the way that works best for you and allows you to still function. At this point I believe I have found a good balance. It is also helping that Juliette and Lorenzo are big believers in a strong nightcap, so I go to bed nicely relaxed and wake up refreshed to the Tuscan sunshine.

This is the most hands on that I've been with an event and I'm loving it. I feel fully invested. Now we have everything for the Ball organised it is time to turn our attention to the chalets and preparing them for guests. Lorenzo has been busy managing the builders, basically keeping them going with delicious refreshments and overviewing their every move. He is friendly but firm with such things, especially as the deadline is fast approaching.

'Today we can finally get into the chalets to start deciding how to decorate and furnish them,' Juliette says excitedly. 'This is my favourite part.'

'Fabulous. I'm looking forward to helping you. I loved decorating my flat when I first moved in. I feel like I'm on one of those makeover programs.'

We both giggle as we make our way over to the row of chalets. Juliette has the clipboard and measuring tape. We are greeted by Lorenzo who is handing out breakfast pastries to the workmen. They are then helping themselves to the coffee at the end of the makeshift buffet table. He offers us both a pastry and Juliette brushes the gesture away.

'Oh, my love, you need your energy.'

'I also need to fit into my dress,' she retorts with a wink.

It is at this moment that I realise that in the midst of everything I haven't got a dress for the Ball. In fact, I don't even have a smart enough outfit with me to get away with. I won't bother Juliette with this yet. She has enough to worry about. Instead, I set a reminder on my phone to order one online later. That would be a classic moment of me helping organise everything else except myself. I turn my attention back to the job in hand, pouring us a coffee. We carry our cups with us as we enter the first chalet.

'They are all laid out the same but I think we'd best measure them. Old buildings are never straightforward.'

'Do you have furniture ready for them?'

'Yes, we have another old barn full of all sorts. I'm hoping we have the right things. If not, we might have to go shopping again.'

'What a shame,' I giggle.

The chalet is adorable. As we walked through the door we entered the living space. It's all open plan with a breakfast bar to the far left, indicating where the kitchen area starts. The kitchen corner is tastefully done in whitewashed wood. Lorenzo was telling me that the carpenter used old pallets to build these. I love how they use what they have and add in the new only when necessary. The new granite effect worktops and a butler sink look great. The mix of new and old works well. To the far right are a set of French doors that look out across the fields and have a patio for sitting out on.

We make our way upstairs. The oak balustrades, Juliette tells me, were made from old dividers that used to be in the stables. They look fantastic, especially with the exposed beams in the vaulted ceiling. There is a bathroom to the left with an impressive roll-top bath and shower over. Juliette tells me that they were found in barn sales over the years and held on to ready for this moment. The toilet and sink are also reclaimed. I voice how impressed I am by the whole thing as I walk across to the far wall and look out the window.

The all too familiar calm washes over me as I stand here for a second sipping my drink. My mind conjures up my imaginary cottage and I smile, knowing that I'm closer than ever to realising this dream. I can literally feel how it will be once I find my Tuscan home.

'That view never gets old,' Juliette says from beside me.

I hadn't even heard her walk over to me.

'I can't imagine it does.' I break myself away. 'So, tell me your plans.'

'This is going to have a big double bed, a day bed and sofa bed. That way it's good for families or just couples. And downstairs we need a sofa and some chairs, bar stools and patio furniture.'

'Awesome, and is it going to be the same in all of them?'

'Yes. Oh and we might see if we can find a couple of new travel cots, just in case. At the moment we only have one between all the rooms. Thinking about it, we may as well get a couple more highchairs while we're at it.'

'There's so much more to consider than I would have thought.'

'You're right. We've learned many lessons along the way, including the extra things that people might ask for. That's why we have put USB ports in the chalets too and have a collection of charging cables. You wouldn't believe how many people forget those when they travel.'

'I bet. It's the first thing I pack now, along with my power bank.'

'That's because you are so organised.'

'I certainly try.'

Actually it's because I'm still trying to work through the guilt about Michelle not being able to contact me because my phone had died. I don't say the words out loud. I'm learning to let these thoughts wash over me, rather than sticking. I'm finding this really interesting, learning about how they set up these holiday cottages. I can't wait to get into the barn and delve into the treasure that they have in there.

'Would you like me to take some photos?'

'Good idea. Then we can do before and after photos for the website - people love that.'

I take a few photos of the rooms and the view from the bedroom window. I then nip outside to take a photo of the front. I go back in and we set about measuring the spaces we need to fill. We do the same with the other chalets and then head towards the barn.

'Wow!'

'Wow indeed,' Juliette says beaming. 'We've been collecting these things for years and if we change anything in the the hotel it comes back in here. Over there are vases, clocks, pictures, those kinds of things. Here are the furniture bits. This wardrobe, drawer and double bed will go together. I think we'll paint it a nice pastel pink. Aha, I have three bar stools and two matching chairs. They'll need reupholstering but that's easily done.'

'I love your enthusiasm.'

'I'm not gonna lie, it took me a few years before I found this exciting rather than overwhelming. The new mattresses are stored over there.' She points. They arrived last week. I just hope I ordered the right sizes. Just like the rooms, old furniture can measure a lot differently to how you hoped.'

'You don't seem worried about that.'

She places a hand on my arm.

'There is little that worries me these days. There is little we haven't overcome before.'

There is something in those words that resonates with me right now. Once I've overcome this obstacle in my life maybe I'll be able to handle other things with greater ease. In comparison to losing my best friend, my hope is that little else will shake me in the same way.

'I've stuck orange sticky notes on the bits for the first chalet. Now the others.'

After an hour or so we have found most of the things we need and go and ask a couple of the waiters who have come on shift to help us move them to their respective new homes. While they are doing that, following Juliette's colour coordinated sticker guide, we go to the other side to find the accessories. This is even more fun. It is like rooting through a hidden attic. We do the same again, choosing pieces for each chalet one at a time and putting the stickers on. This time we pop the smaller pieces into boxes ready to carry across.

By the looks of things we will be spending the next two weeks cleaning these, painting the furniture and reupholstering. I find a pair of brass candlesticks with cherubs climbing the stems and put them in the box. I feel as though a piece of me will live within these chalets. When people admire them I'll have brought them a brief moment of joy.

I consider what Lorenzo and Juliette do not too dissimilar to my job. I bring a few hours of joy with an event and, like Cinderella, the spell is broken and it all returns to normal, but leaves memories that will last a lifetime. I guess one big difference is that people can return to Hotel al Cioccolato. I like the idea of that. Of something that has a more longevity.

I'm thoroughly enjoying myself. Juliette seems to know most of what is here, whereas for me it's all new. I'm digging through each section with an excitement I've not felt in many years. We chat away and I keep calling out to her to show her my finds. With each thing I hold up she tells me about it. Where she found it, how much she paid and, with some pieces, where it was previously located in the hotel. I'm flicking through a pile of pictures that are leaning up against the barn wall when I discover a painting that I remember from my grandparents' home. It's a print of the Monet painting with the lady and girl walking through the poppy fields. I used to stare at it for hours when I was a kid. It just seemed such a perfect moment captured. As I got older I used to wonder what they were talking about as they walked or if they were just happy in companionable silence.

I add it to the pile of decorative items for chalets. I feel that with this hanging on one of the walls that a piece of me will always be here.

Chapter Thirty-Five

Juliette and I are sitting in the final chalet's garden, testing out the patio furniture whilst enjoying coffee delivered by Lorenzo. We have worked relentlessly over the past two weeks. Painting anything that stood still, hanging pictures, revamping the furniture and missioning through hours of upholstering. Even I have become a dab hand with the staple gun. We are feeling achieved.

Somehow, as ever things do, everything has come together just in the nick of time. The deliveries have arrived for the Ball. The chalets are at the final stage. Everyone is feeling exhausted yet confident that the Ball will be a huge success.

'I'm not gonna lie, I don't want to go home. I've had the most fun ever here with you guys. I guess it's what you'd call a working holiday. But I suppose it has to end sometime. Back to reality and all that.'

A lump forms in my throat as the thought of my empty flat pops into my mind. The feeling momentarily overwhelms me and I wonder if I'll ever be able to feel settled back in my old life. Yet I know I have to go home, back to my job and... well, I guess at this point, that's it really. I shake off the feeling. It'll be alright, I'll adapt. I look to Juliette, seeking her wisdom, hoping that she'll say something that will comfort me. However, Juliette looks as though she's going to say something but instead makes a sound to indicate she understands and simply sips her drink.

'Well, shall we get this finished?' she says after a few moments.

'Absolutely. Then I'll nip round and take photos. I can't wait to see them next to the before pictures. Do you have ones from before the builders started?'

'We do. Lorenzo took lots,' she chuckles.

'The guests will be blown away when they arrive. You really do have a talent - now that the chalets are finished, they look so inviting.'

'Thank you. We are lucky you were here to help. We might not have finished in time.'

'I'm pleased to be a part of it all, honoured in fact. It's inspired me to want to try some of these things when I get back home. There's a lovely shop near my flat that sells this kind of stuff.'

Just saying this makes me feel less apprehensive about going home. Perhaps a revamp of my flat is exactly what I need right now to busy myself. We haul ourselves up with the help of the sturdy arms of the wrought iron chairs. Both of us are aching from all the exertion of our work but it's a good feeling, one of achievement. We place our empty cups on the mosaic tabletop and make our way back inside.

It's not until I'm in the shower later that day that I suddenly remember that I still haven't got my outfit sorted for the Ball. I'd stupidly kept snoozing my reminder until it was bugging me so much that I turned it off, and thus forgot. I quickly finish washing the day's sweat and grime from me and get dressed. I tie my hair into a messy bun as I really don't have time to waste on drying it right now. I find Juliette in reception chatting to the young lady behind the desk. They both look over and smile as I approach them.

'Juliette. I'm so sorry to interrupt, but I have a small problem.'

'Oh?' She says something in Italian to the receptionist and turns back to me. 'Problem?'

I nod and explain my predicament.

'That is a problem,' she says, considering it for a moment.

Suddenly she lets out an 'Aha!', causing both me and the receptionist to jump as the sound reverberates around the expansive reception area.

'What's your thinking?'

'This is Sophia,' she says, gesturing to the young receptionist. 'I believe she will be able to help us with this.'

Juliette and Sophia then carry out a quick conversation in fast Italian that I have no hope of following. There are a lot of arm gestures, many of them aimed in my direction, and lots of nodding. I take this as a good sign.

'Your problem is solved. Go get ready,' Juliette instructs. 'We are going out.'

I'm back downstairs within ten minutes and find Juliette there ready with her handbag and light shawl. She always looks so classy. I have literally dried my hair and thrown my jeans, baggy hoodie and Converse on. I wish I'd taken a moment longer to prepare, but I'm here now so it'll have to do.

'Let's go.'

Outside we aim for their new little Fiat 500. It's the modern version that they have treated themselves to after seeing us in the classic one. I smile each time I see it, it is just a happy car. I'm pleased we are going in this. We bop along the winding roads towards the village. Juliette hasn't said where we are going and I haven't asked, but she is giving off excited vibes. I'm just enjoying being out and about.

We park up outside a row of cottages. A lady appears from a side gate to the end cottage and smiles and waves. We exit the car and Juliette makes her way towards her, gesturing for me to follow. She hugs the similarly aged lady and greets her in Italian. This I understand. She then introduces her to me as Anna, Sophia's mother. I go to shake her hand but she pulls me into a welcoming hug too. I laugh. This friendliness is one of the many things I love about Italy. As we follow her through the gate, a cat runs out, obviously not happy to have people invading their space. Instead of entering the cottage we make our way down a thin path to the end of the garden towards a rustic stone outhouse.

As Anna opens the old wooden door a lovely scent of sage and rosemary wafts out. I'm curious now. Whose shed smells that good? Perhaps she's the florist - that would make sense. We've probably come to pick up some of the flowers for the Ball. Although if my memory serves me right they are being delivered the morning of the Ball to ensure they are the freshest possible. They would wilt in the heat if they arrived too soon.

We duck our heads to avoid the low doorframe. As Juliette and Anna move further inside I see a row of beautiful dresses in every colour and fabric imaginable. It appears that we have entered some kind of Tardis as the space inside is much bigger than expected. There is a mannequin modelling a dress that is inside out and looks to be in the process of alteration. The space with a sewing machine to the right looks well utilised with a cutting table and scraps on the floor where they've missed the bin. There are a couple elegant chairs, not dissimilar to the ones we have upholstered. It all looks and smells divine. This is magical, to have this in your back garden.

'Ecco qui,' Anna says with a proud smile.

'Here you go. Have a look. See what you like,' Juliette says as she takes a seat.

Anna gets us all a glass of water from the jug on the side. I wander along the row, running my hand along the fabrics and separating the hangers so I can see the dresses' styles.

I'm not sure what I'm looking for exactly. I have an array of dresses for these occasions back home but these dresses are far more elegant than those. I consider what I need as I work my way along. It needs to be practical in the sense that if I'm needed to quickly run and sort something, I can. I have climbed ladders to fix fairy lights that have come away and carried in cases of wine from the boot of the car that had to race out to get more. Basically, I'm on hand to step in wherever needed. As organised as you think you are, there are always little bits that catch you out on the night. Hence why Bob knew that me being a solver meant this is the perfect profession for me.

'That one,' Juliette calls.

I hadn't even realised they were watching me. They had been catching up, chatting away animatedly.

'This one?'

I pull out a hanger. It's quite weighty and I lift it higher to free it from its space. I hold it up in front of me. It is not at all what I would have chosen. I'm not sure I've ever worn a dress in this shade of jade green.

'Try it on,' Anna says in her thick accent.

She comes over, takes the dress from me, scooping the bottom of it up as she does. She directs me to another doorway that has a curtain to pull across it. She follows me into the little dressing room. It has full length mirrors around it so you can see yourself from every angle. There is a chair and a side table with a simple glass bottle with dried wildflowers in it. Even this space is tastefully decorated. This lady really does know her stuff. After hanging the dress on a hook between two of the mirrors she leaves, pulling the curtain across as she asks my shoe size.

I slip out of my clothes and unzip the dress while it's on the hanger. I step into it, ensuring that I'm not standing on the hem of it as I poke my arms through and slide it up over my shoulders. I zip it up as far as I can at the back and smooth down the front as I look in the mirror. I look so much healthier than when I arrived. Being out in the summer sun has given me a healthy glow. I've filled out again too, lost the gauntness. Juliette has seen to that, keeping me well fed. Yet, more noticeable to me now is my eyes. They have life in them again. The dark shadows are fading.

'Wow,' I whisper.

I feel like I'm in my Cinderella moment for sure. Just hours ago I was up to my armpits in chalet decorating and now here I stand in the most beautiful of dresses. I release my hair from the bun I had returned it to after I quickly blow dried it. Where it was still damp when I put it up, it has curled slightly. As it falls down over my shoulders, it suits the look perfectly. I hear Michelle's voice in my head, 'you scrub up well, girl'. I smile as I know she'd approve of this dress.

'Come show us,' Juliette calls through.

I step out and both ladies smile wide in admiration. Juliette comes over and starts fussing over me like a mother hen, nipping it in at the sides and going round the back to finish zipping me up.

'You look exquisite,' says Juliette.

Anna has placed a tiara on my head. She gestures for me to sit down while she helps me put on some beautiful silver sequined shoes. I am expecting my glass carriage will be arriving at any minute to whisk me off to find my royal soulmate.

Chapter Thirty-Six

Two days later it is all systems go. The Hotel and grounds are a hive of activity. We all worked late into the night and so are grateful to the flow of caffeinated drinks throughout the day to keep us all moving. The flowers have arrived, the decorations are hanging, with everything arranged according to my plans. The extra tables and chairs are being set up both inside and outside. Going along behind them are our team of waiters, who are laying tablecloths and setting the tables with all the necessary things. This is my favourite bit. Where I get to see all my carefully laid plans executed. Standing here on the terrace between the dining room and the ballroom, it literally looks like a dance is taking place. Everyone doing their part to bring the whole show together. I smile, content in the knowledge that it will all come together perfectly.

I continue on, following the people laying the tables and placing the flower arrangements and salvaged mix match of candle sticks centrally on the tables. Guests who are booked to stay over are starting to arrive and Juliette is busy greeting them. She already looks every part a calm, put together owner of a successful hotel and chocolate factory. She's wearing a gorgeous purple kaftan, but I know that her outfit for tonight is even more flamboyant and glamorous.

Lorenzo comes through from the kitchen looking like he's on a mission. He's talking away loudly on his phone and does not seem best pleased if his tone is anything to go by. He still takes a second to pat me on the arm and tell me how wonderful everything is looking before he carries on out the front door. I'm assuming it's a catering issue of some sort. The caterers have been here for hours now and the place is filled with the aroma of delicious food. There is a band coming and I'm looking forward to a good dance later.

'Hayley, I think we are as ready as we can be. It's half four now. Would you like to go and get yourself ready?' Juliette asks.

'Yes. I don't think there is any more I can do at this stage. So it all starts at seven! Make sure to give me a shout if anything comes up.'

Juliette smiles widely.

'Exactly. Meet back here at six thirty?'

'Perfect. I'll see you soon.'

I aim towards the stairs, excited to get ready for tonight. I love my dress so much. Anna worked through the night to alter it to fit me perfectly and Sophia delivered it to me when she arrived for work this morning.

Two hours later I nervously put the last touches of make-up on. My hands are shaky so I'm having to be extra careful at this point with my mascara. I stand back from the full-length mirror in my room once I've slipped my dress on. Even I'm impressed with how I look. A chill runs through me as I imagine Michelle's face if she could see me now. I take a selfie in the mirror which I send to my Mum.

My descent of the stairs is far from dramatic as there is no one to see me. However, I walk tall and am enjoying watching the beautiful green fabric swoosh with each step. I kept my silver shoes off until I was down. The last thing I needed was to trip up now, literally or figuratively. I reached the bottom, aiming towards the sofa to sit and put them on, when I heard a familiar voice call my name. I looked up and there was George.

'Wow. You look amazing! You are the Belle of the Ball,' he says as he leans in to hug me and kiss me on the cheek.

I feel myself blush as I thank him. From over his shoulder I see the team in all their fancy attire. Lauren runs over and hugs me whilst exclaiming over how I look. Josh saunters over and is already looking past me as he says hello to see where the bar is. Lastly, Bob appears in a smart suit and new colour coordinated Converse. On his arm is Debbie in a pink meringue dress that any ugly sister would approve of.

'You don't seem to be surprised,' whispers Bob as he hugs me.

'By what?' I play dumb and try not to smirk.

'By me and Debbie?'

'Oh? Are you two together?' I do hand gestures to add to our whispered conversation's meaning.

'Erm, yes…' he says, blushing from ear to ear.

'Bob.' I elbow him playfully. 'You old dog, you.'

He chuckles loudly, breaking any attempt to have a private conversation. I can't help but laugh along.

'Well, you both look very happy.'

'Aw, thanks. I am. We are.'

I'm genuinely happy for them. I wonder what will happen to Debbie's cats since Bob is allergic. I giggle as I think how Josh would twist this question. It is so good to see the whole gang together.

'Where's Kim?' I ask Lauren.

'The kids got ill so she sent her apologies.'

'Truth be known, she was pissed not to be able to come. She was proper looking forward to it,' Josh says.

We are all chatting away animatedly when I realise someone else has joined our little group. George follows my gaze and turns back as though to say something when the lady stops by him and comfortably puts her arm around his waist. His arm lifts to accommodate her slim figure.

'Hayley, this is Camila. George's partner,' Bob says.

'Lovely to finally meet you.' She smiles. Her perfect teeth are dazzling.

I find my voice and respond. 'Nice to meet you too. Right, you guys come on through. I have to go do a thing for...'

I have no idea what I might be needed for so just allow my voice to trail off and leave them all to it. I head off in the opposite direction towards the kitchen but pause just round the corner out of sight. My breathing is laboured and I lean my back against the wall hoping that this might help even it out. Bollocks. What the hell? I thought I was well past this business trip crush. Apparently, I am not. I'm feeling foolish.

I wish I'd paid more attention to who was coming. Although, I don't remember hearing anything about the team's partners being invited. This is a work trip after all. Lauren and Josh don't seem to have brought anyone. Perhaps Camila took Kim's place at the last minute. I think I'm feeling more upset because when he stood there complimenting me there was an obvious look of admiration in his eyes and a playful smile on his lips. Plus my body reacted to him as it had done before when we were here together. I was just crushed because... well, none of it matters now. He is here with his partner and I'm not about to be 'that' person. Lorenzo exiting the kitchen doors makes me jump. He pauses as he sees me standing there.

'Oh Hayley, you look wonderful,' he says, smiling until he sees the look on my face. 'Is something wrong? Were you looking for me?'

'Thank you. No, everything is fine. I was just taking a minute before all the guests arrived.'

'I always get a bit nervous too. Come, let's get a drink.'

He links arms with me and leads me to the trays of bubbling champagne flutes.

'To Hotel al Cioccolato.'

'To Hotel al Cioccolato.'

We raise and clink our glasses together. The bubbles tickle my tongue and I smile.

'Thank you so much for coming and helping. It truly would not have been so wonderful without you here.'

'Thank you. I was grateful for the distraction,' I smile.

'But of course.' He smiles back kindly. 'You have been good for this place. You helped bring it to life for this evening. Look at this,' he gestures to the room.

'That's kind of you to say. But you two did that. I just sprinkled glitter.'

We clink glasses again and smile broadly.

'Now, please excuse me. I must go find my wife.'

As Lorenzo disappears out onto the terrace. I turn to look around at the beautiful dining room. The decorations, fairy lights and candles make the space look so magical. I could not be more pleased with how it has all turned out. Guests are arriving and I see Lorenzo and Juliette going towards the main entrance to greet them. The waiters have fetched the trays of drinks and followed them. It's showtime!

I find a space over by the doors to the ballroom. These will be opened once everyone has arrived. It looks incredible in there, breathtakingly regal. I'm excited to see the reactions of the guests. The photos of tonight will be a wonderful way to capture the beginning of a new era for Hotel al Cioccolato.

I glance over at the team who are deep in conversation and pointing things out to each other. Bob and Debbie seem genuinely happy together. I'm pleased to see them both having fun. Her whole demeanour seems to have changed. She looks younger and less tense. I wonder if she had feelings for Bob all along and perhaps him for her? Maybe that's why she was always a bit grumpy?

Now that I've had a moment to process it I'm not as bothered as I thought I'd be that George has a partner. I was surprised, of course, and a bit gutted, but I think perhaps mostly because this was the first I'd heard of her. But I'm glad he's not alone in the world. He's a super nice guy.

The band is playing soft Jazz as people are filtering through and filling the space. There's much laughter and buoyancy. I'm in awe of the glamorous outfits and pleased to see them looking impressed with the Hotel's decor. The waiting staff are bringing through the trays and dishes in preparation of the guests being seated.

I've thoroughly enjoyed the last few weeks here. Being part of this process, of the chalets as well as this Ball. It has been inspiring and soul renewing. It has given me time to grieve, in a gentler way, which I think was what I needed. Michelle was such an integral part of my life. Yet being here has made me see that life still has so much more to offer me. The pain of losing her will always be there, I guess. I just hope that it lessens over time and I can instead focus on all the good times we had. I also hope that I can forgive myself for not being able to save her. Perhaps it was not my job to. Maybe it was just her time.

The guests are being directed to their tables and seeing them admiring the table settings and smelling the flowers is gratifying. I watch as a gentleman picks out one of the stems and passes it to his partner, leaning in to give her a gentle peck on the cheek. This warms my heart. The whole occasion. I'm beyond proud of Juliette and Lorenzo and all they have achieved to get to this moment. I'm honoured to have played a part in their journey.

While everyone is busy having their food, I step out of the open doors onto the terrace. I stand by the railings looking out across into the distance. There are strings of lights leading out towards the chalets and chocolate factory for later when darkness falls. I swear I can smell the faint aroma of chocolate on the breeze. The sound of conversation and laughter drifts out to where I'm standing with my back to the hotel. This is the quietest I've known it out here in a while. The builders have stopped work for a few days.

'Don't be a div. This is your Cinderella moment. Get back in there and enjoy it.'

I turn sharply but there is just an empty terrace. I turn back slowly and wrap my arms across my chest.

'But my prince is taken and even the ugly sister has a date,' I whisper.

'Have I taught you nothing?'

I don't reply.

'You make your own dreams come true.'

'That's a Facebook quote.'

'Perhaps.'

Michelle's laughter drifts off. I wipe a tear from my cheek, push my shoulders back and turn on my sparkly high heel, my dress swishing. I head back in to join the team, pulling Lauren up out of her seat.

'Come on,' I encourage her, 'I think I need to dance.'

Chapter Thirty-Seven

The team and I travelled back together. I thoroughly enjoyed the company. I met them in the nearest town where they'd stayed in a lovely Airbnb. Lorenzo and Juliette had dropped me off and we had an emotional goodbye, thanking each other profusely. It had been such a fantastic few weeks that I think if I'd had to travel home alone it would have felt like a harsh come-down. Instead, we made our way from Italy in a flurry of conversation. It was as though we kept the party going.

Arriving home was not quite as cheery. The apartment was cold from being empty for so long. With the thick walls and curtains closed, warmth from the sun had done little to reach the inside. Surprising really as it was turning out to be a hot beginning to the summer for us in London. I popped a cardigan on and lit the fire while I waited for the coffee maker to finish. I'd asked the friendly Uber driver to nip me past a shop so I had basic provisions this time.

For the good it has done me to be away, I can't shake the initial feeling of dread I felt at what I might find upon my return. I wonder if this feeling will ever pass. Taking some deep breaths and fetching my coffee, I sit in the armchair near the fireplace. The warmth and crackle of the wood soothes my worried mind, 'All is well' I keep repeating in my mind. It was a new mantra I had learned from an Instagram reel recently. So far it really has been working. The dark thoughts are clearing faster these days and this mantra gives them that extra shove.

Images from the Ball dance through my mind and I smile. All really was well. Or it was at least, it feels like it's getting there. I curl my feet up under me and pull the blanket over me from the sofa. Looking around my flat, I'm glad I went on a cleaning spree before I left. I still needed to catch up on the washing but hey, the rest of the place looks a thousand times better. I like coming home to a clean house, especially when I've been away for so long.

Pulling my phone from my pocket I drop Michelle's Mum a message as promised. I definitely felt better equipped to be able to help her now. As much as I feel bad for not helping more up until this point, I know that she understands. Plus I believe I'd have been of little use. I could barely function myself. Now I'm feeling so much stronger in myself, I'm ready. Juliette was right. The air in Tuscany was healing. Paula replies straight away with a 'welcome home' and to ask if I am free the day after tomorrow. I run through my calendar on my phone. Tuesday looks pretty clear. Bob had suggested I take a couple of days to recuperate so that works perfectly. He was so chuffed by how the Ball had gone and how much work I'd put in that he would have agreed to anything. I missed my chance there - I could have gotten a big pay rise. I confirm with her and she sends me details of the place and time. Right, I think, I have a day to chill out and clear this laundry and I'll be ready.

Chapter Thirty-Eight

I walk up the steps and greet Michelle's Mum with a hug. She's looking much better lately, wearing her make-up and a smile again. There is still a shadow in her eyes, but it's less pronounced. We're both dressed in trousers and shirts, yet this time we've both chosen something more colourful. More suited to the situation and weather - and probably our emotional state.

'Here we are. What do you think?' I ask her as I open the double doors and switch on the lights.

'It's fabulous!' she says, her hand flying to her chest.

'Isn't it magical? Bob called in a favour from the owner when I told him what we were planning.'

'He did good.'

'He always does,' I chuckle.

The space we have secured for a fundraiser in honour of Michelle is an old theatre from the 1930's. It still has the stage and huge chandeliers. The ground floor chairs had been removed many decades ago. It has lived many lives, one of which was as a dance school. I can see how it would have been inspiring for the young dancers. The thick, dark red velvet curtains are still ready to be pulled back to reveal the stage in all its glory. From the first moment I saw this place I knew it was the perfect venue. In my mind I saw the tables all laid out, theatrical lighting and space for a dancefloor. The projector will show a montage of Michelle's clips throughout the evening and we'll have a podium on the stage for speeches to be made.

After Paula and I had met with the solicitor and Michelle's agent, Grant, we had relocated to the nearest pub garden and spent the next few hours merrily drinking cocktails as the evening drew in. Michelle's solicitor had stipulated that we were to work out what was going to happen to the scholarship program and social media channels. At this point, however, we were more interested in arranging the charity event. I'd had a pad of paper, making notes as we bounced ideas about. Michelle's Mum had found a local charity who supported young individuals struggling with addiction so they had the opportunity to turn their lives around.

'It offers them counselling and a support group to tap into. If it's needed, they even try to find housing and work for them,' Paula explained.

'That's wonderful. Exactly the kind of thing I had in mind.'

'Well, that's their aim but the lovely lady I spoke to, Marianne, said that they struggle to keep funding which means that sometimes people drop off their radar because they can't offer the next step.'

'Well, I think between the GoFundMe and the auctions on the night we can definitely top up their pot of money. Plus it should bring more awareness to their charity, which will hopefully lead to more long term support.'

'That would be fantastic,' Paula said, and I could hear the emotion in her voice.

'And the investors on the night can choose to either invest in the charity or the scholarship fund, is that right?' asked Grant.

'Yes. Or both,' I said with a grin. 'The people Bob has invited are not just well-off, they are ridiculously wealthy. Our hope is to be able to support both the charity and the scholarship.'

'And the revenue from her channel will funnel back into the scholarship too,' Grant said.

'Exactly. Her long term plan was to have it franchised across the world to help as many young people as possible to start and run their own channels in the best way to give them a long term career like she had.'

We took a moment at that point to sip our drinks in silence, the thought of Michelle's career being cut short hanging over our small group.

*

Seeing the For Sale sign being erected as the Uber dropped me home made my heart sink. Mrs Temple met me in the hallway as I entered.

'Hayley, you look very smart.'

'Thank you. Paula and I have just been to look at the venue for the charity event.'

'How wonderful. I have my dancing shoes dusted off ready,' she chuckles.

'I'm so pleased you'll be able to make it.'

'Only just. I fly out a couple of days later.'

'It's come round fast. When you first mentioned staying with your sister in Australia, October seemed so far off.'

'I know and yet here we are saying next month!'

'It's nice to have such exciting things to look forward to.'

'Very much so. Joe was saying he has found an apartment nearer to his children too.'

'That's good.'

'Now, obviously I'm not pushing, but the estate agent thinks this place will sell fast. Any luck with your search?'

'Not yet but I'm working on it,' I say.

I've actually not had much of a chance to look, but it's on the list. This has reminded me of the urgency of the matter. Between arranging the charity event and helping Paula to clear the apartment I have been really busy. Michelle's belongings have now been cleared. There are a few items that Paula thought would be great to auction off. Her gold play button is going to be in pride of place in

Paula's home, and rightly so. Joe handily had a cousin who ran a removals company so when the time came to clear the place they respectfully helped, understanding the tentativeness of the job in hand. They stepped out of the room at points when Paula needed a moment or when we were just sitting on the floor crying tears of laughter going through some of her things. Mrs Temple had scooped them off and distracted them with tea. It had been a team effort and executed with respect for Michelle and her belongings.

'You should keep these,' Paula had voiced as we were going through Michelle's wardrobe.

'No, I couldn't.'

'Why not?'

'It doesn't feel right.'

'Come on. They're yours now.'

I hugged the tracksuits to me, the words 'Juicy' and 'Angel' staring back at me. I smiled as the tears started to fall. It had been days of tears, laughter and exhaustion but somehow going through the process between us ladies and with Joe's help, we had made it through. It felt liberating somehow. As though we were setting her soul free. Once we had finished we ordered in wine and Chinese and sat in the space till late into the evening, regaling stories of her as we had that first visit. By the time we left, it felt right to close the door and hand my key over to Mrs Temple. The cleaners were due first thing in the morning. Our job here was done.

*

Back in the office it is a hive of activity. At the mention of the charity event everyone had stepped up to offer their skills. Bob had made this our top priority event. He had sourced the venue, compiled the guest list of influential wealthy investors. I stand with my clipboard in hand and check in with everyone.

'Josh, how're you getting on?'

'All good, I've booked a couple of bands. One to do classical music for during the meal and a swing jazz one for the dancing later. They also put me in touch with a dance troupe who can show people how to do the moves. I thought that would be fun.'

'I love that idea. Well done. Kim?'

'I'm obviously making most of the desserts myself.' She grins and winks at me. 'But we have caterers booked to provide the rest. The servers are booked too and will all be dressed in black and white to match the movie star theme.'

'Nice. Debbie, are we close to pinning down those RSVPs?'

'Absolutely. I've been on the phone chasing them up today and we only have two of the twelve tables left to fill. That takes us up to full capacity.'

'And you've kept a table for Michelle's family and one for us?'

'Of course. We have 120 guests and then a table for Michelle's family and our table, making 140 in total,' she confirms. A flicker of the Debbie we know and love shows through the glossy demeanour that has been present since her and Bob announced they were officially dating.

'Excellent,' I say as I turn to Lauren.

'The tech team we called in have checked the venue and can set it up so that we have the projection screen set up with the movie clips I'm compiling and live stream. It's looking great, even though I do say so myself.'

'Honestly, it amazes me how you do that. You're an absolute whizz. Bob, anything you think we might have missed?'

'Not by the sounds of it. Debbie, are you still happy to play auctioneer?'

'I certainly am,' she says confidently and smiles at Bob proudly. He responds with a grin.

I swell with pride and excitement at how well the upcoming event is coming together. The team really has come through for me on this. Everyone pitching in like this would normally have me welling up, but there's no time for that.

Chapter Thirty-Nine

The team were good to their word. As I guided Michelle's Mum into the venue on the evening of the charity event I was as impressed as she was. Especially by the fact that our entrance was along a freshly rolled out red carpet. I'd spent most of the day there coordinating and nipped home to get changed. In just that short time the place had been perfected. The chandeliers created a luxurious ambiance. The fourteen round tables, with ten chairs at each, were laid out around the room. The giant martini glasses as centrepieces were lusciously overflowing with red roses, white lilies, and purple irises. They looked every bit as splendid as Lauren's favourite florist had promised. The servers were carefully laying out the place settings with precision.

A semi-circle space large enough for dancing later in the night had been left clear in front of the stage. The stage itself had a simple podium, which could be moved to the side when not in use, which was decorated in matching flowers to the tables. This was for the auctions and planned speeches from Paula, myself and Marianne from the drug awareness charity. The bands were to be situated up there and framed by the opulent curtains. The backdrop was the screen ready to run the videos.

'Hayley, you have outdone yourself!'

Paula pulls me in a hug, both of us trying hard not to crease our dresses or get too emotionally overwhelmed just yet. We are both aware that this is going to tug on our heartstrings - a lot. I'd even sourced tastefully printed tissue packets for each table setting. They were going to be needed for sure.

'I'm just going to go and have one last look round,' I say.

'I need to check Uncle Eric is on his way. That man can get lost even when his taxi driver has the directions.' She chuckles kind heartedly. 'He's been my rock these past few months and is very excited to be attending such a fancy do.'

As I'm up on the stage double checking with Josh that the band has everything they need, I hear two familiar voices. I rush down the wooden steps to greet them.

'Ciao!'

We envelop each other in welcoming hugs. These tears are not going to hold off much longer at this rate and the event hasn't even started. Juliette and Lorenzo are beaming at me.

'It's so good to see you both.'

'We wouldn't have missed it for the world. It looks even more wonderful than our summer Ball.'

As the guests start filtering in, I nip to see that everything is in place ready. Debbie is thoroughly enjoying her initial role as ticket collector. She looks every bit the part standing in the original ticket office. Bob is in his element greeting the guests and guiding them to their tables. Lauren is talking tech with the people providing the sound and screen.

'Kim, I see you're on top of the catering. Not a Tupperware tub in sight.'

She nudges me playfully.

Once all the guests are settled in their seats, the band pauses for me to enter the stage. I stand at the podium in the purple dress that Michelle bought me for my birthday. The tiara from the summer Ball is perfectly placed on top of my freshly styled hair. Chelsea had come to my apartment to do it for me as going to the salon had felt too big a task, even so many weeks later. Baby steps, Mrs Temple had said when I mentioned it to her. Her and Joe are sitting at the table with the team. She is wearing a vintage satin dress in a beautiful charcoal colour, with a shawl to match. Joe is in his best suit and is even sporting a bow tie. From the stage, I look out over the expectant guests. I take a deep breath and smile.

'Thank you all for coming. When we first began planning this event we hoped a few people, such as yourselves, might be interested. Much to our surprise we've been turning people away. So if you are one of the people currently seated comfortably, consider yourselves lucky.' I grin, as chuckles fill the space. 'Thanks to our wonderful team we have a live stream of the evening being broadcasted. Hello to everyone tuning in from Michelle's channels.'

I wave to the nearest camera. Lauren gives me a thumbs up from her makeshift set up to the side of the stage.

'There are several reasons for our gathering tonight. The most important was, of course, for me to wear this fabulous dress. Another, perhaps almost as important, is to raise awareness and support for a local addiction support charity. Many of you may know that in her late teenage years Michelle struggled with drug addiction herself. Thankfully she found a better outlet in creating her YouTube videos and engaging in live streaming her video gaming antics. The more invested she got in her online venture, and the more fulfilment it provided her, the less she found herself drawn to substance abuse. It was a distraction. It was also a connection to communities across the world, through which she discovered both herself and the others who came to join her in her journey. As her channels grew, she founded her scholarship program. The aim was to support and fund young people wanting to become YouTubers and streamers. It has been hugely successful so far, but Michelle had plans to build it to even bigger levels so that it could be franchised across the world. The money raised here tonight will support those accessing the scholarship program in finding their creative self-expression as content creators as Michelle did. We hope that you may find it something you'd like to support long term. We have information packs on the tables and online.'

I look across to the door at the back of the room that has opened. As the figure makes their way across to our team table, they turn and mouth their apology. I smile widely in response to George's apologetic face. I'm so pleased he's made it. He'd moved on to a new project not long after we returned from Hotel al Cioccolato's Ball. It had been strange to not have him around. He'd become every bit a part of the team. I push through the distraction and continue.

'Michelle would have been overwhelmed by your support here tonight. I want to say a massive thank you for all the heartfelt messages that her devoted fans have taken the time to send. Just know that her family have had copies so they could read them.' I gesture to Paula's table. Uncle Eric waves back.

'The GoFundMe that was created in her memory has raised an amount so far that will be greatly received and resourced by our chosen drug awareness charity. You will hear more from their representative later in the night. Know that your kind donations will help change many lives.

'We are honoured that Michelle's Mum, Paula, has chosen some of Michelle's cherished possessions to auction. One of mine and Michelle's favourite local boutiques, Natalie's, have donated several glamorous outfits to the auction list. There will also be a separate online auction for those joining us virtually.

'Lastly, as a special treat we have the Lindy Hoppers here to teach you some moves so you can dance the night away. Thank you all for joining us and helping to continue Michelle's legacy and keep her promises alive. Hopefully her life did not end early in vain. I hope you have a wonderful evening.'

I walk from the stage, head held high, a beaming smile on my face as the music starts playing and someone moves the podium to one side. I glance out across the room from behind the curtain. The servers start making their way through the tables, two plates on each arm. Other servers are keeping the wine topped up. The room is filled with smiling faces, all here to pay homage to Michelle and support everything she had created and wished for. Perhaps she wasn't here to see through the future she had planned, but I'll be damned if I don't see it through for her.

A few months ago, if I had just gotten off stage after delivering a speech, Michelle would have been in the wings to leap on me. She'd squeeze me, rumpling my dress, too intent on congratulating me and glowing with pride. But right now I'm stood alone behind a curtain. My arms are empty when they should be full of her and the warmth she brought to me. I squeeze my eyes shut in a poor attempt at keeping the tears from running tracks through my make-up. Don't worry, babe, I think to myself – to her. I've got you.

Epilogue

Eight months later

I settle at my desk and turn on the computer. I reach over while it loads to move my canvas of a rainy London to one side. As I do so, the sun pours through the window. I take a moment to pause and drink in the view of the rooftops of Florence. I take a deep breath and smile, leaning back in my chair slightly. I lift my cup to my lips and take that first cherished sip of coffee.

So much has changed since I was here with George last May. Yet here, on the anniversary of Michelle's death, I am a mixture of emotions. I miss her every day but feel as though she has been with me every step of the way. Especially this part of my journey. Leaving Notting Hill was easier than I ever imagined it would be. The fact that Mrs Temple had decided to sell the building was definitely a factor. Yet this, renting an apartment in Florence, had happened quite serendipitously. Things had seemed to just flow in the right direction. The synchronicities along the way never ceased to amaze me. The more I followed my intuition the easier each step became.

After the charity event, I'd been discussing with Bob the plans I had to assist with the scholarship fund. When I finished explaining that I needed to find someone to manage their projects he simply asked why I wasn't doing it. Obviously, I had replied that I couldn't put in the hours it would require. His response was that if he only called me in to assist on the bigger events, would that help? I remember being gobsmacked. It hadn't crossed my mind to step back from my day job and be more hands on. I'd been willing to work doubly hard if it meant I could keep spinning all the plates. But Bob, in his wisdom, had offered me a better arrangement.

Funnily enough around the same time I had a similar offer from Juliette. They weren't in a position to be able to have me there full time but asked if I'd consider being their part-time event manager. I had been flattered and went for coffee with Paula to try to find a way to work out how all these small things could be put together in a manageable way. As we spoke, I could see where Michelle had gained her tenacity and adaptability to gain the best from her time and opportunities whilst doing something she loved. She suggested I could work remotely from wherever worked best for me.

Sitting here in my new apartment I may not have found love in the form of a relationship but I had found a love of life. I'm living in the country I'd dreamed of since I was a child spinning that globe lamp. The apartment keeps me in the city where I thrive and is still just a short journey from the beauty of the Tuscan countryside. I was honouring Michelle's legacy as I had promised her Mum by being the project manager of the scholarship fund. I still got to be an event manager for Bob and Hotel al Cioccolato. in my spare time I took the chance to explore this beautiful city. I have many new friends and have even learned to speak very basic Italian.

What I have gained is contentment in my day-to-day life and a variety of things to do that I can put my heart and soul into. More than anything, I get to live my dreams. I spend the evenings in front of my fireplace imagining Michelle sat with me as we chat about the day.

I shuffle to get comfortable in my chair, adjusting the cushion Anna made me from Michelle's joggers. To my delight, it reads 'Juicy Angel'. On my windowsill stands my cherry tree sapling next to my favourite photo of Michelle. It's one we took of us eating ice cream after abandoning our attempt at jogging. Behind it all, I can see the Duomo commanding the Florence skyline. Everything is almost right, and that's good enough for me. I raise my mug to the picture frame.

'Cheers, honey!'

WHERE THE PIECES LAND

Author's Note

Dear Reader,

If you have skipped to the back to read this first, beware - spoiler alerts.

It was after a lot of deliberation that I decided to include some of the heavier subjects experienced by my characters. Originally the story was much lighter, yet as the book developed I felt that the story needed to go to these darker places. Although this is a fictional piece of work, many of the subjects included I have personal or close experience of. As a writer, I tap into these emotional experiences, to the point that when I was writing of Hayley struggling, I too was feeling low. The bonus, of course, was that when she was happy, I felt happier too. In fact, when I was going back through the edits I found it upsetting to even see Michelle's name as I knew what was coming.

Although some parts may have been hard for you to read, my hope is that you saw their purpose within the story. I feel that subjects such as drug misuse and ill mental health can hold such negative stigma. Yet for some people drugs are a form of escapism, sometimes from situations or struggles with mental and they may feel this is the only way to numb the constant negative cycle. Sometimes the only way they can consider themselves fun or worth being around is through alcohol or drug abuse. However, through this cycle harsher issues with mental health and other life areas can be affected; relationship issues, work, financial, etc. Yet, even when individuals manage to find a healthier outlet, the yearning for that old high sometimes rears its ugly head and the risks can catch people up, as they did for Michelle. That 'just one more time' literally became her last.

These are serious topics around which friends or family need to learn how to support and guide the person without judgement so they feel safe to express their struggles and needs.

I find it hard to have voiced some of these things in this book because I feel there have been people in my life who I could have helped and supported better. Yet one thing to remember is that you can offer guidance and support, but only they can take the action that will lead them to recovery. Gaining more awareness and knowledge can assist you to help, not in telling them all the facts, but in having a better understanding of their needs.

I hope that in the writing of this it may help people to consider the severity of such things. On the other hand, opening up Hayley's life choices was enlightening. The workplace structure has changed in so many ways, especially over the last few years. Employers are more open to staff working remotely and, in many cases, discovered that their work is better because they are mentally healthier. I hope the main theme shines through - that you can make your dreams come true and that you are stronger than you ever imagined. And that good things can come out of the worst situations.

Resources that you might find useful:

https://www.youngminds.org.uk/
https://www.talktofrank.com/
https://www.mind.org.uk/
https://www.cruse.org.uk/

Author Bio

Claire Addington can be found writing either from her home in the Cambridgeshire countryside or on trains as she visits her four adult children and granddaughter. She has a BA Hons in Psychosocial Studies and a love of yoga, gym classes and dancing in her kitchen.

Claire has three previously independently published novels and two children's books, under the name Claire Upton. She considered revamping them but has chosen to leave them as they are since people were able to see past any glitches and enjoy the stories. She feels that her latest novel, *Where the Pieces Land,* is the beginning of a new era for her writing.

Keep in touch with Claire:

@authorclaireaddington

@AuthorClaireUpton

Subscribe to Author Claire Addington

WHERE THE PIECES LAND

Author's Note

Dear Reader,

If you have skipped to the back to read this first, beware - spoiler alerts.

It was after a lot of deliberation that I decided to include some of the heavier subjects experienced by my characters. Originally the story was much lighter, yet as the book developed I felt that the story needed to go to these darker places. Although this is a fictional piece of work, many of the subjects included I have personal or close experience of. As a writer, I tap into these emotional experiences, to the point that when I was writing of Hayley struggling, I too was feeling low. The bonus, of course, was that when she was happy, I felt happier too. In fact, when I was going back through the edits I found it upsetting to even see Michelle's name as I knew what was coming.

Although some parts may have been hard for you to read, my hope is that you saw their purpose within the story. I feel that subjects such as drug misuse and ill mental health can hold such negative stigma. Yet for some people drugs are a form of escapism, sometimes from situations or struggles with mental and they may feel this is the only way to numb the constant negative cycle. Sometimes the only way they can consider themselves fun or worth being around is through alcohol or drug abuse. However, through this cycle harsher issues with mental health and other life areas can be affected; relationship issues, work, financial, etc. Yet, even when individuals manage to find a healthier outlet, the yearning for that old high sometimes rears its ugly head and the risks can catch people up, as they did for Michelle. That 'just one more time' literally became her last.

These are serious topics around which friends or family need to learn how to support and guide the person without judgement so they feel safe to express their struggles and needs.

I find it hard to have voiced some of these things in this book because I feel there have been people in my life who I could have helped and supported better. Yet one thing to remember is that you can offer guidance and support, but only they can take the action that will lead them to recovery. Gaining more awareness and knowledge can assist you to help, not in telling them all the facts, but in having a better understanding of their needs.

I hope that in the writing of this it may help people to consider the severity of such things. On the other hand, opening up Hayley's life choices was enlightening. The workplace structure has changed in so many ways, especially over the last few years. Employers are more open to staff working remotely and, in many cases, discovered that their work is better because they are mentally healthier. I hope the main theme shines through - that you can make your dreams come true and that you are stronger than you ever imagined. And that good things can come out of the worst situations.

Resources that you might find useful:

https://www.youngminds.org.uk/
https://www.talktofrank.com/
https://www.mind.org.uk/
https://www.cruse.org.uk/

Author Bio

Claire Addington can be found writing either from her home in the Cambridgeshire countryside or on trains as she visits her four adult children and granddaughter. She has a BA Hons in Psychosocial Studies and a love of yoga, gym classes and dancing in her kitchen.

Claire has three previously independently published novels and two children's books. However, being dyslexic and not having the means at the time to hire an editor, she was left feeling less than pleased with the standard of those works. She considered revamping them but has chosen to leave them as they are – as her practice books – since people were able to see past the glitches and enjoy the stories anyway. She feels that her latest novel, *Where the Pieces Land,* is the beginning of a new era for her writing.

Keep in touch with Claire:

- @authorclaireaddington
- @AuthorClaireUpton
- Subscribe to Author Claire Addington

Printed in Great Britain
by Amazon